It's All About the Moon When the Sun Ain't Shining

It's All About the Moon
When the Sun Ain't Shining

ERNEST HILL

KENSINGTON PUBLISHING CORP.
http://www.kensingtonbooks.com

DAFINA BOOKS are published by

Kensington Publishing Corp.
850 Third Avenue
New York, NY 10022

ISBN 0-7582-0280-6

First Hardcover Printing: June 2004
First Trade Paperback Printing: May 2005
10 9 8 7 6 5 4 3 2 1

Printed in the United States of America

IT'S ALL ABOUT THE MOON WHEN THE SUN AIN'T SHINING

Chapter One

"Maurice, stop it!"

I heard her terse whisper cut through the still darkness and float toward the ceiling. I paused for a moment. My bedroom window was up, and I could feel the breeze from the pond on the back of my neck, and I could hear the crickets chirping and the birds singing and the bullfrogs calling to one another. And she was lying on the bed and I was straddling her. And I looked down at her face and I saw her beautiful brown eyes staring up at me and all I could think of was how much I loved her, and how much I missed her, and how bad I wanted her. And at that moment, I felt my body stiffen at the thought of her and there rose in me an overwhelming desire to possess her as I had done only a few times before. With a movement that was slow and gentle, I eased my sweaty body from atop hers and slid down against the softness of the mattress and, when my mouth was next to her ear, I whispered softly.

"Baby, didn't you miss me?"

I hoped she had, for it was now December and I had not seen her, nor she me, since I had left for the university back in August. But when I asked, I heard her sigh softly then frowned disapprovingly. And in the quiet of the moment, I hesitated, fearing that I had ruined the moment. I glanced at her, but she was not looking at me. Her dainty shoulders were flat against the bed, her knees were propped up, and her flushed face was tilted toward the dark, ominous hall. And I was lying on my side next to her, and my left arm was underneath her head, and my right arm was draped across her midriff, and my face was only inches from hers. Her blouse was open and her breasts were exposed, and I could see her nipples full and erect. I moved forward and when I was close, I opened my mouth and touched her nipple with the tip of my tongue. She cringed, then recoiled.

"No," she whispered. "They gon' catch us."

"They're gone," I said. "Won't be back for a long time."

I tried to kiss her neck but when I did, she recoiled again and pulled away. And I saw her eyes narrow and her forehead wrinkle.

"Maurice . . . I mean it . . . stop it."

"I can't," I whispered. "Baby, I'm aching for you."

I put my hand in the small of her back and pulled her closer to me. I felt her body become rigid. Then I felt her hands pushing hard against my hips. Again, I moved my lips toward hers but at the last minute she turned her head.

"Maurice, I mean it . . . stop it!"

"Honey," I whispered, "don't do me this way."

An awkward moment passed and I gazed into her eyes and I saw her eyes soften, then her lips parted and she spoke again.

"Not here," she said. "Not in your mama's house."

"We're engaged," I said. "Besides, she's not here."

I pressed closer to her, and her hands came between us.

"Engaged ain't married," she said.

I tried to kiss her again. She turned away.

"No," she said. "I'm not comfortable. I want to leave."

"Come on, Omenita," I said. "Don't be like this."

"No," she said. "Not in your mama's house. Now, I want to go up front. If Miss Audrey catch us back here she'll kill us."

"Ain't nobody gon' catch us," I said. "Mama at the church . . . Won't be back for hours."

"I want to go up front," she said.

"Omenita . . . please!" I said. "Don't do me like this."

"I'm serious," she said. "I want to leave."

"Baby—"

I started to say something else, but before I could, she raised her finger to her lips, then looked toward the door.

"What is it?" I asked. I paused, listening.

"I heard something," she said.

Our house was located just off one of the highways leading in and out of Brownsville. We lived well beyond the city limits. I raised my head and looked about, and just as I did a large truck rumbled by. I paused to let it pass and when it did, I heard nothing except the crickets and the birds and the bullfrogs.

"Girl, that's just your imagination," I said.

"No," she said. "I heard something."

I listened again and when I heard nothing, I turned my attention back to her.

"Baby, don't make me beg," I said.

I kissed her on her neck, and she pushed me away.

"Maurice . . . stop it!"

"Okay," I said. "Just let me touch you then."

"You are touching me."

I moved my face closer and instantly I could feel the warmth of her breath upon my face, and I could see the dark pupils of her beautiful brown eyes. And all I could think of was how much I loved her and how much I wanted her and how many hours over the past few weeks I had lain in my small apartment, far from this place, thinking of this moment, longing to feel the touch of her lips on mine and the touch of my fingers on her soft, yearning flesh.

"You know what I mean," I whispered.

I reached for her thigh, and she grabbed my hand.

"No," she said.

"Come on, Omenita," I said.

"No," she said. "I want to go up front."

My room was near the back of the house at the end of a short hall. Mama and Daddy's room was at the other end of the hall. Between the two bedrooms was a bathroom. Directly across from the bathroom was a doorway that led into the living room. My door was ajar, and from where I was lying, I could see into the living room. No one was home except us . . . I tried to reassure her.

"Omenita—" I called to her softly, but before I could say another word she interrupted me.

"I mean it," she said. "If we don't go up front right now, I'm going to leave."

"But baby—"

"That's it," she said, rising from her supine position and placing both of her hands on the bed behind her. "I'm leaving."

"Okay," I said. "Okay . . . we'll go up front."

I slid off the bed and started toward my bedroom door but before I got there, I heard the knob on the front door jiggle.

"Maurice!" I heard Mama shouting my name. "Maurice! You in there?"

Instantly, I fell back against the bed and looked toward the door.

"Goddammit, Maurice," I heard Omenita say. "I told you I heard something."

I looked at Omenita, and her eyes were fiery.

"Now what we gon' do?" she asked.

I looked away, then looked back at her. She was scanning the room, and I knew she was searching for someplace to hide. I paused a minute, thinking. I heard Mama call to me again. Then, suddenly I thought of a plan.

"Go in the bathroom," I said.

She nodded, and no sooner had she bobbed her head yes, than I heard the door jiggle again; then, I heard Mama's key in the lock, and I told Omenita to hurry and she snapped to her feet and raced into the bathroom. I hustled to open the door before Mama could unlock it.

When I pulled the front door open, Mama was standing on the stoop cradling a bag of groceries under each arm, and her keys were dangling from the lock. She looked at me, and I could tell she was wondering what was going on.

"What took you so long to open this door?" she asked, and I saw her looking back toward my bedroom. And when she did, I looked back over my shoulder to make sure the coast was clear. I heard Omenita in the bathroom . . . I heard the toilet flush and then I heard Omenita turn on the faucet and I knew she was pretending she was washing her hands.

"Nothing," I said. Then I was quiet.

"Whose car is that out there?" she asked. And I knew she knew before she asked, but I answered her anyway.

"Omenita's," I told her.

"Omenita!" she said, her voice slightly elevated.

I saw her looking past me trying to locate Omenita. And I knew she was looking toward my bedroom again, and I was angry at myself because I had left my bedroom door open, and the covers were ruffled. At that moment there was in me no doubt that if Mama saw the condition of my bed, her suspicious mind would quickly conclude what Omenita and I had been doing.

"What she doing over here?" she asked.

"Nothing," I told her.

I became quiet, hoping to say as little as possible.

"Must be something," she said after a moment or two then paused, and I knew she was waiting on an explanation.

"Just visiting," I said. "That's all."

Our eyes met, then I looked away.

"You know better than to bring that gal in this house when Nathaniel and me ain't home," she scolded me. "Don't you?"

"Yes, ma'am," I said submissively. Then I became quiet again and Mama looked at me.

"Where is she?" she wanted to know.

"In the bathroom," I said lamely. "Ought to be out in a minute."

Suddenly, I saw Mama looking past me again, and I knew she was trying to decide whether she believed me. She looked for a moment, then spoke again.

"Reverend Turner took sick," she said, still looking about. "Turned prayer meeting out early. Sister Thompson was kind enough to take me to the store before she brung me home."

"Yes, ma'am," I said. "That was kind of her."

Then, before she could say anything else, I took one of the bags of groceries from her and started toward the kitchen, hoping that she would follow. I heard her feet on the floor behind me and began to relax. Then, I heard her stop and instantly I knew she was still trying to figure out what was going on. I turned and looked and as I suspected, Mama was still looking toward my bedroom, and I knew she was trying to spot Omenita.

"What was y'all doing 'fo I come home?" she asked.

"Just watching TV," I said. "Just watching TV and talking."

Mama frowned, then looked about. The lights were out in the living room, but the television was on. As was the hall light.

"In the dark?" she said.

"The hall light's on," I said, then waited, but Mama did not say anything else, and I knew she was letting me know that I wasn't fooling her. I started back toward the kitchen and I heard Mama behind me. Then I heard her click on the switch, and I saw the living room light go on. I was glad that Omenita was still in the bathroom, for now I only wanted to place the bags in the kitchen and leave before she and Mama had an opportunity to have words.

When I made it to the kitchen, I stopped just inside the door and moved against the wall to let Mama pass. Ours was a small kitchen and Mama had to turn sideways to squeeze by me. And when she had passed, I watched her place the bag of groceries on top of the deep freezer, then turn and open the refrigerator door. I knew she would place it there even before she had, for there was neither room on the tiny counter next to the sink nor on the small table at the opposite end of the freezer, which in ac-tuality, was not a traditional kitchen table, but one similar to those found in a soda shop or a fast food place. Our kitchen was too small for a traditional table. In fact, it was too small for any-thing except the old stove, which was crammed in the corner just as you entered the room. And the sink that was directly across from the deep freezer and the old late-model refrigerator that sat in the corner just beyond the sink and just before the back door. And in the center of the room there was a walkway between the sink and refrigerator on one side and the deep freezer on the other. The table sat at the end of that alley. And Mama had been standing near the table when she placed her bag atop the freezer.

I set the bag I was carrying on the deep freezer too. Then I heard the bathroom door open and close. Then I heard Omenita walking toward the kitchen. And when she walked in, I looked at her and she appeared nervous, and I knew she was worried that Mama knew what we had been doing.

"Hi, Miss Audrey," Omenita spoke, her voice low and uncertain.

"Omenita," Mama said, then continued putting the groceries in the refrigerator.

"Can I help you with anything?" Omenita asked.

"No, thank you," Mama said. "I can manage."

There was an awkward silence, and Omenita looked at me, and I could tell she was upset. And I knew she was upset with me because she thought Mama was upset with her. I saw her turn toward Mama again.

"Miss Audrey, you sure look nice this evening," she said.

Mama was wearing a navy blue dress with a belt around the waist and she had on heels and her hair was down and she did look good for her age; she was fifty-eight. But I could tell that she was still dissatisfied with us for she neither nodded nor looked up. Just said "Thank you," and kept putting the groceries away.

And when she spoke, her voice was neither kind nor polite but rather cold and dry. And the fact that she had not tried to conceal her feelings bothered Omenita and I saw Omenita drop her eyes and I knew she was feeling ashamed. She was feeling ashamed because she was thinking that Mama knew what we had been doing back in my bedroom before she had come home. It remained quiet for a few minutes, then I saw Omenita raise her head and wipe a small bead of sweat from the center of her brow, and I realized it was getting hot in the kitchen with all of us standing in such a congested space. I reached over and raised the tiny window just above the sink. Mama saw me raise it, and I guess she must have been warm as well for she immediately opened the back door and, instantly, I could feel the cool breeze through the window and I could hear the crickets and the birds and the frogs. And all I could think about was how nice it would be to sit outside by the pond with Omenita.

"Guess Maurice told you the news," Mama said. I looked up, surprised. She was staring at Omenita.

Omenita didn't answer. Instead, she looked at me, confused. And I saw Mama look at her, then at me. And I saw Mama frown. And I forced myself to smile, though it was the last thing I wanted to do at that moment.

"Maurice, you mean to tell me you ain't told that child yet?" Mama said, her tone indicating shock.

"No, ma'am," I said. "Not yet."

I saw Omenita staring at me, and I wished I were somewhere else because I didn't want to discuss it at the moment.

"Didn't know it was a secret," Mama said.

"It's not a secret," I said. "Just haven't told her yet."

"Pretty sure she want to know," Mama said.

She glanced at me, then started toward the bag of groceries that I had placed atop the deep freezer. I was leaning against the counter, but moved aside to let her pass, then I watched as she removed the other bag and lifted the freezer top. I heard the old rusty hinges screech, then I saw the frosty air rising off the meat when the hot air in the kitchen and the cool air in the freezer collided. I saw her remove some pork chops and neck bones from the bag and stuff them in the freezer. I didn't look, but I could still feel Omenita's eyes on me. And when I remained silent, she addressed me directly for the first time since arriving in the kitchen.

"Know what?" she asked.

"Nothing," I said.

Omenita looked at me, then at Mama.

"He got news," Mama said.

"News?" Omenita said. "What kind of news?"

"Mama, please!" I said, louder than intended.

I saw Mama's head snap. "What did you say?"

"Nothing," I said.

She looked at me hard, menacingly.

"Boy! As long as you still got what little sense the good Lord gave you, don't you ever raise your voice to me . . . You hear?"

"Yes, ma'am," I said. I averted my eyes submissively. Suddenly I was a one-year-old child instead of a twenty-year-old man.

"Damn," I heard Omenita say underneath her breath, and when she did I saw Mama whirl and look at her. Mama's lips were pursed, her eyes narrowed, and her forehead frowned.

"Watch your mouth, missy," she said. "This ain't no bar room."

I saw Omenita's eyes begin to water. Then I saw Omenita's head turn until her sad brown eyes were cast longingly upon my face. And for a brief moment, she looked at me and I looked at her. Then her lips parted.

"I think I better go," she said.

"No!" I said. "You don't have to."

"Maybe that would be best," Mama said.

"Mama!" I said, shocked.

Omenita turned to leave. I followed her.

Chapter Two

By the time I reached the front door, Omenita had already made it outside. And from the doorway, I saw her walking toward the large oak tree just beyond the house and just short of the highway. And I thought that maybe she was going to sit in the swing that Daddy and I had hung from one of the branches but instead she paused in the shadows, and her back was to me, and her tall, slender frame was pointing out toward the darkness, and the moon was bright and the stars were shining. I liked the way she looked basking in the light of the moon. And I liked the look of the soft, subtle glow of the dim light cascading off her long, lustrous hair. And I liked the way her dress was hugging her tiny, delicate waist, and the way it hung off her shoulders and the way it fell down her back and clung to her butt and stopped midway along her full, shapely thighs. And as I looked at her, I wondered why things had to be so difficult between the two of them. Why all the tension? Why all the stress? Why all the strain?

I discretely watched her for a moment, then I stepped out onto the stoop and closed the door behind me. I eased next to her, and when I was close, I slipped my hand about her waist, and my head, like hers, was locked forward. And as I stood beside her, purposely giving her time to collect herself, I could not help but notice that there was a still quietness about and that the night air was filled with the smell of freshly cut grass and that in the distance I could hear the steady hum of rubber tires on the smooth asphalt highway just beyond the yard. As my eyes strayed across the street and beyond the old railroad track, I could see the red glare of the end of a cigarette, and though I could not see the person's face, I knew that someone was sitting on the porch, cloaked in darkness, enjoying the peaceful solitude of a soothing smoke.

And along that street, beyond the tracks, I could see rows of old houses, shacks really, all different, yet all the same. And all following the contours of the street winding unceremoniously through the quaint, depressed, black neighborhood with which I was all too familiar. As I gazed out upon the horizon, I was anxious to talk to Omenita, but she was still angry, and when she was angry she was mean-spirited, and somewhere deep inside of me a wiser voice cautioned patience, so I remained silent, waiting for some sign from her that she was ready to speak calmly about that which had just transpired. I was secretly afraid that when she did decide to speak, I would not like what she had to say. I would not like it at all.

A moment or two passed and when she remained speechless, I decided, against better judgment, and spoke first.

"You okay?" I asked, then waited.

She pulled away, ever so slightly, and turned toward me, but she was not looking at me. She was looking at her car, which was sitting in the yard, on the grass, just off the seashells that were the driveway. I saw her looking and I knew she was contemplating leaving, and I knew she was wishing that she had never come to see me, and that she had never gone in the back room with me and that she had not heard the words that Mama had spoken to her. And she was thinking all this and at the same time, she was trying to hold her face straight and keep her eyes dry, and not let on how bad Mama's words had hurt her.

"What's she so anxious for you to tell me?" she finally asked. Her voice was low, but I could still hear the pain.

"Nothing," I said.

"Must be something," she said. "Something else for Miss Audrey to throw in my face. What is it?" she continued to push. "Did you win another award? Did you find out you're graduating at the head of your class? Did some big company offer you a job? Please tell me. What is it?"

"Nothing," I said again.

She looked at me, and I could tell that my answer had not satisfied her.

"Must be something or else Miss Audrey wouldn't be carrying on so."

I remained quiet. I had said all I planned to say.

"What is it?" she asked again, then waited.

I remained quiet.

"I'm leaving," she said.

"All right," I said. "I'll tell you."

She waited for a moment but when I remained silent, she spoke. "Well," she said.

"I'll tell you later," I said, "when the time is right."

She turned to leave. I grabbed her hand.

"Come on, Omenita," I said. "Don't act like this . . . It's nothing . . . I swear. Mama's just pulling your chain."

"It's something to me," she said.

"Come on," I said. "Let's just talk about something else. We haven't seen each other in over four months. . . . Please, let's talk about something else. Okay?"

I felt the tension in her arm loosen and I released my grip, and she turned toward the street and stared far off into the darkness.

"Can't take Miss Audrey no more," she said. "Can't take her trying to make me feel like I'm nothing."

"She doesn't know what she's doing," I said. "It's just her way."

"She know," Omenita said.

"No," I said. "It's just her way."

Omenita looked at me, and her eyes began to water.

"Why are you taking up for her?"

"I'm not," I said.

"You are," she said. She had been fighting back tears, but now she could not fight them any longer, and as the tears descended her face, I could feel my insides churning, and I could feel my heart aching, and all I wanted to do was put my arms around her and pull her close to me and make the pain and hurt that was making her cry dissipate.

I reached for her and she pulled away, and I saw her eyes narrow and I saw her nose begin to run and I saw her drop her head and I saw her wipe her nose with the back of her hand and I could see that her hand was trembling and I could hear her sniffling and I knew she was trying to stop crying. I wanted to put my arms around her but I knew she would not let me.

"She know," Omenita said, sobbing heavily. "And you know she know. You were there. You were there just like me."

"I was where?" I asked, confused.

"You saw the way she treated me."

"Treated you when?" I asked. I was at a loss. She was not making sense.

"Could've let me know that she was proud of me . . . seeing how me and you were a couple . . . and seeing how I was the first in my family to graduate."

"Graduate," I mumbled to myself. Then it dawned on me. "High school," I said. "Girl, you talking about high school?"

"But no, she had to be mean. She had to let me know I wasn't nothing."

"She was proud," I said. "She was proud of both of us."

"No," Omenita said. "She wasn't proud. That was the happiest day of my life, and she just had to let me know that I wasn't good enough. Always been that way with Miss Audrey. I graduate from high school and she got to let me know you the val. I go to junior college and she got to let me know you going to the university. I take a job around here so I can be close until we can be together and she got to let me know I didn't need to go to school for no job like that. She know alright. She know just what she doing."

"No," I said. "It's not like you think."

"Yes, it is," she said. "And you know it just as well as I do."

Omenita started crying again and I put my arms around her and pulled her close. She leaned her head on my shoulder, and my heart was aching because I could hear the hurt in her voice.

"It's not like you think," I said again.

And when I said that, she buried her head into my shoulder, and her tormented body began to pulsate and the tense muscles in her back began to shake. And I could feel her warm tears seeping through my shirt, and I wanted to comfort her, but I didn't know what to say. I pulled her closer and held her tighter and suddenly it seemed quiet again. We were in a dense haze and I could hear the birds singing and the crickets chirping and the bullfrogs calling to one another. And then, in an instance, I heard her voice, above it all, calling my name softly, tenderly.

"Yes," I answered her call, and I looked down and her glazed eyes were wide, gazing out into the darkness of the night. Suddenly, she looked up at me, her face wet with tears.

"When you graduate in a few weeks . . . and find a job . . . and we get married. Promise me we'll move away from here."

"She'll always be my mother," I said.

"But you won't always be her boy," she said, her eyes full of tears. "You'll be my man . . . and we'll have our own family . . . and we'll have our own lives . . . Promise me . . . Promise me we'll move away . . . I can't take her always downing me . . . Promise me."

"I promise," I said.

"No," she said. "Say it like you mean it. Say it like it's true."

"I do mean it," I said. "It is true."

I looked at her as tenderly as I could, and her sad eyes grew wide, and the flesh of her brow furrowed, forming an angry frown.

"How she gon' judge me?" she asked. "And she just a maid."

"That's my mama," I said.

"And I'm your woman."

"She doesn't mean any harm," I said for the third or fourth time.

"The hell she don't," Omenita said, and I heard her voice trembling with a rage that seemed to have emanated from a strange place deep within her soul.

"Shouldn't cuss in front of her," I said.

"So, now it's my fault?"

"I didn't say that," I said.

"Sure sound like it to me."

"Omenita," I said, "you know how she is."

"And!" she said.

"You shouldn't give her a reason," I said.

"What did I do?" she asked.

"You know she's a churchgoing woman," I said.

"So?"

"Just need to watch your mouth," I said. "That's all."

"No," she said. "You need to be a man."

"I am a man," I said, feeling my anger rise.

"No," she said. "A man would protect his woman. He wouldn't duck his head and hide."

"What do you want me to do?" I asked.

"Stand up to her," she said.

"I don't want to talk about this anymore," I said. "I am a man."

In the distance, I saw headlights approaching fast, and when the car was close, it slowed, and as it passed, I recognized the car as belonging to Deacon Fry, and from the appearance of things, Miss Cora had gone to prayer meeting, too, and Deacon Fry was bringing her home, for when he pulled into her yard next door and she got out, she was carrying her Bible and wearing that cream-colored dress that she only wore to church or funerals or prayer meetings. Miss Cora was a portly woman, and it took her a while to get out and when she walked toward her porch, she kept her hand on the car, bracing herself until she was close to the steps that led into her house. There was a vacant lot between our houses, and as she hobbled up the steps onto her porch, I told myself that I was going to mow that lot in the morning because the grass was getting just tall enough to draw snakes. And Omenita was scared of snakes. And tomorrow evening I was going to make some sandwiches and fry some chicken and we were going to sit in the backyard on one of the picnic tables underneath the pecan tree. At least, that was my plan, before all of this confusion with Mama.

I was standing half-dazed watching Deacon Fry back out of the yard when I felt Omenita pull away from me and start toward her car, and I knew that now, not only was she angry at Mama, but she was also angry at me. For in her mind, the conversation was not supposed to be over. I was supposed to tell her that I was going to talk to Mama and that I was going to make things right. She was my woman and I was going to make it right.

"Wait!" I said.

Suddenly, I saw her stop and wheel around, and when I was closer, I looked into her eyes, and in those eyes was anger and sadness and pain.

"Wait!" She repeated my request in a voice tinged with sarcasm.

"Yes," I said. "Wait."

"I'm tired of waiting," she said, and I saw the tears rolling down her face. "That's all I been doing since I met you. Waiting on you to finish college. Waiting on you to find a job. Waiting on you to be a man."

"I am a man," I said.

"Prove it," she said.

I became quiet.

"I'm tired of waiting," she said. "And I'm not going to wait any longer."

"Baby."

"No," she said. "From now on if we're gon' be together, we gon' be together. No more waiting."

"Fine," I said.

"And we gon' start with Miss Audrey," she said. "Either you gon' be her son or you gon' be my husband."

"I won't choose between the two of you," I said.

"You're gon' have to," she said, "if you want me."

"No," I said. "I won't."

"Then it's over," she said.

She turned to leave and I grabbed her arm.

"Don't do this," I said.

"Choose," she said.

I became quiet again and she started to leave.

"Okay," I said. "I'll talk to Mama . . . and I'll make her stop. I will."

"And if she don't?" she said.

"I'll choose."

Chapter Three

I watched Omenita back out into the street and drive toward the night until the taillights of her car disappeared into the darkness. And when I could no longer see her, I turned and started back toward the house, and as I walked I told myself that I would talk to my mother, and I would make her understand, and if she refused to understand, then I would choose. And though I would rather not, I would, because I was a man.

Resolute and determined, I climbed the steps to the front door, and when I reached the door, I pulled it open, and all at once, the savory scent of coffee and sweet rolls drifted to me from deep within the house. I was surprised, yet I do not know why. For as long as I could remember, Mama had followed the same routine. Every Wednesday night, she went to prayer meeting, and as soon as she returned home, she made a pot of coffee and baked a pan of sweet rolls, and then, Daddy and her would sit in the kitchen around the old table with the broken leg and argue about the Bible and the church and men like Deacon Fry who ran more women once he got in the church than he ever ran when he was out of the church. And while they talked, the back door was usually open and if you were outside, anywhere within range, you could smell the scent of sweet rolls and coffee lingering heavy in the crisp night air.

Once inside the house, I noticed that Mama had changed clothes and was no longer in the kitchen, but was now sitting in the living room on the old sofa, and her sewing can was next to her, and a pair of Daddy's work pants were across her lap, and the lamp was on, and she was leaning close to the light, working a piece of thread through a needle. And though she was pretending to concentrate on the thread, in actuality, I knew she was waiting for me. I stopped before her to say something, but before I could, she spoke first.

"Sweet rolls in there," she said, "if you want some."

I nodded, but I did not speak. I wanted her to know that I was angry with her, and I wanted her to know that from this point on, things were going to be different and that if she forced me to choose, I would choose Omenita. I paused for a moment and waited, but when she did not budge, I knew that she was letting me know that she was not going to give me the satisfaction of looking into my face.

I waited a moment more, but when it was obvious that she would not look, I made my way toward the kitchen, and as I walked, I glanced at her, and out of the corner of my eye, I saw that she had threaded the needle and was busy at work mending Daddy's pants. And I looked at her face, and there was no discernible expression, but I could hear her humming, and when I heard her humming, I knew that she was pleased that Omenita was gone.

In the kitchen, I saw the pot on the stove, percolating, but I ignored the coffee and looked about, searching for the sweet rolls. I wasn't much of a coffee drinker, in fact, I rarely drank it at all. I did not particularly like the taste nor did I find it necessary to get me going in the morning or to keep me going at night. For me, there was just no need. No need at all.

For a brief moment, I stood gaping in the middle of the floor until I finally located the sweet rolls. They were still on the cooking tin and Mama had placed them on the windowsill just above the sink to cool, and I could tell they had not been out of the oven long because I could still see the heat rising from them. And as I moved toward them, I knew that I would not take many, for I really wasn't that hungry and besides, I knew that when Daddy and Grandpa Luke made it home, they were going to sit around the little table with Mama, and eat sweet rolls, and drink coffee, and talk about the church, and about the money Daddy and Grandpa Luke had received for the load of aluminum cans they had taken to Arkansas, and about Omenita and me, and about how foolish I was for wasting my time with a girl of her caliber.

I took a few sweet rolls from the tin and a paper towel from the holder and I considered going outside to sit on the back stoop but at the last minute, I changed my mind. Instead, I sat at the table and placed the sweet rolls on the napkin before me. The back door was still ajar and from the light of the moon, I could see the faint outline of the large catfish pond nestled safely behind the tall hurricane fence. Because it was dark, I could not see the water, but I could see the high mounds of dirt that formed the banks and jutted along the pond, following the water until they finally disappeared into the darkness of the woods on the side farthest from our house. And out near the pond, I could see the faint outline of several horses grazing along the banks, and I could hear the insects calling from the trees, and as I sat looking out across the pond I asked God to please give me the strength to do what I had to do and grant me the words to make Mama understand.

The sweet rolls looked good. I lifted one from the paper and carried it to my mouth, and as I chewed it, savoring the taste, I tilted my head back and closed my eyes, and I could feel the breeze blowing off the pond, and the cool, crisp air felt good on my warm, moist skin. And as my eyes were closed, I wondered again, why Mother and Omenita could not get along. And why were they forcing me to choose between the woman who gave me life and the woman to whom I planned to give my life.

I opened my eyes to take another bite of the sweet roll, but just as I was about to sink my teeth into it, I turned my head and I saw my mama standing in the doorway, watching me.

"Guess you told her," she said, looking at me with dark, piercing eyes.

"No, ma'am," I said. "Not yet."

Instantly, her face furrowed and her piercing eyes clouded. "Why not?"

"Just didn't," I said.

I took another bite of the sweet roll and pretended to look out the back door. A quiet moment passed and though I could feel her eyes on the side of my face, there was deep inside of me the faint hope that she was going to let things stand, but no sooner had I completed that thought, Mama spoke again.

"Son, that gal don't mean you no good," she said. "She just trying to get between you and where you trying to go."

"That's not true," I said.

"It is true," she said. "Might not want to hear it but it's the truth."

I shook my head. "No, Mama," I said louder than intended. "It's not."

She looked at me intensely, and instinctively I dropped my eyes. An awkward moment passed, then she spoke again.

"You best watch yourself, Maurice." She issued a vile threat. "Lest you forget who you talking to."

I sighed deeply, but did not speak.

"Tell her . . . Next time you see that gal . . . you tell her . . . you hear?"

Omenita was right. Mama was handling me like a child, and that realization touched something inside of me and I felt myself become angry, so angry, until I felt that if I answered her, I would speak to her in a manner that would only make things worse. So, I didn't answer her. Instead, I turned my head toward the back door and looked out. High in the pecan tree, I saw a raccoon dangling from one of the branches. It had strayed out too far and the weight of the limb could not support him, and his shoulders were hunched and his body was curled and his wide eyes shone yellow, reflecting the light of the moon. I was watching him struggling, wondering if he was going to fall when I heard her stern, starchy voice cut through the silence.

"Boy, you listening to me?"

Her words smacked hard against my bruised ego, and instantly I felt warm blood pulsating through constricted veins.

"Yes, ma'am," I uttered through tightly clenched teeth, then it got quiet. She had called me a boy; but I wasn't a boy, I was a man. I waited for her to say something else and when she did not, I spoke again: "Why do you treat Omenita like that?" I said. My voice was forceful and Mama hesitated before she answered.

"Ought not to act the way she do," Mama said matter-of-factly "What kind of girl go traisping through folks' houses when they ain't home?"

"I told you we were just visiting."

"In your room?" Mama said.

I looked at her defiantly, but I did not speak.

"Maybe you got more on your mind than just visiting."

My eyes wanted to stray toward the floor but I would not allow them. Instead, I looked at her directly and I reminded myself that I was a man.

"Is that what you been learning in school?"

She paused and stared, but still I said nothing.

"Boy, you better answer me," she said.

"I love her," I said.

"Love . . . what you know 'bout love?"

"I know enough," I said.

"Keep living," Mama said. "You gon' find out what you don't know."

"What has Omenita ever done to you?" I asked.

"Never said she did anything," Mama said.

"Must of done something," I said, "for you to hate her so."

"Hate!" Mama said, shocked.

"Omenita say you think she ain't good enough for me."

"You can do better," Mama said.

"Don't want to do better," I said. "I just want Omenita."

"That gal gon' be yo' downfall," Mama said. "You mark my words."

"You just don't know her," I said. "If you did, you wouldn't talk like that."

"Know her better than you think," Mama said.

"Why you hate her so?" I asked again.

"I don't hate her," Mama said. "I don't hate nobody."

"But you don't like her," I said.

"Not her," Mama said. "Her ways."

I tilted my head and looked at her strangely. "What ways?"

"That gal her mama all over."

"That's what you got against her?" I said. "Her family."

"She is who she is . . . and her family is her family."

"So what," I said, perplexed.

"So what?" Mama said. "Honey, family is everything."

"Maybe to you," I said.

"And to you too," Mama said. "You just don't want to admit it."

"One thing I will admit," I said, "I don't like mess. And that's all this is. A bunch of silly old mess."

"No," Mama said. "This ain't about mess. This about your future."

"My future is just fine," I said.

"Could be," Mama said. "If you leave that gal alone."

"Don't want to hear this," I said.

"Might not want to hear," Mama said, "but it's true."

"Why are you doing this?" I asked.

" 'Cause you my child," she said. "And I'm responsible for you."

I sighed again, heavy this time.

"I'm not a child," I said. "I'm a man."

"You my child," Mama said. "You gon' always be my child."

I shook my head. "I'm a man."

"You got some important decisions to make," Mama said.

"And I'll make them," I said.

"Don't want that gal influencing you."

"She's not a gal," I said. She's my fiancée."

Mama looked at me and shook her head.

"I had hoped this thing between you two would pass. But since it hasn't, there's something I need to say."

"I just wish you would let things be," I said.

"You say I don't know Omenita."

She talked on as if she had not heard me. I sighed again and looked out of the back door and pretended that I was not there. I heard her, but I was not listening to her. I was looking at the trees and pond and the starlit sky.

"Well, that couldn't be farther from the truth," she continued. "We all come up together . . . Me and your daddy and Omenita's folks."

I stared high into the pecan tree. The raccoon was gone now and a gentle breeze was blowing, and I could see the leaves stirring and the smaller branches swaying back and forth, riding the invisible currents of the wind. I did not want to hear what she had to say and it angered me to know that I had no choice but to indulge her.

"We went to school together," I heard her say. "We worked in the fields together . . . and we all lived in the quarters together." Her voice seemed distant and faint, and I told myself that this was but a bad dream that I simply had to ignore. I focused on the tree and I tried to ignore her. But I could not. I leaned back in the chair, frustrated. I heard her but I was not listening. "Back then they used to call Omenita's daddy Tipsy Russell . . . Called her mama Run-Around Sue. Of course, they wasn't married back then. None of us were."

Suddenly, I felt her hand on mine, and my eyes strayed from the tree and I looked at her. She paused briefly, then started again.

"Son," she called to me softly in a voice tinged with tenderness and cloaked with compassion. "Them people ain't never wanted nothing out of life 'cept what they could beat folks out of . . . and them ain't the kind of folks you need to get yo'self tied up with . . . they ain't the kind of folks at all."

Her words touched something in me and I felt myself reacting in a way in which I had not planned. My heart raced; my skin tingled. Then, suddenly my mouth opened and I spoke in spite of my secret vow to remain silent.

"I'm not interested in her folks," I said. "I'm only interested in her."

Mama stopped, then looked at me contemplatively.

"She drink?" she asked.

"Some," I stammered. Her question caught me off guard.

"Curse?"

"A little," I said.

"Had many boyfriends?"

"She dated a few guys," I said. "But she's had only one other steady boyfriend besides me."

"Like they say," Mama said. "You know the parents . . . you know the child."

"I love her," I said.

"You can do better," Mama said again.

"Don't want better," I said for the second time. "Just want her."

"Ain't lived long enough to know what you want," Mama said. She was talking down to me again. I felt my anger rise, and inside my head I heard a voice screaming: *I'm a man.* "Besides," she continued, "wants don't matter much in this life . . . folks be wise to study on what they need. Right woman will come along someday. When she do, you'll know."

"I'm going to marry Omenita," I said.

Mama didn't say anything.

"She and I have already talked about it," I said.

"Talk is talk." Mama broke her silence. "Done heard plenty talk in my life. Most of it ain't never 'mounted to nothing."

"We're going to get married," I said adamantly. I waited for Mama to say something, but she remained quiet. I waited a little longer. Still, she did not speak.

"I mean it, Mama . . . Omenita and I are going to get married."

"I know you thanks so," she said.

"I know so," I said, leaving no doubt.

"Well you remember this," she said. "There's many a slip between the cup and the lip." She said that, then she didn't say anything else.

"I love her, Mama," I said. "I love her with all my heart."

"You love them long legs," Mama said. "But once you been in this old world a while, you gon' find out it's more to life than that. Might have to find out the hard way . . . I don't know. Some folks is like that."

"Like what?" I asked defensively.

"Hardheaded," Mama said.

"My head's not hard," I said bitterly.

"You just like Brother," she said.

"I don't know what you're talking about," I said.

Mama walked across the floor and sat at the table. The entire time she had been standing just inside the door next to the deep freezer.

"When Brother was 'bout your age," she began, "he brung home a little old yellar gal from 'cross the river. And she had them old long legs just like Omenita. And she'd bat them big old eyes of hers at Brother, and he'd look like he'd lose what little sense he come here with. Then one day that crazy boy up and told Mama how much he loved that gal and how they was fixin' to marry. And I remember Mama pulled him aside and talked to him, just like I'm talking to you. Told him he needed to take a little time and think about what he was doing. Told him marrying was serious business . . . But his head was too hard and too full of foolish notions. Told Mama he know all he needed to know. Told her he was gon' marry that gal and all he wanted her to do was to buy a little old gown and put it on whenever he came home. And let him tell it, that's all he wanted out their life together. Just wanted that gal to put on that gown when he come home. So he went against Mama and he married that gal with them big legs from 'cross the river. And they got a little old rent house in the quarters close to that grudge ditch. And he took to working in the fields, hauling hay, and driving tractors, and digging taters and working hisself like a dog whilst that gal sat up in the house all day and did next to nothing. And sho 'nuff, after they first married they tell me he'd come home all covered in dirt and that gal'd be sitting up in the house watching TV, and he'd tell her 'baby, why don't you go put on that gown.' And sho 'nuff, she'd put it on and they tell me them two would carry on so. Well, that went on 'bout a week or two. He'd come home and tell that gal to put on that gown and then them two would carry on like wasn't no tomorrow. Then one day, a few weeks later, he come from work and he didn't have to tell her nothing. She was standing there with that gown already on. But, they'd been married 'bout a month now, and he'd been having to work harder and harder to try to meet the bills . . . Tell me he didn't even hardly look at that gal good, just come on in the house and fell down in his old chair, looking like he was 'bout half dead from working in that hot sun all day, and they say after a minute or two he took one look at that gal standing there half naked, and said, 'Woman, you better take off that gown and put on some peas.' "

Mama became quiet a minute and I knew she was giving me time to absorb what she was saying. And when she thought enough time had passed, she started up again. "Naw," she began, "I ain't got nothing against Omenita . . . Just don't want you making the same mistake Brother made. Don't want you making the same mistake me and your daddy made. You'll be graduating from LSU in a few months . . . got a chance to do something with yourself. Need to get you somebody you can do good with 'cause Lord knows you can do bad all by yourself."

"Mama, I'm not Brother," I said.

"Don't fool yourself," she said. "You got his ways alright."

I looked at her, then looked away.

"Omenita and I will do just fine together," I said.

"Don't know why your head so hard," Mama said.

"My head's not hard," I said.

"Well, maybe your daddy can tell you something," she said. " 'Cause Lord knows I can't."

"Daddy," I said.

I looked toward the door. Daddy had arrived.

Chapter Four

I followed Daddy with my eyes, watching him as he passed through the door and made his way deeper into the kitchen. He was a big man, but not a fat man. He stood somewhere close to six feet tall and weighed well over two hundred pounds. And though he had never touched a weight in his life, he had the unmistakable look of a seasoned power lifter: broad shoulders, powerful arms, bulging biceps. And yet, as I sat looking at him, I could not help but notice how at this moment, he neither appeared powerful nor strong. The trials of the day had sapped him of his energy and now he appeared haggard and tired. I rose and moved back against the rear door just in case he wanted to sit at the table with Mama, but he did not sit. Instead he stopped before the sink and I saw him turn on the faucet to wash his hands. He had just leaned over the sink when I heard Mama call to him.

"Didn't hear you come in," she said, then pushed back from the table as if she was about to stand, but at the last minute seemed to change her mind.

"Door was open," I heard Daddy say. His back was to her, but from where I stood I could see him scrubbing his outstretched hands underneath the steady stream of water. "Didn't see no need to knock."

I saw Mama looking at him and I watched her wait patiently

until Daddy had shut off the water, and when he had, she called to him again.

"How you make out?" she asked him.

Daddy turned around and I saw his roving eyes look toward the far wall. There was an old dishcloth draped across the rack just beyond the sink. I saw Daddy remove the cloth and begin drying his hands.

"Awright, I reckon."

"Just awright," Mama said. She paused and looked at him strangely. When he left, the truck was loaded with cans. She had expected more.

He nodded. "Price dropped a little."

"Dropped!" I heard Mama say.

For an answer, Daddy nodded again, then leaned back against the counter and for the first time, I could see his eyes clearly. They were dull and drowsy, and though I was some distance from him I could see that they were bloodshot. Yes, it had been a long day and he was tired. I saw him look at the empty chair and I thought he was going to sit, but before he could Mama spoke again.

"How much?" she asked.

I saw Daddy tilt his head and look at her, confused. And I knew he was wondering if she was asking how much he had made or how much the price had dropped. He had not understood because he had been looking at the chair, not listening to her.

"How much what?" he asked.

"How much it drop?" she asked.

I saw Daddy shift his weight, then rub his hand across his face. Yes, he was tired. I looked at the empty chair again. Oh, how I wished he would sit down.

"Half a cent," he said.

Mama paused and shook her head, and I could see that she was disappointed.

"It's always something."

She said that, and then she paused again. And in that split second I looked at Daddy. And I thought about asking him if he wanted to sit. But they were having a conversation and I felt it would be rude to interrupt them, so I remained quiet.

"Wonder why the price dropped so."

"Don't know," Daddy said. "Just the price he give me."

"Highway robbery," Mama mumbled.

Daddy didn't say anything.

"Nathaniel, sometimes I wish you would quit fooling with them people," Mama said, "especially if they ain't gon' do no better than that."

"Got to sell somewhere," Daddy said. "Don't know of no other place."

"Just hate to see you drive way up yonder for them kind of prices."

"Well it beats nothing," Daddy said. "Even with the price being what it was, we still cleared right at two hundred dollars. At least that'll be enough to cut the phone back on and put a little gas in the truck for the rest of the week." Suddenly, Daddy paused and looked at me, then smiled.

"How you doing, son?" he asked.

"Fine, Daddy," I said.

I looked at Mama and saw her looking at me, and I knew she wanted to tell Daddy about Omenita. And for a brief moment I thought she would. But to my surprise she remained quiet. I was still looking at her when Daddy spoke again.

"You interested in making a little pocket change while you home?"

His question caught me off guard. I looked around and hesitated, then when I fully understood what he had asked me, I smiled and answered him. "Yes, sir," I said, then waited.

"We a man short in the kitchen," he said. "Silas done took sick. Ought to be out better part of the week."

I opened my mouth to speak again, but before I could Mama spoke first.

"Ain't nothing serious, is it?" she asked.

"Naw," I heard Daddy say. Then I saw him turn toward Mama and shake his head. "Way I hear it, he done come down with the flu or something like that. Doc Sims put 'im on bed rest. Told 'im to take it easy for a few days. Ought to be awright soon as he get his strength back."

"When I start?" I asked. I was broke and the idea of earning some money appealed to me.

"First thing in the morning if you want to," Daddy said. "Already talked to the boss man. He said it's up to you. Didn't know if no college man would be interested in working in the kitchen washing no dishes."

"He interested," Mama said.

"Let the boy talk for hisself," Daddy said. "He might need to sleep on it 'fo he decide . . . You know, roll it around in his mind, mull it over."

Mama looked at me, then frowned.

"Mull it over, my foot. He interested . . . Besides, maybe that'll keep him way from trouble whilst he home."

I saw Daddy look at Mama, then back at me and I knew he was trying to figure out if something was going on.

"Don't imagine that's no big concern," he said. "Probably couldn't find no trouble round here if he wanted to."

"Hunh," Mama said, grunting. "Don't fool yourself."

She looked at me again, and I looked away.

"Well, it's up to him," Daddy said. "Whatever he want to do."

"Where's Grandpa Luke?" I tried to change the subject.

I saw Daddy look toward the living room.

"Went to lie down . . . said he feeling poorly."

Mama rose, and I saw her look toward the door, then back at Daddy. She was concerned; I could see it in her eyes.

"Think I ought check on him?" she asked.

Daddy shook his head, and I could tell from his expression that he wasn't the least bit concerned.

"Let him be. He just a little tired. That's all."

"You sure?" Mama asked, her eyes still cloaked with doubt.

"I'm sure," Daddy said. "He slept most of the way home. He'll be alright after he rest a while. Ain't no sense in making a fuss."

"Long as you sure," Mama said.

"I'm sure," Daddy said again. "Just let him be . . . He done got old and need to take his rest, that's all."

I looked at Daddy and before I knew it, I heard myself calling his name.

"Daddy," I said.

"Yeah, son." He looked at me, then waited.

"How old is Grandpa Luke?" I asked.

I saw Daddy pause, then look up toward the ceiling.

"Well, let's see," he said, then paused again. "Mama was born in twenty-four . . . Papa four years older than her . . . So, he'll be eighty come January."

"Didn't realize he was making eighty," Mama said.

"Well he is."

I saw Mama look at Daddy.

"Ought to do something special for him. It's a blessing to live that long."

Daddy shook his head.

"He wouldn't want you to make no fuss."

"Wouldn't be no fuss," Mama said. "Just thought we could have a few of his friends over and eat a little cake and ice cream. Just something to show him how much we love him."

"Papa know we love him," Daddy said. "Besides, most of his friends done passed on. Can't be no more than one or two of 'em left."

In the other room, we heard the loud, exaggerated sound of Grandpa Luke snoring.

"Told you he was tired," Daddy said.

Mama frowned.

"He didn't try to help you unload that truck, did he?"

"Naw, but he might as well."

Mama squinted. "What you mean by that?"

"Spent just as much energy fooling 'round with that old camera."

"Snapping pictures?" Mama said. Hers was more of a question than a statement.

"Like they was going out of style," Daddy said. "Would of been home long time ago if I didn't have to drive all over Eudora so he could take pictures of the strangest things. You know that man made me stop the truck so he could take a picture of a railroad track."

"Hope you was patient with him," Mama said. " 'Cause, Nathaniel, I swear sometimes look like you the most impatient man on Gawd's green earth."

"I didn't bother him," Daddy said. "Just thought it was funny. What in the world he gon' do with a picture of a railroad track?"

"Well if that's his pleasure."

"I didn't bother him," Daddy said again.

"Must be missing Mama Lu."

"I imagine so," Daddy said.

I saw Mama look at Daddy, then shake her head.

"Sometimes I feel so sorry for him."

"Don't 'spect feeling sorry for him gon' do much good."

"Might not," Mama said, "but that's how I feel. And I guess sometimes I just wish I knew what to tell 'im."

She paused, but Daddy didn't answer. I looked at her. She had been looking at Daddy but now she was staring off into space.

"I can always tell when he thinking about her," she said.

Daddy had been gazing down at the floor. Now he raised his eyes and looked directly at Mama.

"How?" he asked.

Mama paused before answering. She was still staring off into space.

"First thing he do is go to snapping pictures. Then he steal off to hisself."

"Hunh," Daddy said contemplatively. Then he was quiet.

Mama paused, then shook her head again.

"Must of been a terrible thing. Her getting up every day and not remembering nothing or nobody. And him watching the whole thing and not being able to do nothing about it. I just can't imagine it. Can't imagine it at all."

"Just one of them things," Daddy said.

"One of them terrible things," Mama corrected him.

"Terrible or not," Daddy said, "we all got to deal with it one way or the other. And I guess them pictures is Daddy's way. Deep down, I reckon he figure if he wake up one morning, and his mind gone, them pictures'll help him remember who he is and where he come from."

"Must be a scary thing," Mama said. "Living with that every day."

"Grandpa Luke knows that we're here for him," I said. "I'm sure that counts for something."

"Count for a lot," Daddy said. "It do him all the good in the world to be around family—family count for everything."

When he said that, I felt Mama's eyes on me, but I didn't look. I wouldn't look. Daddy paused for a moment. Then resumed. "Just appreciate the way you and your mama done made him feel at home since he been here with us."

"Feel at home," Mama said. "He is at home."

Daddy smiled, then it was quiet again. I saw Mama rise. The pot was still on the stove. I saw her looking at it.

"Ready for your coffee?"

Daddy looked at the pot, then at her.

"Not tonight," he said. "I'm too tired. Just want to take a bath and go to bed."

"Ain't you gon' eat?" she asked. "Your supper in the oven. Some sweet rolls over yonder cooling in the window."

"Too tired to eat," he said. "Been a long day."

"Need to eat something," Mama said. "Can't go to bed on a empty stomach."

"Just want to soak in a hot bath," Daddy said, "Then go to bed."

"After you soak, you need to eat something," she said again. "Can't work all day then go to bed without eating." I saw her take a couple of sweet rolls from the tin and place them on a saucer. Then I saw her turn and look at Daddy. And I saw Daddy stoically standing before her. He had made his feelings known, and for him the conversation was over and her subsequent actions, however well intended, were futile. He stood, silently gazing upon the sweet rolls. And in that instance the full force of fatigue fell upon him and his weary mind drifted; his heavy head began to tilt forward. Mama called to him softly.

"Nathaniel."

He lifted his eyes.

"Why don't you go on in yonder and lie down whilst I run your water."

Daddy nodded. Yes, he was exhausted—too exhausted to answer. He pushed away from the counter, then turned toward the door.

"I'm gon' put these sweet rolls in the room in case you change your mind."

"Suit yourself," Daddy said. He turned to leave again, then paused and looked back at me. "Good night, son."

"Good night, Daddy," I said. "See you in the morning."

They left the kitchen, and I went to my room and once inside, I closed the door and switched off the light, then stretched out lengthways upon the bed. In the stillness, I heard Mama fill the tub; then I heard her go back into the bedroom. I heard Daddy's voice rise above the silence.

"What you and Maurice was talking about when I come in?"

I heard feet shuffling about, and I figured Mama was gathering Daddy's things before he headed into the bathroom to take his bath.

"That gal," I heard Mama say.

It was quiet again and I knew Mama was waiting for Daddy to say something, but when he did not she spoke again.

"You know that boy had that gal in this house while we was gone?"

"Well, he at that age," I heard Daddy say.

"That's all you got to say?"

"All there is to say . . . Maurice a grown man. We done raised him once. We can't raise him no more."

"Just don't know what he see in her."

"Ain't for you to know," Daddy said. "That boy got to find his own way. And part of finding his own way is making his own choices."

"Just hate to sit by and let him throw his life away."

"Well, it's his life," Daddy said. "You just gon' have to let him live it."

"Told me him and her still talking 'bout marrying."

"That shouldn't surprise you none. They been talking about marrying since high school."

"Well, I don't like it. And I don't think I'd be much of a mother if I sat by and let him make the same mistake we made."

"And what mistake was that?"

"Slipping off and getting married."

"So our marriage was a mistake?" Daddy asked.

"No," Mama said. "Getting married wasn't a mistake. The mistake was getting married too soon. We should have waited. We should have got prepared for life. That boy gon' need his education, and if he get tied up with that gal, it will never happen."

"A man'll be alright . . . long as he'll work."

"Mo' to it than that, Nathaniel."

"We did alright," Daddy said.

"Could've done better," Mama said, "if we'd had got a education."

"Well, it's his life and his choice. You best accept that."

"I can't . . . and I won't."

Chapter Five

The talking ceased and through the stillness I could hear the occasional sound of water splashing in the bathroom next door, and from the living room, I could hear the soft steady hum of Mama's smooth soprano voice rising delicately above the quietness that was the night. And as she hummed, I listened intently, trying to place the tune, but try as I might, I could not for she was humming a song of which I was not familiar. It was soft and soothing, and though I could not see her, I assumed that she had returned to the living room to resume her task of mending Daddy's pants. And as I lay prone across the bed listening to her, I only wished that she would accept that which I had told her, for if she did not, I would have no other recourse but to choose. And if I chose, I would choose Omenita.

Outside, a strong breeze had risen, and on the closed window shades I could see the faint outline of shadows cast from dangling limbs dancing wildly under the glare of the full, bright moon. I closed my eyes, summoning sleep but before my active mind could surrender to a somber state of unconsciousness, I heard upon the front door the faint sound of a soft, steady knock, which quickly gave way to the gentle ring of a woman's voice.

"Audrey . . . you home?"

There was a moment of silence. Then Mama called back to her. "Cora Lee . . . is that you?"

In the darkness of the room, I turned over on my side and raised up to my elbow, listening. All was quiet save for the sound of Mama's feet shuffling across the floor. Suddenly, I heard the screen door creak open. Then I heard my mama's voice again.

"Cora! What you doing out here this time of night?"

There was a brief pause and it sounded like Miss Cora was trying to catch her breath. And I figured she was good and tired because of all the weight she was carrying. And by the way she was breathing I figured she must have walked to our house at a pretty fast gait because she sounded tired, real tired.

"It's Miss Hattie," I heard her say. Then her voice trailed off and I heard her breathing again.

"Miss Hattie!" I heard my mother say. "What about Miss Hattie?"

I swung my feet to the floor and stood. Mama cooked and cleaned for Miss Hattie. She had done so for years.

"Say she tried to call you," Miss Cora said, still panting heavily.

"Telephone out," Mama explained. "Been out better part of a week now."

"Well, when she couldn't get you she called me," Miss Cora said, still breathing hard. "Told me to give you a message quick as I could."

"She ain't sick is she, Cora?"

"Naw. Just going on and on 'bout being in a fix."

I eased forward and leaned against my bedroom door. From where I stood I could see the living room clock. It was almost nine. Down the hall, I heard Daddy snoring. He had finished his bath and he was sleeping sound and snoring the way a man snores when he's dead tired.

"What kind of fix?" Mama asked. Her voice seemed to relax a little.

"Something about her daughter."

"Danielle!" I heard Mama say.

"Un-hunh," Miss Cora said, then paused and let out a deep sigh. "Lord Jesus, I ain't young as I use to be. Look like I can't go from here to there 'thout giving out."

"You want to come in and sit down," Mama said. I heard the

hinges on the door squeak, and I knew she had opened the door wider.

"Naw," Miss Cora declined. "I'll be alright . . . soon as I catch my breath."

"Can I get you a drink of water or something?" Mama asked.

"Naw," Miss Cora said, then paused. "Just give me a minute."

There was a brief silence, then I heard Mama's voice again. "Why Miss Hattie send you over here this time of night when she know I got to be at her house first thing in the morning for work?"

I heard Miss Cora struggling with her breathing.

"Told me to tell you don't come to work in the morning."

"Don't come!" Mama said. "Why not?"

"Say she want you to do her a favor."

"What kind of favor?"

"Say she want you to pick Danielle from the airport."

"Miss Hattie know I don't drive," Mama said.

"She wanted to know if Maurice made it in."

I heard my name, and I moved farther out into the hall next to the door leading into the living room. I poked my head through and looked. Mama's back was turned toward me, and though I could not see her face, I could see that she was standing on the porch with the screen door cracked opened, and Miss Cora was standing on the top step. I could not see Miss Cora clearly. Just the side of her head.

"Made it in this morning," Mama said. "Why?"

"Well, she say maybe he can drive you to the airport to pick Danielle up."

"Thought Mr. John was supposed to pick her up," Mama said. "Least that's the way I understood it 'fo I left there this evening."

"He was, but Miss Hattie say he called little while ago and said he was stuck in Chicago. . . . Something come up and he won't be able to get home 'til sometime tomorrow night. . . . Don't want her sitting at the airport or trying to catch a cab all the way from Monroe."

"Well, I can't talk for Maurice," I heard Mama say. "Besides Nathaniel got to have his truck to git back and forth to work."

"She say for you to send Maurice over her house."

"For what?" Mama asked.

"She say he can get they car and y'all can go in it."

It was quiet again and I knew Mama was thinking.

"What time Danielle due in?" she asked, and I could tell from her tone that she was trying to figure things out.

"Little bit before six," I believe she said.

"In the morning?" Mama asked.

"That's the way I understood it."

"Well, that ain't gon' do," Mama said. "Nathaniel expecting Maurice to go to work with him in the morning."

Mama said that, and it was quiet again.

"Maybe Nathaniel let him come in a little late," Miss Cora said, "seeing how he the head man down there in the kitchen."

"I don't know," Mama said.

"Why don't you ask him," Cora said. "I can wait."

"Hate to wake him up," she said.

"He gone to bed already?"

"Was taking a bath, but I 'spect he in the bed by now."

"Well, you got to tell Miss Hattie something."

"Aw right," she said. She turned to leave, then stopped and turned back. "Sure you don't want to come in?"

"No, thank you," Cora said. "I'll wait out here."

"Aw right," Mama said again. "Oughtn't be but a minute."

Mama started back toward the bedroom, but she made it as far as the hallway. I stepped from the shadows.

"He's sleep." I said.

"Well, I guess I'm gon' have to wake 'im up."

"Ain't no need in bothering him," I said. "Crowd ought to be light . . . 'til after lunch. We ought to be back by then."

"Well," Mama hesitated. "I don't know."

"I'm sure it won't be a problem," I said again. "There's no sense in bothering Daddy. I'm sure it's alright."

I saw her look at the closed bedroom door, then at me.

"Well, if you think it'll be aw right."

"It will," I said.

"Aw right," she said. And though she was giving in, I could tell she was still a little uneasy with the decision. "Let me go tell Cora."

She turned to leave and I went back inside my bedroom.

"Tell Miss Hattie we'll be there first thing in the morning," I heard her say.

"I'll tell her right now," Miss Cora said.

"Be careful on them old steps," I heard Mama say.

"I will," Miss Cora told her.

I heard the door shut and I heard Miss Cora's feet on the steps. Then I heard Mama in the hall walking toward the kitchen.

Chapter Six

It was a quarter 'til five when we exited the house and headed toward Daddy's old pickup truck. It had been my intent to walk to Miss Hattie's house (it was just a little over two miles) to get the car, then pick Mama up on the way out, but Daddy wouldn't hear of it. Just kept saying it didn't make any sense for me to walk when we could catch a ride with him. And as soon as we had stepped outside, I was glad he had made the offer. Overnight, the temperature had dropped and the unseasonably warm climate had given way. And not only was I thankful for the ride but I was also glad that I had brought my heavy clothes home with me from school. Up until this point the weather had been mild, but now it was cold. Freezing cold.

When we reached the truck, Daddy climbed behind the wheel, and I followed Mama to the passenger side, and when she was ready, I opened the door and helped her in. She slid next to Daddy, then I climbed in next to her and hurriedly closed the door. It was cold in the truck. Real cold. I saw Mama look at Daddy.

"Now, Nathaniel if this gon' throw you off, me and Maurice can walk."

"Ain't no sense in that," Daddy said. "Besides, it's too cold to walk."

"Well, me and Maurice both bundled up pretty good," she said. "I imagine we can manage if we have to. Just don't want you to be late."

She was wearing her long, gray coat and her heavy winter shoes. I was wearing my tan jacket that stopped just below my waist.

"I got time," Daddy said.

I saw Daddy put the key in the ignition. I heard the old engine turn over slow a couple of times before it finally started. It was cold inside the truck and I saw Daddy release the steering wheel and blow on his hands, then I saw him step on the gas. I heard the engine roar, then fall, then roar again. I buried my hands in my pockets, then leaned forward, shivering. I saw Daddy looking at me.

"Soon as the engine warm up a little, I'll turn on the heater."

I nodded, then dug my hands deep in my pockets. It was quiet a moment, and I saw Mama slide a little closer to Daddy. I don't think it was conscious. Just think she was reacting to the cold.

"You sure you can make out without Maurice for a little while?" she asked.

I saw Daddy nod, then turn on the wipers. Overnight, there had been a light freeze and a thin sheet of ice had formed on the windshield.

"We'll make out just fine," he said.

"Hate to leave you shorthanded."

"We'll be fine," Daddy said again.

"Well, I know Miss Hattie appreciate it."

"Un-hunh," Daddy said. He depressed the accelerator again. The engine roared.

"Nice of her to give me a whole day's pay for a couple hours work," Mama said. "She ain't had to do that."

"This ain't about you," Daddy said. Out of the corner of my eye, I saw him pull the truck into gear and peer back over his shoulder. "This about Maurice."

I had been leaning forward looking down toward the floor but when I heard my name I leaned back and turned toward Daddy.

"Me!" I said.

"Yeah," Daddy said. "You!"

I continued to look at Daddy, but he was no longer looking at me. I watched him back the truck out into the street. Then, I heard the gears grind, and I felt the truck lurch forward.

"What this got to do with me?" I asked.

"Miss Hattie just making sure she teach you a lesson she figure you ain't learned in school, that's all," Daddy said.

"A lesson!" I said.

"That's right," he said. "A lesson."

I looked at him, confused.

"What lesson?"

He didn't answer me immediately. Instead, he stared at the highway for a moment like he was thinking about something. Or like I was supposed to figure it out. And when I didn't he decided to tell me.

"Your place," he said.

Suddenly, I felt the seat move.

"That ain' true," Mama said, turning toward Daddy. "And Nathaniel, you ought to be shame of yourself for saying such a thang."

"It is true," Daddy said. "And you the one ought to be shame."

I saw Daddy lean forward and turn on the heater. I heard the fan rattle, then I felt the warm air from the vents on my cold, throbbing fingers.

"I don't understand," I said, still confused.

"Ain't nothing to understand," Daddy said. "Miss Hattie just trying to teach you that no matter how much education you get, you still ain't fit for nothing but to run white folks' errands."

"Nathaniel!" Mama said. "Miss Hattie ain't like that and you know it. . . . And for the life of me, I can't understand why you'd go and say such a mean, hateful thing."

" 'Cause it's the truth," Daddy said.

"It ain't the truth," Mama snapped, "and you know it."

"I don't know no such thing," Daddy said.

"Miss Hattie been good to us," Mama said. "Her and Mr. John both. And you ain't got no cause to sit here and drag her name through the mud like that, no cause at all. She been good to us."

I saw Mama looking at Daddy. But he wasn't looking at her; he was looking straight ahead.

"When you ever knowed Miss Hattie to mistreat anybody?" Mama asked him.

Daddy didn't answer.

"I tell you when," Mama answered for him. "Never, that's when. Miss Hattie asked Maurice to go on account I don't drive. And that's the only reason."

"Woman, this ain't about you," Daddy said again.

"I done known Miss Hattie and Mr. John my whole life," Mama said. "And they good people. . . . They good people through and through."

"Never said they wasn't, just said this ain't 'bout you."

"If you didn't want Maurice to go," Mama said, "why didn't you say so?"

"Maurice a grown man," Daddy said. "He do as he please. He got to find his own way. Got to make up his own mind."

"It's no big deal to me," I said. "I don't mind going."

"Nathaniel, you wrong about Miss Hattie," Mama said. "Dead wrong."

"Been wrong 'bout lots of things in my life," Daddy said, "but I don't figure this one of 'em."

"Well it is," Mama said. "You wrong, I tell you. Wrong as wrong can be."

"It's no big deal," I said again.

Then all was quiet save for the sound of the heater blowing warm air through the vent. I had said it, but I was sure they were not listening to me. Both had retreated within themselves. Daddy clutching the steering wheel looking far up the road and Mama sitting statuelike between the two of us, her hands folded across her pocketbook, her eyes staring straight ahead. I looked at them for a minute then turned my head. It was early yet, and though there were but a few people out and about; inside their homes they were beginning to stir. Through the darkness, I could see the occasional glow of a burning light illuminating a distant window or a front door or a back porch, and I knew that those were the domiciles of people like my father who had to be up and about long before the rest of the world had begun to stir.

I was staring at the house when I felt the truck slow. I turned my head back toward the windshield and looked. We had reached the intersection at Main Street. Daddy paused a minute to let a car pass, then turned right and headed out of town. A block or two before Main Street, Daddy turned right at what had once been the Ford dealership. The building was still there—boarded up and abandoned—but the business was not. Like so many others, it had gone under when the plant closed and the locals who had worked there moved away in search of a place that could offer them what Brownsville no longer could: employment. And after they had gone, what was left for a town was mostly a collection of poor and old people, mixed in with a few wealthy white folks like Miss Hattie and Mr. John who had amassed their wealth during more prosperous times. Back then, Mr. John had been a lawyer; he was now a judge. And Miss Hattie, his wife, had simply married well.

I had rarely ventured into this section of town. Very few blacks had unless like my mother, they did so to cook or clean, or attend to some other folks' children. For this section was the domain of that elite class of whites who had been born into old money and had come of age wedded to old ways. No, I rarely came unless there was some unusual occasion in which there was a task Mama had to perform that was beyond her—something too heavy for her to lift or too big for her to move. Then and only then, did I come.

Miss Hattie's house was located toward the end of the street. It was a large plantation-style house with four impressive pillars and a beautiful second-story balcony. It wasn't exactly on the street, rather it set well off the street on a moderate side lot and was partially hidden by several large trees. Oak, I believe. And if I wasn't mistaken, I heard at one time or another while I was still living in Brownsville that those trees were well over one hundred years old and had been planted there by Mr. John's father, the late Theodore Shaw.

Just as we approached the house, I could see the long driveway leading up to the carport, but Daddy didn't turn into the driveway, instead he pulled to the shoulder and stopped. I could tell that Miss Hattie was waiting for us. The porch light was on, and in

the house I could see a second light burning in what I knew was
the parlor.

When I opened the door and stepped out, I felt the ice-cold
wind engulf me. I pulled my hood over my head, covered my
ears, then ran my hands deep into my pockets and when I did I
felt myself involuntarily sucking in cold, dry air through numb,
chattering teeth. And each time I released the air, I saw my breath
flow out, then dissipate into the frigid morning air.

I heard the springs in the seat creak and I saw Mama climb
from the passenger side and ease to the ground. I pulled my
hands from my pockets and reached out to assist her. And when
she was on the ground, I quickly jammed my hands back into my
pockets and followed her up the long sidewalk until we stood
boulderlike before the front door. Mama pushed the button. The
doorbell rang, then from deep inside the house, I heard quick-
ening footsteps, then I saw the curtain move and I saw Miss
Hattie's shifty gray eyes peering out at us.

"Who is it?"

"Miss Hattie," Mama called back to her, "it's me. Audrey."

The chain rattled and the door swung open.

"Land sakes," she said. "Y'all come on in out of this weather."

Mama stepped into the foyer. I followed her.

"Good morning, Miss Hattie," I heard Mama say.

I heard her because I was not looking. My shoulders had been
hunched against the cold, but now that we were inside the warm
house my shoulders relaxed, and I removed my hands from my
pockets and began rubbing them together. I had been rubbing
them together when Mama spoke

"Morning, Audrey," I heard Miss Hattie respond.

And when she did I looked at her. She was a petite lady whom I
guess was only a few years older than my mother. She stood about
five foot three or five foot four and weighed somewhere around a
hundred pounds. She had dark, straight hair; an oval face; and
dark brown eyes. And though it was early, she was already
dressed. She wore a beige dress and a pair of ruby red slippers.

"Miss Hattie," Mama called to her again, "you remember Maurice?"

Mama stepped aside and I felt Miss Hattie studying me.

"Well I do declare," she said. "If you didn't grow up to be a handsome one."

"Morning, Miss Hattie," I said.

She smiled and looked at Mama, then back at me.

"And polite too."

I forced a faint smile, then looked away.

"Henry got a fire going in the parlor," I heard Miss Hattie say. Henry was the handyman. He had been with the Davenports for years. "Y'all come on around to the fire and warm up." I turned toward the parlor, but before I had a chance to move, the sound of Mama's voice stopped me.

"No, thank you, Miss Hattie," she said. "Like to be at the airport when Miss Danielle step off the plane, if I can. It's almost five now. If we gon' get there in time we best be on our way."

I saw Miss Hattie look at her watch.

"Didn't know it was so late," she said.

"Yes, ma'am," Mama said again. "We best be going . . . hate to have Miss Danielle waiting."

I saw Miss Hattie look at her watch again, then at Mama.

"Well, let me get the keys," she said, "and you can be on your way."

I watched her go down the hall and turn into the parlor. Though I had not been in there in years, I could remember the room well. It was a quaint space, not too large and not too small. There were hardwood floors and oriental rugs and a large fireplace surrounded by a small sofa and two antique chairs. There were also a couple of lamps and a few pieces of art—and only a few—Mr. John was an outdoorsman and on the wall were mostly the heads of large exotic animals that bore testimony to that fact. From where I stood, I could hear Miss Hattie moving about in the parlor, and when she returned she was carrying the keys in one hand and a small white envelope in the other.

"Tank should be full," she said, "but here's a little something in case you have any trouble . . . although I don't expect you will." She handed the keys and the envelope to Mama.

"Yes, ma'am," Mama said.

"Insurance and registration papers ought to be in the glove box."

"Yes, ma'am," Mama said again.

Then Miss Hattie turned to me.

"I hope you're a careful driver."

And after she had said it, she looked at me as if to let me know that she was entrusting me with something valuable. No, something precious.

"Yes, ma'am," I said. "I am."

She looked at me like she didn't know whether to believe me.

"You had much experience?" she asked, and when she did she never took her eyes off me, and the fact that she didn't made me uncomfortable.

"Yes, ma'am," I said. "Been driving since I was thirteen."

"Thirteen!" she said.

"Not on the highway," I said. "On Mr. Levi's farm."

"But you do have highway experience?"

"Yes, ma'am," I said. "Plenty."

"No tickets or anything like that?" she asked.

"No, ma'am." I said.

I looked at her, and she was still watching me, and I felt myself becoming a little nervous. I wanted to glance away, but I did not. She looked at me a little longer, then turned back toward Mama.

"Now Audrey, there's no need to hurry."

"Yes, ma'am, Miss Hattie," Mama said.

"If you get there a little late, Danielle knows to wait for you in the baggage area. Okay?"

"Yes, ma'am," Mama said again.

We turned to leave, but Miss Hattie stopped us again.

"One more thing," she said.

Mama stopped and turned back toward her. "Yes, Miss Hattie," she said.

"There may be a little ice on the road between here and Monroe, so do be careful." She was looking at Mama as she spoke, but I knew she was talking to me.

"We'll be careful, Miss Hattie," Mama said. She turned back toward the front door to leave, but before she could, Miss Hattie stopped her.

"Be closer to go out through the kitchen," she said. "The car is still in the garage. I had Henry warm it up a little while ago."

Mama and I followed Miss Hattie through the large, spacious kitchen, and when she reached the rear door, she pulled it open, then stepped aside. And no sooner had she opened the door that I once again felt the cold rush of air whipping through my clothes, chilling my bones. I pulled my coat tight and buried my hands in pockets still warm from our brief sojourn in the house and made my way toward the car. And as I walked, I looked it over. It was a 2002 Lincoln Town Car. Dark, sleek, top of the line. I turned and looked. Miss Hattie was still watching me. Maybe this was why she was so uptight. She was uneasy entrusting such an expensive vehicle to someone like me. She knew she could trust Mama, but of me she could not be sure.

I went around and opened the door for Mama. She handed me the keys and the envelope, then gathered the hem of her dress in one hand and the back of the seat with the other, then slide inside. When she was settled, I handed her the envelope and shut the door, then stepped back to make my way to the driver's side. And when I stepped back, I glanced toward the kitchen door. Miss Hattie was still watching and at that moment, I wondered if I had slammed the door too hard. Feeling clumsy and ill at ease, I walked stiff-legged to the door, opened it, and gently slid under the wheel, aware of Miss Hattie's menacing stare. I closed the door and looked up. Yes, she was still watching. With nervous hands, I grabbed the seat belt and pulled it across my shoulder. I stole a quick glance. She was still watching. I inserted the metal clamp into the tab. It clicked. I paused, then looked up at Mama.

"Wish she would quit staring at me," I said.

"Mind your manners," Mama said. "You hear?"

"Yes, ma'am," I said and inserted the key into the ignition, then switched it on. I heard the low, steady hum of the well-tuned machine. I glanced up again. She was still watching. And like a nervous kid taking a driver's test, I put the car into gear and eased off the brake, ever mindful of the fact that I was clutching the wheel too tight, and that my shoulders were too stiff, and my back was too straight. I pulled out of the drive and into the street. And in the rearview mirror I could see the garage door slowly coming down. At the stop sign I made a left onto Highway 17, traveled two blocks and made a right onto Main Street. I cleared one signal light then the other, and when I was well outside of town, I leaned back into the seat and stared headlong through the windshield. I adjusted the radio. Then, I heard the sound of heavy breathing. I looked to my right. Mama was sound asleep.

Chapter Seven

It was 5:00 A.M. when I drove across the railroad tracks into the small village of Mer Rouge. And when I did, I did not slow enough, and the wheels of the car elevated slightly, then landed with a thud on the opposite side. Instantly, I heard Mama's sleeping body bouncing on the seat next to me. I stole a quick glance at her out of the corner of my eye and I saw her head tilt forward, then her eyes flew open.

"Be careful," she said.

She looked around to see where we were, then she looked at me hard and menacingly to let me know that she was not satisfied with the way I was driving.

"Yes, ma'am," I said.

I eased my foot off the accelerator and the car slowed, and as we eased through the center of town, I could feel her eyes on the side of my face and I was sorry that I had awakened her for now she would want to talk and what she would want to discuss would be Omenita. And I did not want to talk and I did not want to be talked to. I leaned back into the softness of the seat and looked headlong through the windshield. This was not much of a town. It was more like a village. And a small village at that. There was the one caution light through which we had just passed. And on either side of the street were several nondescript businesses. There was a police station, a post office, a service station, and a small hamburger stand all contained in an area considerably smaller that a city block. At the end of the block was a small residential area of no more than four or five luxurious houses with large beautiful yards with well-manicured lawns. It was twilight and in the distance seemingly well beyond this universe, the large orange sun sat low on the horizon casting off the dawn's early light.

"Look like it's gon' be a pretty day," she said.

"Yes, ma'am," I said.

I glanced at her again, making sure to avoid her eyes. She had been looking out the window, but now that daylight had broken and we could finally see that which heretofore was concealed in darkness, she busied herself scanning the inside of the car. It was a beautiful vehicle. It had a sleek leather interior, large bucket seats, a navigational system, a telephone, a CD player, the works. She saw me looking at the car and she spoke again. "This some automobile, hunh."

She waited for me to respond, but I kept quiet. I did not want to talk and I did not want to be talked to. I continued to stare at the road. And when she realized that I was not going to speak, she continued. "When I was your age black folks couldn't dream. Oh, we could pray and we could hope that things would get a little better, but we couldn't dream."

She paused again and I could feel her eyes on me. And I sensed she was looking at me, but she was not seeing me. She was seeing her past.

"No," I heard her began again. Her voice was low, distant. "It ain't like it was when I was coming up. . . . Back then living was hard. Wasn't no whole lot of choices. Folks did good just to get by." She paused and looked out the window. "I can remember on days like this, it'd be so cold you could hardly stand it, and Mama and Papa would have Brother and me out in the woods picking up wild pecans to sell so we could have winter shoes. Most times we didn't have salt to go in bread. No, it ain't like it was when I was coming up."

She paused again and I glanced at her. She had turned her head and was staring out of the window. I turned my head back toward the road.

"Didn't think things was ever gon' get better for us," she said. "Then one day Mr. Harvey just up and quit farming. Told everybody they was gon' have to find something else to do. That's when Mama and Papa moved to town. Papa found a few odd jobs here and there. And Mama went to work for Miss Lindsey, Miss Hattie's mama. And that's where she worked for the rest of her days. And that's how me and Miss Hattie come to know each other. I was too little to stay at home by myself, so I would go to Miss Lindsey's with Mama. Miss Hattie would be there sometimes. And while Mama worked, me and Miss Hattie would play together. Then later on in life when we was both adults, Miss Hattie married Mr. John and I married your daddy—too early, I might add. But it ain't like I wasn't warned. When Miss Hattie found out about it, she was some upset. And said I ought to go to school and make something out of myself before I got tied down with a husband and a bunch of children. But I was hardheaded and couldn't nobody tell me nothing. So I went on and married. Then you come along. And shortly after that, me and your daddy fell on hard times. So, I went to Miss Hattie, and she give me a job. And I been working for her ever since. And I gotta say she been good to me. And she been good to this family. And I owe her and Mr. John so much. Much more than I can ever pay 'em." She paused a minute, and I saw her looking far up the road. Her mind had drifted and I could tell she was deep in thought. "Don't know if your daddy understand that," she finally said. "Don't know if he ever will."

We reached the small town of Bastrop and drove past the courthouse and as we did, I gazed up at the large, beautiful steeple, high atop the building and suddenly I noticed the hands on the huge white-faced clock. It was a quarter 'til six. And I also noticed that traffic had thickened, and for a minute I was baffled until I remembered that this was a mill town and that the residents were shift workers and right now was shift change. I slowed a bit, following the traffic, and as I neared the paper mill I smelled the foul, pungent odor that was indigenous of the mill and in the distance I saw the huge white clouds of billowing smoke emanating from the tall, far-away towers. Mama stopped talking and I knew she had grown concerned by the increased traffic.

"Reckon we'll make it in time?" she asked me.

"We'll make it," I said.

After I answered, I did not look at her. Instead, I continued to stare ahead. Her southern demeanor had little to do with Papa. I knew that. And I knew that she knew I knew. This was about me and Omenita and the choice I was making. And because this was about Mama challenging my right to choose the course of my own life, I felt myself becoming angry. So angry until I convinced myself that it would be better that I not comment at all. I looked farther up the road at the long line of cars, and as we slowed even more, I could not help but wonder if this was more than work traffic. The road was a little slick. And the weather was less than favorable. Maybe there had been an accident. I looked at my watch again. *We'll make it,* I told myself. *If nothing else happens, we'll make it.*

I was still looking ahead when Mama spoke again.

"Hope you think about what I'm saying before you jump up and do something you gon' regret."

"I have thought about it," I said.

"Then you need to think about it some more."

She paused and waited for me to say something else. But I kept quiet.

"Son, you got choices me and your daddy never had." She paused again, and I could feel her eyes on the side of my face. I tightened my grip on the wheel and continued to stare ahead. "But if you don't make good on the choices you got, then them choices won't mean a thing. Now you need to think about that . . . and you need to think about it good."

She became silent again. And without a clear picture in my mind as to what she was doing, I stole a quick glance at her out of the corner of my eye. I saw her gather her purse in her lap and lean back against the seat. I shifted my eyes back toward the highway. I did not want her to see me looking at her. For now, I was convinced that she was thinking about me and Omenita, and pondering what she needed to do to persuade me to see things her way.

We crept along a minute more until just past the turnoff to the mill; the traffic cleared, and instinctively, I pressed the gas pedal and instantly the car accelerated. Relieved to be moving freely again, I relaxed my grip on the wheel and watched the open road unfold before us as we passed beyond the city limits and onto the final stretch of highway leading into Monroe.

In Monroe, I did not bypass the city as I would have normally. Instead, I turned left just before the overpass into a residential area just west of campus and followed the street leading to the university. Normally, I would have stayed my course, but this was a shortcut, and because we had been unexpectedly delayed in traffic, I now feared that we would be late.

I saw Mama fidgeting, and I knew she was wondering what I was doing. I started to explain, but quickly reconsidered. I did not want to engage her and give her an excuse to start up again. She was quiet, and I wanted it to stay that way.

I saw the back of the campus come into view, and I followed the road past the old library and through the center of campus. And as I eased through the campus, I looked about. There was very little activity. Most of the parking lot was empty, and the only people I saw milling about was a lone officer standing outside the security building and a couple of students walking along the bayou; but other than that it seemed desolate and deserted, which for me was no surprise for like my own school this one was also closed for winter break. I followed the road through the campus and when I was on the opposite end, I turned left onto Desiard Street and followed the highway to Airport Boulevard. I turned right onto Airport Boulevard and when I did, I saw Mama pull down the visor in front of her and begin primping in the small mirror. We were close now, and I saw her checking her hair and her eyes and her lipstick, and when she was satisfied that all was as it should be, she flipped the visor into position and sat back in her seat, clutching her purse on her lap and staring straight ahead.

At the airport, I parked in front of the terminal just across the street. I put some coins in the meter, and we hurried inside out of the cold. And from just beyond the entrance, I could see the terminal in its entirety. To the right were the ticket counters. To the left down a short hall were the restrooms, several telephones, and a small concession area. Straight ahead was the waiting area and just beyond that behind a glass wall and through a security entrance was the boarding area. To the left of the boarding area was another short hallway that stretched past the rental car counter and opened into the baggage claim area. As we stood searching for Danielle, I figured her plane was either late or had already landed. For even though no one was in the lobby, I could distinctly hear the dull, low rumbling sound of chattering people emanating from the baggage claim area. I looked at Mama. She wore an expression of concern.

"Must be in baggage claim," I said. And when I said it, I did not wait for Mama to respond, instead I started toward the area and she followed.

When we got there Danielle was standing next to the conveyor belt. Her back was to us, and I would not have known her from any of the others crowded around the conveyor belt. I had not seen her since we were children and even then I had seen her only once, and from a distance at that. I watched Mama ease next to her and tap her lightly on the shoulder. She turned quickly and I heard Mama call to her in an uncertain voice.

"Danielle?"

There was a brief hesitation, then her eyes widened and the corners of her mouth turned up.

"Mother Audrey!"

She threw her arms about Mama's shoulders and hugged her, and as she did, I observed her. She wore a long coat with fur about the collar. On her hands were a pair of brown leather gloves and on her feet were a pair of stylish leather boots that stopped just below her knees. And though the coat partially covered her, I could tell that she was tall and slender with long blond hair. They held each other for a moment or two, then I saw Mama pull away and look at her.

"How was your flight?" she asked, still smiling.

"Long," Danielle said, "but pleasant."

"Haven't been waiting long, I hope."

"No, ma'am," Danielle said. "As a matter of fact we just walked into the building."

Mama looked at me and I knew she wanted me to come closer. I had been standing back, but now I stepped forward.

"This is my son, Maurice," she said. "Maurice, this is Danielle."

She smiled, removed her glove, and extended her hand. I gently took it into my own and to my surprise her hand, like mine, was cold.

"Pleased to meet you," she said.

"Likewise," I said. And no sooner had the words passed through my lips, a horn blared and a light flashed.

"Oh, thank God," she said, turning back toward the conveyor belt. "Our luggage is here."

She moved closer to the conveyor belt and Mama moved next to her. I hung back just behind them.

"Hope they made it," I heard her say.

I saw a couple of bags dart through the chute and fall onto the conveyor belt and make their way past us.

"Got many bags?" I heard Mama ask.

"Just two," she said. "A trunk and a small suitcase."

I looked at the conveyor belt again. A couple of cardboard boxes passed. I watched them circle until a tall stranger wearing a large cowboy hat lifted them off and set them on the floor next to him. I looked at Danielle again. Her cheeks and nose were still red from the cold. I was still looking at her when Mama spoke again.

"Just point 'em out when they come 'round," she said. "Maurice'll get 'em off for you."

I moved close to the belt, and Danielle looked at me and smiled. We watched a few more pieces pass, then I saw a large gray trunk dart through.

"That's it," she said.

When it was within reach, I grabbed the handle and lifted it off the belt. It was heavier than I expected and before I realized it, I grunted and let it fall hard to the floor.

"Oh," she said. "Are you alright?"

I felt her hand on the back of mine. I nodded, then looked away, embarrassed.

"I'm sorry," she said. "I should have warned you. It's quite heavy."

I saw Mama looking at the trunk, concerned. And I knew she was wondering if I had broken something when I dropped it. She looked at me with cold, stern eyes to let me know that she expected me to be more careful. A few bags passed before Danielle identified the other one belonging to her. And when she did, I retrieved it and placed it on a cart along with the trunk. We then made our way out to the car, and I popped the trunk to load the luggage. Suddenly, I heard Danielle shivering. I looked up. Her body was stiff against the cold and her arms were folded across her chest. I saw Mama looking at me, agitated.

"Oh, I'm sorry," I said. "Let me get the door for you."

I started around the car but Mama stopped me.

"We'll sit in the back," Mama said. "That way, we can visit."

I quickly opened the back door and Danielle slid in first, then Mama slid in next to her. And when they were out of the cold, I loaded the luggage into the trunk and climbed behind the wheel. And as I buckled my seat belt I saw Danielle's reflection in the rearview mirror. Our eyes met, and she smiled.

"Thanks for picking me up," she said. "I knew Father wasn't going to make it, but I didn't know I was going to have my own personal chauffeur."

I smiled, but did not speak. Inside, I felt my blood run hot. No, I wanted to say. I ain't your damn chauffeur. But because I couldn't, I chose to say nothing. I paused for a few minutes to collect myself, then I started the car and pulled out into the street. As I drove, I looked toward the highway. The hour had grown late and the traffic leading from the airport had stiffened but was still relatively light. I looked at my watch. It was six-thirty and I could not help but wonder if Daddy was getting along alright at the diner and if I might not make it back in time to help him with the breakfast dishes.

I turned onto the highway. Behind me I heard Mama and Danielle talking, about what I could not say. I was not listening to them. I was watching the road. I was thinking about Daddy. I was thinking about Omenita. On the way back, I did not cut through the campus; instead, I bypassed it and connected with the main highway leading back to Brownsville. We were well on our way, and I had settled in comfortably behind the wheel when I heard Danielle's soft, jovial voice call to me from the back of the car.

"So Maurice," she said, "tell me about yourself."

I looked at her reflection in the rearview mirror. She had slid toward the center of the seat and was leaning forward, looking directly at me.

"Nothing to tell," I said.

"Maurice!" I heard Mama call my name. I did not look back, but I could tell from her tone that she was not happy with the manner in which I had answered. I am sure that she thought my response had sounded smart, too smart.

"Just going to school," I said.

"May I ask where?" Danielle asked me.

"LSU," I said.

"Really?"

"Really," I said.

"He graduates in May," I heard Mama say. And when she said it, I could hear the pride in her voice. Traffic slowed and I pulled into the fast lane and passed the car in front of me, then changed lanes again. I looked in the mirror. Danielle's soft blue eyes were looking at me.

"Married?"

"Not yet," I said, "but working on it."

"Well, I tell you," she said, "you'll be a fine catch for some lucky woman. As a matter of fact, I have a couple of black girlfriends back East who would love to meet you . . . you interested?"

"He ain't got no time for such talk, missy," I heard Mama say. "He still got things to do yet."

Danielle chuckled. Mama became quiet and I stared at the road.

"Tell her 'bout your plans," Mama said.

I sighed softly to myself but did not speak.

"Go on, son," she said again. "Tell her."

"Might be too personal, Mother Audrey," Danielle said.

"Aw, ain't nothing like that."

"I was accepted to law school," I said.

"Law school."

"Yes," I said again. "Law school."

"Congratulations," she said. "That's fantastic."

"Thank you," I said. I looked at the road and wished I could will the miles passed. I looked in the mirror again. Danielle had turned toward Mama.

"Mother Audrey, I know you must be so proud until you don't know what to do," Danielle said. "Have you told Mother?"

"Hadn't told nobody," she said. "Except Nathaniel and Papa Luke."

"When she finds out she'll just die."

There was silence.

"What kind of law would you like to practice?"

"I don't know for sure," I said. "Criminal, perhaps."

"You want to be a trial lawyer?"

"Maybe," I said.

"You should speak to Father."

"I wouldn't want to bother him," I said.

"It wouldn't be a bother. In fact, I'm sure he would enjoy it . . . Tell him, Mother Audrey."

"Might not be a bad idea," Mama said. "Never hurt to talk to somebody who already been where you trying to go."

"That settles it," Danielle said. "We'll talk to Father. Boy, won't he be surprised?"

Chapter Eight

I drove on, and as I did, my mind was blank, and my eyes were unfocused, and I was fully caught off guard when I regained awareness and saw that we were crossing the city limits into Brownsville. And instantly I realized that this was crazy, for I neither knew when Danielle had ceased talking nor when or how I had traversed the vast terrain stretching between Monroe and home.

And in the mirror, I could see Danielle, and she was leaning comfortably against the seat, and Mama was next to her, and Mama's head was tilted back, and her arms were folded across her pocketbook and her mouth was open and her eyes were closed. And as the road unwound before us, I was glad that it was quiet, for in the solitude of the moment there was for me a brief respite from the haggard turmoil that had depleted my spirit and left me feeling drained. And in the distance, I could see the light from the sun illuminating the town and I could see the rows of houses lining each side of the highway and I could see the deep curve approaching fast, signaling our impending entrance into downtown proper.

And now that we were close, I saw Danielle lean forward and begin to fidget with the contents in her purse. And I saw her remove a brush and begin brushing her hair and I saw her check her lipstick in a tiny mirror. And her movements awakened Mama, and I saw Mama's head slowly tilt forward and I saw her eyes open and I saw her look about unknowingly, trying to get her bearings. And I refocused my attention on the highway. For now that we were back, I had planned to drop Mama off first, then take Danielle home, then walk back to work. And I shared my plan with Danielle and to my surprise, she vehemently voiced her opposition saying that it was nonsensical for me to lose more time from work driving them home when she was perfectly capable of taking care of that herself. And I did not argue with her for my mind was neither on her nor work. But it was squarely on Omenita and the dreaded conversation that stood ominously before us like some unknown phantom lurking silently in the deep, dark stillness of the night.

In Brownsville, Danielle motioned me over, and I pulled off the road into the parking lot behind the diner and stopped. And I unbuckled my seat belt and reached for the door and just as I was about to open it, I heard Danielle call to me from the backseat. And she called to me not in the tone of a stranger, but in the way that old friends use when calling each other. And it surprised me, and I hesitated, then looked back at her.

"Thank you," she said. There was in her eyes a soft, gentle glow and there was upon her face a warm, pleasant smile.

"You're welcome," I said.

I cracked the door open and she spoke again.

"Hope this wasn't too much of an inconvenience."

I looked at her and smiled.

"It wasn't," I said.

Through the rearview mirror I saw her bend low and retrieve her purse from the floor, then snap it open.

"I'd like to pay you for your trouble," she said.

But before I could answer her I heard Mama chime in from the backseat. "I won't hear of such a thing," she said. "I won't hear of it at all."

I saw Danielle release her grip on the purse and lean against the seat. And I saw her look at Mama with soft, pleading eyes.

"But, Mother Audrey," she said, "I would like to do something to show my appreciation. After all, Maurice did go out of his way . . . and besides, he's been so nice. Please," she said. "Let me do something."

"No need for that," I said, sliding out of the car. "It wasn't any trouble . . . It wasn't any trouble at all."

"Let me take you to lunch," she said.

I bent low and looked at her.

"That's not necessary," I said.

"But I want to," she pleaded.

"Really," I said. "It's alright. You don't owe me a thing."

"It doesn't have to be today," she said. "It could be anytime. Please. Let me do this for you."

I looked at Mama. She nodded and I quickly looked away. I felt the cold wind whip through my pants. And I was tired of the conversation and wanted desperately to get out of the weather.

"Okay," I said. "Lunch it is."

Danielle smiled and leaned back, satisfied.

"Fantastic," she said. And when she said it, I figured that must have been a favorite expression of hers for that was the second time she had used it. "I'm glad that's settled," she said, continuing to smile. "Thank you so much."

"You're welcome," I said.

I opened the door for her and she got out, then climbed behind the wheel. And after she was inside, I closed the door behind her and stepped away. But she did not leave immediately; instead, she rolled down the window and poked her head through.

"Let me know what day is good for you," she said.

"I will," I said.

"Now, don't forget."

"I won't," I said.

She smiled and waved good-bye, and I waved back. And as she pulled out of the parking lot onto the highway, I made my way to the rear entrance of the diner and pulled the door open. Daddy and two other men, Jake and Mr. Reuben, were standing before their stations working. Each of them wore a rubber apron around his waist and a pair of rubber gloves on his hands. Daddy's back was to me and he did not see me come in. I approached him quietly.

"Hi, Daddy." I said.

He turned and looked.

"Hi, son." His hands were in the soapy water. He continued to work as he talked. "Glad you made it back," he said. "Had a big rush this morning. Don't understand it. Must be the holiday crowd."

"Whatever it is," Jake said. "Dishes piling up."

I looked over my shoulder. Jake was standing before a large stainless-steel sink just like the one my father stood before. There was a huge stack of plates piled high on the counter next to him. His hands were submerged in the water. His face was covered with perspiration. I looked at him for a minute, then back at Daddy.

"So, what you want me to do, Daddy?" I asked.

"Apron on the wall there." He nodded toward the far wall. I saw a long rubber apron hanging on a nail. "Gloves under the cabinet. Grab that cart next to the door. And see what you can do with them."

I looked at the cart then back at Daddy.

"Where you want me to work?"

Daddy nodded toward Jake.

"That's Silas's station over yonder," he said. "You can work there."

I grabbed the cart and moved it to the sink next to Jake. And after I had donned my apron and gloves, I began working. It was cold outside but it was burning up inside. Our work area was next to the kitchen, and I could feel the heat from the grill. And I could see Tommy, the short-order cook, through the window in the door that separated the kitchen from our area. He was frying bacon on one side of the grill and scrambling eggs on the other. I had just sunk my hands into the tepid water when Jake spoke to me.

"How's school?" he asked. He smiled and his gold tooth showed.

I opened my mouth to answer, but before I could, the door swung open and a young waiter poked his head through.

"Need more plates out here!" he yelled.

Daddy turned toward us. "Come on, men," he shouted. "Let's get the lead out."

"Clean plates in the corner," Reuben yelled from his station. I glanced at him. He was washing a stack of glasses and a pile of silverware. And like the others, his face was covered with sweat. I saw the waiter grab the cart and hustle through the door. And no sooner had he left than a busboy hurried through with another tray of dirty dishes.

"Where you want 'em, boss?" he asked Daddy.

Daddy nodded toward an empty cart. The boy set the dishes down and turned to leave, but before he could make it out of the kitchen, Jake called to him. "How's the crowd?"

"Still heavy," the boy said.

"What in the hell's going on today?" Jake asked. He looked at me, then at the busboy. "Where all these goddamn people come from?"

"Some kind of training session at the plant," the boy said. "Bunch of big shots from the corporate office. Must not of ate 'fo they come down here," the boy said. "They ordering flapjacks like it ain't no tomorrow."

"Let's go, men," Daddy said. "Let's hussle. They gon' need more plates."

Suddenly the door swung open. The busboy had returned.

"Need mo' glasses."

"Goddammit, boy," Jake yelled again. "Hold your horses. They coming."

"Leave 'im alone, Jake," Daddy said. "He just doing his job."

"Well damn, boss man," Jake said. "We moving fast as we can."

I saw Reuben push a cart of glasses to the center of the floor. The busboy grabbed them and disappeared through the door. The door swung in, then out. I lowered my hands back into the soapy water; so did Jake.

"You say school alright, hunh?" he asked me.

"Yes, sir," I said.

I quickly removed a plate and held it under the steady stream of water falling from the faucet then placed it on the tray next to me.

"No complaints?" he asked.

"No complaints," I said.

I lowered my hands back into the water and grabbed another plate. As I worked, Jake continued to talk.

"Well that's good, I reckon. 'Cause, from my experience, complaining don't do no good no way. What will be will be. Ain't that right, boss man."

"You telling him right," Daddy said.

I finished the plate and placed it on the tray next to me. I saw Daddy stack a pile of dishes on a cart and roll them out toward the center of the room.

"He telling him a lie," Reuben called from across the room.

I heard Daddy chuckle. I saw Jake look over his shoulder.

"Nigger, who you calling a lie?"

"You, nigger," Reuben said. "You know well as I do that you don't do nothing but complain."

"Never said I didn't. Just said it don't do no good."

"Well, if you know that, why the hell you complain so much? And how the hell you gon' tell him not to?"

" 'Cause my situation's different," Jake said. "I got a wife. . . . He don't."

I heard Daddy laugh again. I saw Jake looking at me.

"You ain't got no wife, do you?" Jake asked me.

"No, sir," I said. "I don't."

"Well, that's what I thought" Jake said, then added. "And if you know like me, you'll keep it that way. 'Cause far as I'm concerned the ruination of man is matrimony."

"Don't listen to 'im, son," Reuben said. "He don't know what the hell he talking about. He just a confused old man."

"I know what I'm talking about," Jake said. "And God knows I know."

"Jake," I heard Reuben call to him. "You ain't one of them homosexuals, is you?"

"Is you?" Jake asked Reuben.

Daddy chuckled and so did I.

"Y'all can laugh all you want to," Jake said, looking at no one in particular, "but that's why I don't respect God."

"Watch yourself," Reuben said. "Watch yourself now."

"I mean it," Jake said. "Why didn't God give Jesus a woman? Think about it. Jesus his own flesh and blood. And God could have given him anything he wanted. Anything in the whole wide world. Why didn't he give him a woman? Tell me . . . Why?"

"Nigger, you crazy." Reuben said.

I heard Daddy laugh, but he didn't say anything.

"I'll tell you why," Jake said. " 'Cause God knowed Jesus couldn't handle it, that's why. Just think about it. Jesus been out all day healing the sick and raising the dead and casting out demons. And when he come home he dead tired and all he want to do is sit down and take his shoes off. You know, prop his feet up. But when he get there, his old lady standing in the do' with her eyes all bucked and her mouth poked out. Now Jesus see her, and he know she ready to act a fool, but like something crazy he speak anyway.

"'How you doing baby?' he say. But his old lady don't say nothing. Just keep on staring at him. You know how they do." Jake said. "So Jesus come on in the house but before he can get in good, she put her hand on her hip and holler like something crazy."

"'Where you been?'"

"Jesus just look at her and smile."

"'Working.'"

"'Working!' she say."

"'Yeah, baby,' he says, 'working.'"

"Then she looks at him like he lying."

"'All this time?'"

"Jesus try to play it off."

"'Yeah, baby,' he say. 'Had a pretty good day too. Met some folks down by the river. They was pretty nice people. But, boy, they was some hungry.'"

"'Down by the river,' she say. 'Down by the river. When you left here this morning you ain't said nothing 'bout going to no river. What you doing way down there?'"

"'I told you,' Jesus said. 'Working.'"

"'Working.'"

"'Yeah, baby.'"

"'Ain't no work down by no river.'"

"Then Jesus tried to explain hisself."

"'I told you,' he say. 'I met some people down there. And they was hungry, so I fed 'em.'"

"'Fed 'em!'"

"'Yeah, baby. They was hungry, so I fed 'em. What's the problem?'"

"Then she looked at him like she wanting to fight."

"'Fed 'em what?'"

"'Fish and bread,' he say."

"'Fish and bread! What you feedin' them fish and bread for? We ain't got no goddamn bread in this house and sho' ain't got no goddamn fish. Where my fish?'"

"'Didn't bring you no fish,' he said."

"Now she sho' 'nuff mad."

"'I know you lying,' she said."

"Now Jesus backed up against the wall, 'cause he tired and want to sit down."

"'Naw, baby,' he say. 'I sorry. But I ain't brought you no fish.'"

"'Why not?' she pressed him."

"'I don't know,' he say. 'I just forgot.'"

"'Forgot!' she hollered like something crazy."

"'Yeah, baby. I just forgot, that's all.'"

"'Well, I know one thang, mister. You better hop right on back down there and get me some fish. That's all I know.'"

"'You want some fish. I'll go get you some fish.'"

"'I know that's right,' she say. 'And another thang. I better not catch you walking on that goddamn water no mo' either. Slip down and break your neck if you want to. It's gon' be hell to pay 'round here. I mean it goddammit. Ain't nobody playing with you.'"

I saw Daddy lay his head down on the sink and laugh.

"Jake," I heard Reuben say. "You sho' is one crazy nigger."

"You can say what you want to," Jake said, "but I'm serious. . . . All that talk about thorns and thistles and having his side pierced and not saying a mumbling word is all fine and good. But you show me where Jesus put up with a woman and held his peace, and I'll join church tomorrow."

"Son," Reuben called to me.

"Yes, sir," I said.

"If I was you," he said. "I would move. Wouldn't want to be too close when that lightning bolt strike."

Chapter Nine

For lunch, Daddy stayed at the diner with Jake and Reuben, and I met Omenita at the little diner on the opposite end of town. I had not seen or spoken to her since the day before and I was a little concerned about her frame of mind for I did not know if she was still angry about the events of the day before or if time had rendered things moot.

It was just before twelve when I parked Daddy's truck just west of the diner and I was still sitting behind the wheel waiting when I saw Omenita pull up in her Hyundai. She saw me and pulled next to me. I got out and held her door open for her. She was wearing her long leather coat, a pair of gloves, and a hat. I kissed her quickly and we hurried in out of the cold. It wasn't a fancy place nor was it large. Toward the front, just as you walked in, were tables with checkered red-and-white tablecloths. In the center of the room was the counter. On one end of the counter was the register and on the other end was the serving line for those who ordered the buffet. There were probably fifteen or twenty people sitting at the tables. Omenita and I looked about for a moment, then moved near the back and sat in one of the empty booths along the west wall next to the window. It was more secluded and a bit warmer since in was situated farther from the cold draft that blew in each time someone opened the front door.

I assisted her off with her coat, then removed my own. She slid in on one side and I slid in the other across from her, and no sooner were we seated than a hostess presented us with two menus and told us that someone would be with us in a few minutes. I had just opened the menu and began reading when Omenita interrupted me.

"You talked to Miss Audrey?" she asked.

"I talked to her," I said.

"About us?" she asked

"Un-hunh," I said.

"What she say?"

"Didn't say nothing," I said disdainfully.

"Must of said something," she pressed me.

"I told you . . . she didn't."

A waiter came to our table and placed silverware and napkins before us.

"Ready to order?" he asked.

"What's good?" I asked.

"Well, lots of folks seem partial to the stew."

"What kind of stew is it?" I asked.

"Beef tips," he said.

I looked at Omenita.

It's nice and hot," he said. "Warm your bones on a cold day like today."

She nodded.

"Stew's fine," I said.

"For both of you?"

I nodded again.

"Anything to drink?"

"You got lemonade?"

"We got lemonade," he said.

"What about tea?"

"Got tea too," he said. "Sweetened or unsweetened?"

"Sweetened tea for her. Lemonade for me."

"Anything else?"

I shook my head.

"Alright then," he said. "Two stews coming up."

He left, and I saw an older couple come in and sit in the booth behind us, and before they were seated good, the waiter returned with our drinks, then quickly attended to them. I took a sip from my lemonade, then looked at Omenita.

"Did Miss Audrey say she gon' leave me alone?"

I nodded.

"Because you promised."

"I know I promised," I said.

"I ain't playing with you, Maurice. I can't take her no more."

"I told you she's not going to bother you anymore," I said.

"She said that?"

I nodded again.

"What else she say?"

"Didn't say anything."

I saw her gazing at me, and I knew she did not believe me. But, there was something in her that wanted it to be true. I saw her look out the large bay window, then back at me.

"Wish you would tell me what she was talking about."

"I'm going to," I said, "if you give me a chance."

"Alright," she said. "You don't have to bite my head off."

"Just like to have a nice lunch," I said. "Talk about all that stuff later."

"Fine!" she said.

I looked around to see if our food was ready. When I didn't see the waiter, I turned back toward Omenita. I could see that she was getting upset so I decided to change the conversation.

"Work going alright?" I asked.

"Kind of slow today," she said. "Not many people out with the weather and all. Guess they all hugging the heater."

"Well that's understandable," I said.

"I must say, I'm kind of surprised to see you in town on such a cold day," she said. "Seeing how you a warm weather man."

"Helping Daddy out at the diner."

"Washing dishes!" she said.

I nodded.

"Why?"

"Mr. Silas took sick. Just helping out 'til he's back on his feet."

"And how long will that be?"

"Just for a few days," I said.

"Maurice," she said, "I swear. Sometimes I just don't understand you."

I furrowed my brow and looked at her.

"What is it that you don't understand?"

"Oh, forget it."

"No," I said. "Tell me."

"I just don't understand why you would disgrace yourself washing dishes, that's all."

"Disgrace!" I said. "What's the disgrace?"

"Well if you don't know I'm not gon' tell you."

"Now who's being snobbish?" I said.

"That's different and you know it," she said. "I ain't looking down at nobody, I just don't want nobody looking down on us."

"Because I'm helping my Daddy at the diner?"

"Forget it," she said.

"No," I said. "I won't."

"You don't understand," she said. "You just don't understand."

"Well make me understand," I said.

"How can I," she asked, "when you won't listen?"

"Just open your mouth and tell me," I said. "That's how."

I looked at her but she remained quiet.

"What is it?" I asked.

She looked out of the window, took a deep breath, then looked back at me.

"Maurice," she said, on the verge of tears, "I been catching hell all my life because of my mama and daddy. Now I'll be damn if I'm gon' spend the rest of my life catching hell because of you."

"Because of me!"

"Because of you," she said.

"I don't know what you're talking about," I said.

"Maurice, you a college man. You ain't no goddamn dishwasher."

"You need to quit worrying about what everybody think," I said.

"Forget it," she snapped. "Wash all the goddamn dishes you want to. See if I care."

"You need to lower your voice and watch your mouth," I said. "I swear I don't know why you have to curse so much."

"Hope this ain't the big news you had to tell me," she said. "You got a goddamn job washing dishes."

"Watch your mouth, Omenita," I said. "I mean it!"

"Don't handle me, Maurice," she said angrily. "You ain't my daddy, and I ain't no child, and you ain't gon' talk to me like that."

The waiter brought our food and placed it on the table before us. Two large bowls of steaming hot stew and a large square of corn bread. I unrolled my silverware and placed the napkin across my lap. Omenita did the same. I looked at her, then at the waiter.

"Looks good," I told him.

"Need anything else," he said, "just let me know."

"I appreciate it," I said.

He left and I saw Omenita dip the edge of her spoon in the stew and lift a small portion of the pot liquor to her mouth.

"Well," I said after she had tasted it.

"It's fantastic," she said.

Suddenly, I laughed.

"What's so funny?" she asked.

"Nothing," I said.

"Must be something," she said, "or else you wouldn't be laughing."

"Just reminded me of somebody, that's all."

"Who?" she asked.

"Just a friend," I said.

I dipped my spoon in the bowl, and when it was full, I lifted it to my mouth and I felt my body tingle as the warm stew slid across my tongue and down the back of my throat. The stew was good, but the warmth was even better. In the silence of the moment, I watched Omenita eating from the bowl. Her soft brown eyes danced in the light of the room. She saw me looking at her.

"Well," she said, "you gon' tell me or not?"

"I got into law school," I said.

"What!" she said, then dropped her spoon and stared at me.

"I applied a few months ago," I said. "Just heard last week."

"Law school!" she said. "I don't understand."

"LSU," I said. "I got back in, and get this, I was awarded a scholarship, which was surprising because they don't usually award scholarships for law school. But there's this new program aimed

at keeping some of Louisiana's brightest young lawyers from leaving the state. I applied for one and won. It pays full tuition, plus a
small stipend to cover my living expenses while I'm in school.
The only catch is that I have to agree to practice law in Louisiana
for at least three years after graduation. But, that's no big deal
though, because this is where I planned to live anyway . . ." I
paused and looked at her and I saw her eyes had begun to water.

"Do you love me?" she asked.

I squinted and looked at her strangely. I thought the question
odd. "Of course I do," I said.

"Do you want to be with me?"

"More than anything in the world."

"Then why are you doing this?"

"For us," I said. "I'm doing this for us."

"This ain't got nothing to do with us," she said. "This all about
that tack-head cousin of yours, and your obsession with getting
him out the pen."

"Let's talk about something else," I said.

"I ain't gon' do it," she said.

"Ain't gon' do what?" I asked.

"Let this happen," she said.

"Let what happen?" I asked.

"You go off to school again while I sit around and wait my life
away."

"I don't want to talk about it anymore," I said.

"We gon' talk about it," she said.

"Keep your voice down," I said.

"I mean it, Maurice. I ain't gon' wait no more. Either we gon'
be together or we gon' be apart. But I ain't gon' be in one place
while you in another one."

"Omenita!" I said.

"No," she said. "I ain't gon' do it. And I mean that. I swear,
Maurice, all you think about is yourself."

"Myself," I said. "This is for us. Why can't you see that?"

"This ain't got nothing to do with us," she said again.

"It has everything to do with us," I said. "Everything."

"Tell that lie to somebody else," she said.

"Hold on," I said. "Hold on now."

"Hold on, my foot," she said. I knew she wanted to say something else, but couldn't on account we were in a public place.

"I guess it would be asking too much for a little support," I said.

"Support!" she shouted.

"Keep your voice down," I said again.

"How dare you say that to me," she said.

"Well it's how I feel," I said.

"I don't give a damn how you feel," she said.

"Don't cuss at me," I said. "I mean it. Don't cuss at me."

I looked around and saw that the old couple was staring at us.

"Don't tell me how to talk," she said. "You just like my goddamn daddy. Want to control everybody and everything."

"I mean it," I said. "I'm not playing with you."

She looked at me, and I saw her eyes water again.

"Maurice," she said, "how you gon' sit here and talk to me about not supporting you. Hell, I been supporting you for the last four years. But Maurice, this is my life too. And I'm tired of not having nothing. Now, you need to be a man and get a job and think about us if you want to be with me."

"You telling me I can't go to law school?"

"You a grown man," she said. "I can't tell you what to do. Go where you want to. Just don't expect me to be here when you get back."

"Oh, I see," I said. "If I go, it's going to cause problems between us."

"If you go," she said, "ain't gon' be no us."

"I can't pass up this opportunity," I said.

"And I can't wait no more," she said in a voice laced with finality.

Chapter Ten

We finished lunch and agreed to continue the conversation later that evening after we had both calmed down. I walked Omenita to her car and kissed her good-bye and headed back to work. I made it back to the diner just before one and when I got there Jake, Daddy, and Reuben were still sitting at the little table in the corner talking. They had finished eating and were simply waiting for their lunch break to end. I looked at the clock. We still had about ten minutes left so I joined them at the table. I sat next to Reuben; Daddy and Jake sat across from us.

"Had a good lunch, son?" Daddy asked.

"Yes, sir," I said.

"Got so busy this morning that I didn't have a chance to ask you about your trip. How did it go?"

"Went alright," I said.

"Did your mama go to work?"

"No, sir. She went home."

"Didn't walk in this cold, did she?"

"No, sir," I said. "Danielle dropped me off then took her home."

I saw Jake looking at me as if he was trying to figure out who I was talking about. I started to avert my eyes but before I could I saw Jake's lips part and I saw his mouth open, then I heard his deep, surly voice addressing me. "That's Mr. John's daughter, ain't it?" he asked me.

"Yes, sir," I said.

"Had 'im playing chauffeur this morning," I heard Daddy say.

"Well," Jake said, "a man got to do what a man got to do."

"I reckon," Daddy said.

"It wasn't like that," I said. "She was nice. Even offered to pay me."

"You didn't let her, I hope," Daddy said.

"No, sir," I said, "but she did lasso me into lunch."

"You gon' go?" Daddy asked.

"Yes, sir," I said. "Don't guess I have much choice."

"Well now you watch yourself," Jake said. "Them white girls is real friendly. And if a fellow ain't aware of that fact, he can wind up with mo' trouble than he know what to do with."

"Just lunch," I said. "That's all."

"Well," Jake said, "maybe. And then again, maybe not."

"Aw, Jake," I heard Reuben say, "what the hell you talking about now?"

"Just trying to help the boy," Jake said. "That's all."

"I might be wrong," Reuben said. "But I didn't hear 'im ask you for no help. Did you, boss man?"

I saw Daddy smile but he didn't answer.

"Ain't got to ask," Jake said. "That's the difference between me and you, Reuben. I see a man need help, I help him. I don't wait for 'im to ask." I saw Jake shift his eyes toward me. "Now, son," he said, "I know what I'm talking about. Them white girls is friendly. And 'fo you get tied up with 'em, you got to be sho'."

"I ain't gon' get tied up with nobody," I said. "Just going to lunch."

"Well that's how it start," Jake said. "First it's lunch, then it's dinner . . . and next thang you know you got a situation. Tell 'im, boss man."

"Aw, I reckon you telling him right," Daddy said.

"Aw, boss man," Reuben said. "Don't encourage that foolishness."

"Foolishness!" Jake said.

"That's what I said," Reuben lamented. "Foolishness!"

I saw Jake look at Reuben, then at me.

"Son," Jake said, "you can listen to Reuben if you want to, but if you got the kind of sense I think you do, you'll hear what I'm telling you. Now, I know what I'm talking about. I done seen this thang before. Seen it with my own eyes."

He paused and looked at me. I remained quiet.

"See, I was working out in California at this loading dock for one of them big old trucking outfits. Don't exactly remember which one 'cause I worked for several. But I do remember it was a pretty good job. Paid about nineteen dollars a hour, which was good money in them days."

"Aw hell," I heard Reuben say. "Here we go again."

Daddy laughed. Jake looked at Reuben then continued. "Well, they hired this young fellow from Arkansas. I guess that must of been right after the war."

"What war?" Reuben asked.

" 'Nam," Jake said.

"Nigger, you ain't fought in no war."

"Like hell I didn't."

"Guess that explain it," Reuben said.

"Explain what?" Jake asked.

"Why you so goddamn crazy."

"Crazy," Jake said. "Nigger, who you calling crazy?"

"Who!" Reuben said. "You . . . that's who."

"Anyway," Jake said. "It fell on me to train the young buck."

"Train!" Reuben said. "You!"

"Yeah," Jake said. "You know, show him the ins and outs of the business."

He paused, but no one spoke.

"Well," he continued. "Over the course of time, me and that boy got to know each other pretty good. Matter of fact I took a liking to 'im. I can't really tell you why. I guess I took to 'im mainly because he was from Arkansas and I was from Louisiana. You know how it is. Well, anyway, after he got to know his way around a little bit, he took to hanging 'round the office. Well, I didn't think much about it 'til he come to me one day and said, 'Jake, I thank one of them girls up there like me.' Well, I didn't know what the hell that fool was talking about, so I asked him what girl.

At the time we was in the break room and he nodded toward the office, so I looked where he was looking and when it come to me what he was carrying on about, I looked at him like he was crazy 'cause I knowed ain't nothing worked up in that office but them little ole white gals.

"Now, normally, I would have just minded my own business, but he was young and green and straight out the country. And I could see that he was letting hisself get all worked up and excited, so I tried to calm him down, you know, talk some sense to him. I pulled him aside and I said 'boy, these white girls out here is different. They real friendly. Now you can't go getting yourself all worked up 'cause they smile at you. It don't mean nothing . . . they just friendly, That's all.'"

"Crazy Boy bucked his eyes and went to shaking his head.

"'Uh-unnh,' he said. 'She like me. I know she do.'

"'She told you that?' I said.

"'Naw, but I know.'

"'I'm telling you,' I said, 'They just friendly.'

"'Naw, sir,' he said. 'You wrong. It's mo' to it than that. . . . She like me. . . . She wanting to go to lunch. . . . She asked me the other day.'

"'Don't mean nothing,' I told him. 'Everybody out here go to lunch. She just being friendly,' I said.

"'Naw,' he kept saying. 'She like me. I know she do.'

"'Boy,' I said, 'they just friendly. Now I'm telling you what I know.'

"Well, that old crazy boy got mad and went to raising his voice.

"'Naw sir,' he said. 'She like me . . . she do.'

"'Alright,' I said. 'But you better be sho'.'

"'She like me,' he kept saying. 'I tell you she do.'

"Well, I left it alone. And sho' 'nuff, they went to lunch. And when they got there that white gal went to talking real nice to him and patting on him and such. You know how they do. Well, that crazy boy got excited and took that girl off to herself and up and drawed his thang on her."

"What?" Reuben said.

"Sho' as I tell you," Jake said.

"What happened?" Reuben asked.

"Well, that gal got all upset and told the big boss. And he called that fool in the office and next thang you know, that boy done lost that good job and all them benefits. I seen him 'fo he left. Walking 'round looking all crazy and confused like he don't know whether he coming or going. And I didn't say nothing to him. Just shook my head. That's how I know what I'm saying is true. Them white girls is friendly, and when you go to fooling around with 'em you got to be sho'. Now, son, I tell you, if you think that gal like you, don't you jump up and draw on her like that ole crazy boy out there in California did. Naw, you let her reach in there and get it herself. . . . Now, that'll stand up in any court of law."

I saw Daddy laughing, then I heard Reuben call to him.

"Boss man," I heard Reuben say, "Jake talking 'bout hisself. He the one drawed hisself on that girl and lost that good job. That's why he back down here in Louisiana washing dishes. Ain't that right, Jake?"

"Nigger, you can believe what you want to," Jake said. "Ain't nobody talking to you no way. I'm talking to the little boss man. Now, son, you better listen to me . . . them girls is friendly . . . Don't you lose your mind and draw on that gal . . . don't you do it."

"I got a girl," I said defensively.

And when I did Daddy shook with laughter. So did Reuben.

"Aw, leave him alone, Jake," Reuben said. "You done had your fun."

I saw Daddy rise to his feet, still laughing.

"Come on, men," I heard him say. "Let's go back to work."

I rose and went back to my station. The dishes had stacked up, and from what I could tell the crowd had not varied much from breakfast. I donned my apron and gloves and sunk my hands into the warm, soapy water. I heard Daddy and Reuben behind me, and I could see Tommy flipping burger patties on the steaming hot grill. Jake did not return to his station. Instead he went out into the diner and when he came back he was pushing a cart stacked high with dirty plates and glasses, and I figured he must have left them there just before lunch.

"How's it looking out there?" Reuben asked him.

"Not too bad," Jake said. "Few stragglers. But most of the crowd done cleared out."

"How the dishes holding up?" Reuben wanted to know.

"So far, so good." Jake said.

He made his way to his station and donned his apron. "Reckon we might get out of here early today, boss?" Jake asked.

"All depends," Daddy said.

"On what?" Jake asked him.

"Flow of customers."

"And?" Jake said.

"How fast we get done."

"Can't do nothing about the first," Jake said, "but damn sho can do something 'bout the second."

"Can't see too many people coming out in this weather," Reuben called from the other side of the room.

"Son." I heard Daddy call me.

"Yeah, Daddy."

"If you got time," he said, "like for you to go with me and Papa to find a tree sometime this evening."

"Yes, sir," I said. "I got time."

"Good," Daddy said. "We'll go after work."

Then all was quiet save for the sound of water splashing and dishes clanging.

Chapter Eleven

The thin crowd held, and we washed the bulk of the dishes and mopped the floors and cleaned the grill, and Daddy let Reuben and Jake go. And he and I stayed back to wash up behind the stragglers. And at five we stacked the chairs on the tables up front and made sure that everything was in order. Then, he and I headed home to pick up Grandpa Luke. And I drove because Daddy was bushed, and while I drove, he sat leaning against the passenger door. And I did not say much to him nor he to me. For his eyes were closed and my mind was on Omenita.

As I watched the road unwind before us, there was a strange thought in my head. I was in an unfamiliar place and Omenita was there and there was a man standing before us. And upon his face was a smile, and he was gazing at her and she was gazing at him, and there was some secret between them. I saw him stretch forth his hand. And then, as quickly as the image had appeared, it was gone. And I could feel the sweat on my face and the numbness in my hands.

Then I realized that there was a large shadow over us. I looked outside and we were passing beneath the large oak trees and I slowed the truck, for this was a residential area. And I watched the sidewalks for playing children and as I did so, I could feel my mind straying again. And I was thinking of Omenita and how I did not want to lose her. And how in my mind there were no words I could find or actions I could take that could move us beyond this impasse.

At home, I turned off the highway into the yard. And when I did, I heard the seashells crunch and I saw Daddy open his eyes and gaze about, dazed. And I saw the old house sitting back off the highway, partially concealed by the large, billowing branches of the old cypress tree.

"Must of been more tired than I thought," he said. "Guess I dozed off."

"Yes, sir," I said. "It's been a long, hard day."

I killed the engine and waited. I saw him look at his watch and then I saw him lean forward and peer up toward the sky.

"Ain't much light left," he said. "Be dark soon."

I had been thinking the same thing. It was a few minutes after five. That gave us less than forty-five minutes to reach our destination and find the tree. I opened the door and stepped out and waited for him to make his way around the truck, and while I waited, I glanced up. Yes, the sun had long since descended from its perch high above it all and now it felt as if the cold weather had gotten even colder. Involuntarily, I felt myself shiver. I tucked my chin and folded my arms across my chest. I looked up; Daddy was watching me.

"You gon' need on warmer clothes," he said. "Bring any with you?"

I shook my head. I had not thought to bring any. I figured it might get cold, but not this cold. After all it had been so warm, unseasonably warm.

"Gon' be cold out there in them woods," he said. And I figured he meant to say colder because it was already cold. "Ought to be a extra pair of coveralls in there if you want 'em."

"Yes, sir," I said, and I could feel my voice trembling from the cold as the words rolled from my quivering lips. "I do."

"Well, gone in the house and tell your mama to get 'em for you. I'm gon' be 'round back. Got to get the ax and a couple of flashlights out the toolshed. I'll meet you and Papa back at the truck."

"Yes, sir," I said.

I turned to leave but the sound of his voice stopped me.

"And, son . . ."

I turned back toward him and hunched my shoulders against the cold.

"Yes, sir," I said.

"Tell your grandpa to hurry," he said. "Ain't much daylight left."

"Yes, sir," I said. "I will."

I shoved my hands into my pockets and hurried into the house and got Grandpa and, when we returned, Daddy had placed the ax in the back and was sitting behind the wheel. I pulled the door open and slid in next to Daddy; Grandpa Luke climbed in next to me. I had hastily pulled the coveralls on over my clothes. Inside the truck was cold again. I slid my hands deep inside the pockets.

"They fit?" Daddy asked.

I nodded.

I saw Daddy look at Grandpa Luke.

"How you doing, Papa?" he asked.

"Making out," Grandpa Luke said. "And you?"

"Aw, I'm aw right," Daddy said. "Just bushed."

He backed out into the street, stopped, put the truck into gear, and headed north. I had never made this trip with them before, but I very well knew where we were going. There was a stand of wild pine trees buried deep in the woods some ten miles outside of Brownsville. The woods were on Old Man Harper's land, well beyond the pasture where he grazed his cows. Grandpa Luke had worked for him on shares years ago, and every year since Grandpa Luke was a young man, Old Man Harper had allowed him to select three Christmas trees off his land—one for Old Man Harper, one for Grandpa Luke, and one for us. I was looking out of the window when I heard Daddy yawn.

"Hard day, son?" Grandpa Luke asked him.

"Papa, I ain't seen that many folks at the diner in years," Daddy said.

"What's the occasion?" Grandpa Luke asked.

"Some kind of convention out at the plant," Daddy said. "At least that's what they tell me."

"I hadn't heard nothing 'bout no convention."

"Caught us all by surprise too," Daddy said. "Good thing we

had old Maurice here or we wouldn't of made it. He did a fine
job, a real fine job."

I felt Daddy's hand on my knee. I looked at him and smiled.

"Don't surprise me none," Grandpa Luke said. "That boy never
was scared of work. But then again, I ain't never met a Dupree
who was. Hell, all of us worked night and day, and then some.
That boy ain't no different. It's in his blood. He come by it nat-
ural . . . He a Dupree aw right."

"Well he did a fine job," Daddy said again. "Even managed to
put up with ole Jake."

"Jake!" Grandpa Luke said. "That crazy SOB still up there?"

"Still there," Daddy said.

"And still crazy as hell, I reckon," Grandpa Luke said, smiling.

"Ain't changed one bit," Daddy said.

Grandpa Luke shook his head and chuckled. "Well, I'll just
be," he said. "If that don't beat all."

"Ought to come up there one day," Daddy said. "I'm sho Jake
and Reuben would get a big kick out of seeing you again."

"Might just do that," Grandpa Luke said, "when I get a little
time, that is."

"Speaking of time," Daddy said, "what you do all day?"

"Went by the house for a little while," Grandpa Luke said.
"That's 'bout all."

"The house?" Daddy said. "What house?"

"My house."

I saw Daddy look at him, confused.

"How'd you get over there?" he asked.

"I walked," Grandpa Luke said.

Daddy frowned. "In this weather?" he asked.

"I bundled up good," Grandpa Luke told him.

"But Papa, you shouldn't be out in this weather like that . . .
least not by yourself. Suppose something happened. You'd freeze
to death 'fo anybody could get to you. Why didn't you just wait 'til
we got home?"

"Just needed to get out to the house," Grandpa Luke said.

I saw Daddy looking at Grandpa Luke, and I knew he was waiting for him to say more, and when he didn't, Daddy spoke again.
"I don't want you going off like that by yourself," he said.

"Don't know why you carrying on so," Grandpa Luke said. "Last time I looked I was still able to cross the street 'thout a wet nurse. I'm old, but I ain't helpless."

"I know you ain't helpless," Daddy said. "Just worry about you. That's all."

"Well, don't," Grandpa Luke said.

"Don't see how we can help it," Daddy said.

"Well," Grandpa Luke told him, "I wish you would."

"Papa, wishing ain't gon' stop us from caring about you."

"Don't want you to stop caring," Grandpa Luke said. "I appreciate your concern. I really do. You and Audrey and this boy here been more comfort to me than you'll ever know . . . but sometimes . . . I . . . aw, never mind."

"No Papa, what?"

Grandpa Luke grew pensive. I heard him sigh. I saw him turn his head and stare out of the window.

"What is it, Papa?" Daddy asked again.

Grandpa Luke didn't answer.

"Is something wrong, Papa?" Daddy asked him. "Something you ain't telling us. You ain't feeling poorly, are you?"

"Feel just fine," Grandpa Luke said.

"Then what is it?" Daddy asked again.

"Nothing," Grandpa Luke said.

"Papa, if you don't tell us," Daddy said, "we can't help you."

"Nothing to tell," he said.

"Must be something," Daddy said, "or else you wouldn't be carrying on so."

"Just let it be," Grandpa Luke said. "Son, please just let it be."

"Just let what be?" Daddy asked him.

"Just wish we could talk about something else," Grandpa Luke said.

"But Papa . . ."

"Son, please!" Grandpa Luke said. "Is that too much to ask?"

"Aw right, Papa," Daddy said. "I'll leave it alone."

There was silence, and I felt Grandpa Luke squirming on the seat next to me. I pulled my legs closer together to give him more room.

"Sometimes it just gets a little lonely." Grandpa Luke broke the silence. He paused and Daddy looked at him, but did not speak. "And when it do," Grandpa Luke continued, "it helps to be close to your mama." His voice broke, and he opened his mouth to say something else, but when he couldn't, he turned his head and stared far up the road.

"Papa," Daddy called to him gently, "Mama gone . . . and she ain't coming back, and we just gon' have to face that."

"I know she gone," Grandpa Luke said. "God knows I do, but even though she ain't here in body, look like I can feel her over there." Grandpa Luke paused and looked at Daddy. "Son, I can't feel her at your place. I just needed to be close to her today." His voice broke again, and he turned his head. "I just needed to talk to her, that's all . . . I just needed to talk to her."

It was quiet a minute, and I saw Daddy staring up the road statue-like. He fumbled with the wheel a moment, then turned his head and looked at Grandpa Luke. "We just worry about you, Papa," he said again. "Would hate for something to happen to you out there on that road all by yourself."

"Ain't even a good mile from your house to mine," Grandpa Luke said. "Done walked it a million times. Ain't no cause to worry 'bout that . . . no cause at all."

"Can't help but worry," Daddy said.

"Well I wish you wouldn't," Grandpa Luke said again. "I'm fine . . . just missing Lucille, that's all."

There was a lull in the conversation, and I stared straight ahead, watching the passing landscape. We were well outside of the city limits, and there was nothing to see but open land and untilled fields of recently harvested cotton. I glanced at Daddy and he, too, was staring ahead.

"Anything we can do?" Daddy asked.

Grandpa Luke shook his head, then paused. I saw him look out across the landscape. "Don't reckon it's nothing nobody can do." His voice was low . . . flat . . . lifeless. "Just got to work it out," he said. "Just got to work it out somehow." He had his camera around his neck. I saw him reach down and began fiddling with it. His eyes began to water. I saw Daddy look at him, then back at the highway.

"Just gon' take time, Papa," he said.

"I know, son," Grandpa Luke said, "but to be perfectly honest with you I been thinking about moving back home."

I saw Daddy look at Grandpa Luke and shake his head.

"No, Papa," he said. "I can't go along with that. I can't go along with that at all."

"Just want to sleep in my own bed," Grandpa Luke said. "Just want to be around my own thangs."

"Don't like the idea of you being in that house by yourself," Daddy said. "What if you take sick? What if you need something?"

"I'll be alright," Grandpa Luke said.

"I don't like it," I heard Daddy say again. "I don't like it at all."

"I'll be alright," Grandpa Luke said a second time. "Ain't no cause to worry 'bout me. I'll be alright . . . you'll see."

"Why don't you think about it a little while?" Daddy said. "You know, give this thing a chance to work itself out."

"I have thought about it," Grandpa Luke said. "Thought about it long and hard. I done made up my mind. I need to go home. I need to be close to Lucille."

Up the road, I saw the turnoff leading on to Delvin Harper's place. I felt the truck slow and when he were close, Daddy pulled onto Mr. Harper's place and followed the narrow road past the large brick house and out past what used to be the sharecroppers' quarters when black folks like Grandpa Luke worked the place on shares. Now the place was mechanized and in the distance were the large tractors and cotton pickers and trailers and other farm equipment that had rendered obsolete the need for but a few laborers to work the massive fields that made up Mr. Harper's plantation. Daddy guided the truck through the fields and along a slough and stopped half a mile hence at the mouth of the woods.

"This close enough, Papa?"

Grandpa Luke nodded, and we climbed out and made our way across the slough and eased our way deep into the thick woods. Most of the leaves had fallen from the trees and the damp forest floor was covered with dried leaves and brittle twigs, and as we walked, all was quiet save for the sound of twigs snapping and leaves crunching under the weight of our heavy shoes. Daddy, clothed in coveralls, had one ax and Grandpa Luke, clothed in overalls and a heavy coat, had the other one. I didn't have any-thing—my hands were in my pockets.

"Reckon it's still out there?" Daddy asked Grandpa Luke.

"It's out there," Grandpa Luke said.

"When the last time you seen it?"

"Week or two ago," Grandpa Luke said.

"Hope ain't nobody cut it."

"Ain't nobody cut it down," Grandpa Luke said. "Put my mark on it. Besides, J.D. ain't gon' allow nobody to cut a blade of grass up yonder but me."

"Well, I sho' hope not," Daddy said.

"It's out there," Grandpa Luke said again. "Trust me. It's there."

"How much farther?" Daddy asked.

"Just over that ridge yonder."

"What kind of tree is it?"

"Nice little old fir," Grandpa Luke said. "I saw him pause and raise his hand to his eye level. " 'Bout yea high. Gon' make a good tree . . . been watching it for two years now. It's a beaut."

"Hope we find it soon," Daddy said, looking up as we walked. "Ain't much light left. Be pitch black before long."

"Ain't much farther," Grandpa Luke said. "Ain't much farther at all."

We made our way through dense brush, trampling through weeds and kicking past old briars and hanging vines until finally we found ourselves in a small clearing. Suddenly, Grandpa Luke stopped and pointed.

"There she is," he said.

Daddy and I stopped and looked.

"Ain't she a beaut?" Grandpa Luke said.

We inched forward and when we were close, I saw Daddy lean his ax against an adjacent tree, then I saw him circle the fir, in-specting the branches.

"It's a nice one, Papa," I heard him say. "The nicest one yet."

I saw Grandpa Luke smile, satisfied.

"Cut her down square," he said. "Don't split the trunk. Whatever you do, don't split the trunk."

"I won't, Papa," I heard Daddy say.

"What you think, son?" Daddy asked me.

I eased forward and gazed at the tree. It was about six feet tall with nice full branches and a beautiful green color.

"Nice," I said. "Real nice."

I turned and looked. Grandpa Luke was staring off into the distance. He no longer seemed interested in the tree. His mind had drifted to something else. Something well beyond the ridge. I saw Daddy looking at him.

"What is it, Papa?" he asked Grandpa Luke.

"When we was young," Grandpa Luke began, "and working the fields, used to be a little spot just over that ridge yonder where Lucille and I used to slip off every now and then and picnic under a old oak tree. Used to be so quiet and peaceful back there . . . Hadn't seen that spot in years. Like to see it again . . . snap a few pictures if I can."

"I don't know, Papa," I saw Daddy look up toward the sky again, then back at the tree. "We ain't got much time left. It'll be dark soon."

"Asked your mama to marry me under that tree," Grandpa Luke said. "And when she said yes, I carved our initials in it with my old pocketknife." I looked at Grandpa Luke, then at Daddy. Grandpa Luke was still staring out across the rise; Daddy had bent low under the tree. "Wonder if it's still there," Grandpa Luke said.

"Is what still where?" Daddy asked. I saw him rise to his feet and look.

"That old oak tree."

"Don't know, Papa," Daddy said. "Maybe."

"Think I'll take a look."

"It's getting late, Papa," Daddy said. "Shouldn't go traipsing off in the woods alone this close to dark."

"Just over the rise," Grandpa Luke said. "Won't take but a minute. I'll be back before you know it."

Grandpa Luke turned to leave. I saw Daddy look at him, then at me.

"Go with your grandpa," he told me.

I started to move but Grandpa Luke stopped me. "Like to go by myself, if you don't mind."

I saw Daddy look at him.

"Aw right," he said, "but be careful."

"I will," Grandpa Luke said, walking toward the rise. "Don't worry . . . I will."

We watched him climb over the ridge and disappear into the dusk, and when we could no longer see him Daddy turned to me. "You been awful quiet since we left work," he said, moving toward the ax he had propped against the tree. "Something on your mind?"

"Same old, same old," I said. I eased forward and he lifted the ax, then looked at me.

"Omenita," he said.

I nodded.

"Trouble, I guess," he said, then crossed next to the tree.

"Just pressing me a little," I said, "that's all."

"I see," he said. He was not looking at me. He was looking at the tree, and I knew that in his mind he was examining the trunk, mentally marking the spot at which he would swing.

"I just don't know what to do," I said.

I saw him brace himself steady, then swing. The blade of the ax whistled through the air, then hit the tree with a heavy thud.

"Well, what you want to do?" he asked.

"Mama say I ought to leave her alone."

"Ain't for her to say one way or the other," he said. Then I heard the thud of the ax crashing against the tree. I heard him grunt, then speak again. "You got to figure that out for yourself."

"Wish I could," I said.

He paused and looked at me.

"Will she share a crumb with you?"

"Sir?" I said, confused.

"That was always the thing I looked for," he said. "Wanted to find a woman who would share a crumb with me. I guess, in my mind, I figured if she would do that she was a good woman. Does that make sense to you, son?"

"Yes, sir," I said. "It makes sense."

"Old folks used to say hard times will come and hard times will go but a good woman'll stick with you through thick and thin. And I guess that's the kind of woman I was looking for."

He swung the ax again.

"Did you find her?" I asked.

I saw Daddy smile.

"You better believe it," he said.

"Mama," I said, then I smiled too.

"Now don't get me wrong," he said. "Your mama and me got this little song and dance we do sometimes, but when it's all said and done and the chips are down, I know I can depend on her and she can depend on me. Now, she complains a little every now and then, but what woman don't? But one thing about your mama. Come hell or high water she's gon' be there for me and she's gon' be there for this family." He paused to catch his breath. "Son, I been married to your mama over twenty-somethin' years, and I can't ever say I found myself in a situation where I was pulling one way and she was pulling the other. Now, if I believe in something—I mean believe in it hard—and I go to her, she's gon' take a interest in it. And she's gon' support me any way she can."

"Even if she doesn't agree?" I asked.

"Even if she doesn't agree."

"I guess that's the way it ought to be, right?"

He was about to swing the ax again, but when I said that he stopped.

"Well, now, I don't profess to know all there is to know about the happenings between a man and a woman. Truth be told I'm still learning myself, so I can't tell you what ought to be. All I can do is tell you about the woman I got and how things are with us."

"And how are they?" I asked.

I saw him smile again.

"Better than I ever expected," he said. "I love your mother but more importantly, she loves me. Now she may not say it very often because that's not the kind of woman she is, but you can bet your life she's gon' let me know."

"How?" I asked him.

"By letting me know her."

"I don't understand," I said.

"Well, son, let me explain it like this," he said. "I know that when we get home tonight, if I were to go out in the backyard and start staring up at the sky, ain't gon' be long before your mama gon' ease out there, and when she get close she gon' say 'Nat, what you doing?' And I'm gon' say 'looking up at the moon.' And she gon' say, 'what you doing that for?' And I'm gon' say 'I was just thinking. I'd sure like to go there one day.' And when I say that, she ain't gon' bat a eye and she ain't gon' say 'nigger you crazy standing out here in the dark looking up in the sky like you done lost your mind.' Naw, she ain't gon' do that. But you know what she's gon' do?"

For an answer, I shook my head.

"She just gon' tilt her head back and take a long look. And then she gon' look at me and say, 'well, you better take a coat, 'cause I hear it get cold up there.' That's how I know she loves me. Because she'll stand behind me. No matter what I try. And she won't throw it in my face if it don't work out." He paused again and looked at me. "Son, a man needs a woman who can help him get where he's going and who will give him a soft place to land if he fall along the way. Now, I don't know Omenita that well. I just know you and her been at this thing a long time. Now, if you love her and you say she the one, then I love her too. The only thing I say is just make sho' she'll share a crumb with you."

He paused again and brought the ax down hard against the tree, and no sooner had the blade struck the tree than it fell crashing hard against the cold, frozen ground. I moved close to the tree and so did Daddy.

"Papa was right," he said. "This gon' make a nice tree."

I smiled and nodded but I was not thinking of the tree, I was thinking about what he had said; I was thinking about Omenita. I saw him kneel and inspect the tree closer. I looked up. Over the crest of the ridge, I saw Grandpa Luke approaching and when he came into full view I saw that the ax was in his left hand and his right arm was extended behind his back. He was dragging something behind him. He came closer and I could see that it was a tree.

Chapter Twelve

We dragged the trees out of the woods and at Grandpa's insistence, we dropped the one he had cut by his house before taking ours home. And at home, the three of them sat down to supper, but I did not stay, for I had promised Omenita that we would spend some time together this evening, and I was anxious to see her and hold her and make her understand that regardless of the momentary tension between us, I loved her in ways I never thought possible and with a strength and depth that not even I understood. And that this love was not something that either of us should take for granted, but it was something that we should cherish and nourish. And that this thing of which we had to speak was but a small obstacle—the importance of which could not and should not pose a threat to either that which we now have or that which we longed to have in the not too distant future. Yes, I had heard Daddy speak of love in a way I had not considered. And now that I had, I wanted Omenita to understand the importance of us being there for each other, and not just today, or through this crisis we now had to navigate, but for all eternity—through good times and bad.

I pulled onto her street, feeling swarmed by emotions with which heretofore I had not been familiar. I parked on the shoulder just beyond the small cluttered yard that extended a few feet from the three concrete steps leading onto the small wooden porch that jutted out from her parents' house. She was home; so were her parents. I could see their vehicles parked in the yard just east of the house. Her father's truck was parked up front, and her car was parked directly behind his. I ambled out of the truck and marched forward with my head angled down against the wind and my anxious heart pounding in anticipation of gazing into the beautiful brown eyes of this woman for whom I so desperately yearned, and as I walked, I noticed in the yard next door, several men cloaked in coats, standing around an old trash barrel. The fire within could be seen flickering just above the rim, and I saw one of the men tilt his head back and drink from a bottle, then pass it to the man standing next to him.

I climbed the stairs and knocked on the door. And instantly, it swung open and Miss Jones stood before me.

"Hi, Miss Jones," I said. "Is Omenita home?"

"She here," Miss Jones said politely. "Come on in out the cold. She ought to be ready in a few minutes."

I entered the house and as I did, I looked around. Mr. Jones was sitting in his recliner before the television watching the evening news and from the rear of the house I heard the sound of a radio, and I figured it was coming from Omenita's room for I did not believe that either her brother or her two sisters would be listening to such a tune. It was too mellow, too sedate, too sophisticated. I entered the room and stopped before the sofa and when I did, I looked at Mr. Jones but he did not look at me.

"How you doing, Mr. Jones?" I said.

"Aw right," he said, grunting. And when he said it he still did not look at me and I could tell that something was wrong. And I was wondering if it was me, or if he and Miss Jones had been quarreling or if he was just in a bad mood. I was looking at him pondering the possibilities when I heard Miss Jones's voice again.

"Can I get you anything?" she asked. "Coke, water, a cup of coffee?"

"No, thank you, " I said. "We gon' get something a little later."

"How Audrey?" she asked.

"She's fine," I said.

"And Nathaniel?"

"He's fine too," I said.

"Well, when you see 'em again be sho to tell 'em I send my regards."

"Yes, ma'am," I said. "I will."

I saw her look toward the hallway, then back toward me.

"Well, sit down and make yourself at home," she said. "I'll tell Omenita you here. She ought to be out in a few minutes."

"Yes, ma'am," I said again.

I removed my coat and sat warily upon the sofa. And as I watched Miss Jones walk away, I hoped that Omenita would not take too long for I sensed that Mr. Jones was in a foul mood, and I felt uncomfortable sitting alone with him. I looked at my watch. It was almost seven and though I had not given a lot of thought to what Omenita and I were going to do, it had occurred to me that it might be nice to drive to Cedar Lake. There was an inexpensive motel overlooking the lake, and if Omenita agreed, I thought that we might pick up some takeout and go there and get a room and spend the evening together in the peaceful solitude of a quiet, cozy room with nothing to disturb us but time. I was thinking that when she entered the room, and immediately I stood and looked at her and at that moment she looked more beautiful than I could ever remember. Her hair was hanging about her shoulders and her face was made up and she was wearing a pair of designer jeans that hugged her waist and revealed the incredible shape of her amazing body. And when I saw her, this feeling came over me and all I could think about was that hotel in Cedar Lake and how anxious I was to get her there and hold her and touch her and love her.

"Ready?" she said.

"Ready," I said.

She turned her back to me, and I assisted her with her coat.

"We going, Daddy," she said. He grunted again, but did not look.

We made our way to the door and Miss Jones followed us.

"You kids have fun," she said.

"Yes, ma'am," I said. "We will."

I pulled the door open and we stepped out onto the stoop. A gust of cold wind swept us. I saw Omenita cringe. I put my arm around her and drew her close. Then, I heard the door shut be-hind me. And as we slowly descended the steps, I saw that the men were still huddled around the barrel, only now there were four of them instead of three and from all outward appearances the liquor they were consuming had taken hold, for now their laughter had grown louder and their inebriated bodies more ani-mated. I slowly guided Omenita to the truck, enjoying the fact that her head was on my chest and her arm was about my waist, and when we were close, I opened the door and helped her in, then quickly scurried around to the other side and climbed in next to her. I started the truck and immediately switched on the heater.

"You hungry?" I asked.

"A little," she said. "Why?"

"Well, I thought we might stop by Wongs and pick up some takeout and drive to Cedar Lake to spend a little quiet time to-gether, if that's alright with you."

"Sounds nice," she said.

"Good," I said. I pulled out into the streets. And as I did, I looked at her. She was sitting close to the door and her baby doll face was angled away and there was a far-away look upon her face.

"Something the matter?" I asked.

"They just at it again."

"What happened?"

"He was drinking. And Mama said something about it, then all hell broke loose." Her voice trailed off as if she were about to cry.

I paused a moment, not knowing how to respond.

"You okay?" I asked.

"I guess," she said in a sad, unsure voice.

"Anything I can do?" I asked.

She paused and turned toward me. Her eyes were moist.

"Tell me that you love me," she said. And at the moment I could tell that she needed to hear me say it. She was vulnerable and hurt, and needed to be reassured.

"I do," I said. "More than anything on this earth."

"Tell me that we will never be them."

"We won't," I said. "I promise."

I saw her reach up and wipe her eyes.

"Don't know why she put up with him."

"He's her husband," I said.

"Should've left him a long time ago."

"You don't mean that."

"I do," she said. "She weak and she just let him walk all over her."

"Might not be weakness," I said. "Might just be love."

"Love!" she said.

"He seems to be alright when he's sober," I said.

"She should have left him," she repeated.

"Why doesn't he consider enrolling in a program?" I asked.

"A program!"

"Yeah," I said. "A program."

"You joking, right?"

"No," I said. "I'm serious."

"My daddy," she said, "in a program?"

"Why not?"

"He'd die first."

"Really?" I said.

"Really," she said. "Daddy stubborn as hell."

"Well, I'm sure they'll work it out."

"No they won't," she said. "He'll keep doing what he doing and Mama'll keep taking it." I saw her dab her eyes again. "I just want to get away from this place," she said "Far, far away."

We stopped at the restaurant and purchased the food, then drove the eight miles to Cedar Lake. At the intersection, leading into the city, I turned right and followed the road along the lake until, in the distance, I saw the bright flickering lights of the Lakeside Motel. We pulled into the lot and as always had been our custom, she waited in the truck while I went in and paid for the room. And like always, we both knew that we would stay but a couple hours and when we departed we would not check out, rather we would simply leave the key on the nightstand next to the bed and be on our way.

The Lakeside Motel was small—only two levels high—but Omenita and I preferred it because it was affordable and because the rooms were only accessible from inside the building. And once inside, we were always at ease, for we felt with a certain degree of confidence that anyone visiting the lake or passing by would not be aware of our presence.

I secured the key and we went to the room, which was located on the second floor on the side of the building overlooking the lake. And once we were situated, we sat at the small table next to the window, and the curtains were open and it was dark outside and we could see the glow from the lights cascading along the far bank of the lake. And as I watched her remove the cartons from the bags and place them neatly on the table, I could not help but think how much I loved her and how certain I was that she was the one with whom I wanted to spend the rest of my life. While I was looking at her, she looked up and our eyes met.

"What?" she said softly, flirtatiously.

"Nothing," I said.

"No," she said. "Really . . . what?"

"You just look nice," I said.

She lowered her eyes and looked away, embarrassed.

"I look a mess," she said, "sitting here crying like some kind of silly old fool. My eyes are puffy, my mascara's running."

"No," I said. "I mean it. You look absolutely beautiful."

She smiled and slid a container of food next to me. "Here," she said. "Eat before your food gets cold."

"Have to do something first," I said.

I pushed away from the table and rose to my feet. On the way to her house, I had stopped by the corner store and purchased a couple of candles. Not fancy. But candles nonetheless. I retrieved them from one of the bags that I had hid among the food, and I placed them in the center of the table. And when I was sure that they were where I wanted them, I turned off the lights and lit one candle and then the other. And instantly, I watched the flame flicker and grow until the dim light cut through the darkness casting about us a warm, soft glow. And I looked at Omenita through the flickering flame and her eyes sparkled and her skin shone and through the window by which she sat, I could see the moon sitting high in the heavens, full and bright, keeping watch over the stars and the lake and the night. I smiled at her and she smiled back. And I felt rise in me a warmth that engulfed my being and made my emotions spiral and sent soaring my desire to hold her, to touch her, to possess her.

There was a small radio on the stand next to the bed, I tuned in to a station and adjusted the volume. It was jazz. The music was low and soft and soothing. I turned my face again toward her, and when I was sure that the music met her satisfaction, I returned to my seat at the small table across from her and again gazed longingly into her beautiful brown eyes and there was pulsating in me the joy of the moment and the unabiding love I felt for this woman—the one I had loved since the long gone days of high school. I was sitting there, taking her in when she stretched forth her hand and took my hand into her own.

"Thanks," she said. "This is so nice of you."

"Glad you like it."

I lifted my fork and I began to eat.

"Maurice." She called my name softly.

I looked up and gazed into her soft brown eyes.

"I do love you," she said. "You know that, don't you?"

"I know," I said.

"I mean it. I know I don't always show it, but I am deeply in love with you. It's just that sometimes—"

"Shhh," I said. "No speeches. I don't want to think right now," I said. "I just want to be with you and enjoy this moment. I missed you so much when I was away. More than you can ever imagine. I don't want to get into anything heavy . . . not now, not tonight."

I saw her lower her head and look away; she was crying again. I took one of her hands in both of mine.

"Don't cry," I said. "I don't ever want you to cry."

"I can't help it," she said.

"Things gon' work out," I said. "They always do."

"I just wish we could go away," she said. "Just me and you. And start our life together just like we always planned."

"We will," I said.

"Do you mean it?"

"Of course, I do," I said.

"When?" she said.

"Soon."

"How soon?"

"I don't know," I said.

"What about May?" she said.

"May!" I said.

"Yes . . . May. Right after you graduate. It's perfect."

"I don't know," I said.

"Why not?" she asked. "It's the way we always planned it. We'd finish school, then we would get married."

"I know," I said.

"You've changed your mind?"

"No," I said. "Don't be ridiculous."

"Then what?"

"Law school," I said.

She pushed from the table and walked next to the window.

"I have to make a decision soon," I said. "They'll only hold the scholarship until the first of the year. I need to let them know in a few days."

"I won't put my life on hold for you or no other man," she said. "I won't."

"I'm not asking you to," I said.

"You are," she said.

"Baby."

"No," she said. "I won't."

She turned toward me, and I could see the tears.

"I don't understand," I said.

"All my life, I seen my mama struggling because she was living somebody else's life . . . operating behind somebody else's dream. That ain't for me, Maurice. It's two of us in this relationship, and what you talking about don't work for me. You want to go to law school, go, but like I said before, when you leave, don't come back 'cause won't be nothing here for you."

"You don't mean that."

"I do," she said. "As much as it pains me to think about it, I do."

"I'm sorry about your folks," I said. "I know it's been hard on you, but I ain't your daddy," I said. "You need to understand that."

"Don't fool yourself," she said. "You daddy all over. You just don't know it yet, that's all."

"What's that supposed to mean?"

"You a dreamer," she said. "And your dreams come first. To hell with me or anybody else. It's all about you and what you want to be."

She lowered her head and began to cry again.

"This is about us," I said. "And our future. Why can't you see that?"

"You ever heard Daddy sing?" she asked.

I shook my head.

"Ever hear him play the guitar?"

I shook my head again.

"I'll tell him to play for you one day."

"What's this got to do with us?" I asked.

"Tell me in his day he was a guitar playing fool . . . and could sing. Lord, they say he could sing a woman right out of her draws on his worst day. And that's what him and Mama hitched they horse to. He was gon' sing them right out of the projects, so he took to playing that guitar and running all over the place while she pittled on one dead-end job after another trying to make ends meet. In the meantime, the babies kept coming . . . Guess he couldn't give up his dream and find a job to take care of his family, but he could quit long enough to climb on top of Mama and try to knock a hole into next week. Naw, Maurice, that ain't for me. Now, I put my life on hold for you to go to college, and you did that. Now, it's time for you to find a job and start providing."

"But—"

"But nothing," she said. "I'm tired, Maurice. I'm tired of living with my mama and my daddy, I'm tired of dealing with their drama, and I'm tired of waiting on you."

"Baby," I said, "it's just three more years. Can't you wait three more years?"

"Three mo' years!" she said. "I ain't waiting three more minutes."

"Baby, please," I said. "Don't be this way."

"No, Maurice. I mean it."

"But why?"

"Why!" she said.

"Yes," I said. "Why?"

She turned her back to me, crying. I placed my hand on her shoulder. She turned back and faced me.

"Okay, Maurice, let's say I agree to wait three years, then what? Halfway through you come to me and tell me you made a mistake. You don't want to be no lawyer. What you really want to be is a goddamn astronaut . . . Naw, Maurice, I can't do it. I love you, it's true, but I love me too."

"That's not gon' happen," I said. "I know what I want to be."

"And I know what I want you to be too," she said.

"What's that?" I asked.

She looked at me; I saw her lips part. "Employed."

"I will be," I said. "Soon as I finish law school."

"Take me home," she said.

"Omenita!"

"Take me home," she said.

"Can't we talk about this?"

"I've said all I have to say."

"Why do you always do this?" I asked.

"Do what?" she asked.

"Draw a line in the sand."

"I don't know what you talking about," she said.

"Maybe it's you that's like your daddy," I said.

"Take me home," she said.

"Aw, so that how it's gon' be?" I said.

"Take me home," she said, again.

"Baby, please," I said.

"Decide," she said, "and when you do, you know where to find me. In the meantime, leave me alone."

"I have decided," I said. "I'm going to law school."

"Is that right?" she said.

"That's right," I said.

"Well, I don't reckon I'll be needing this."

She twisted the ring from her finger and threw it at me.

"Aw right," I said. "If that's the way you want it."

"That's the way I want it," she said.

"Fine!" I said. "Home it is."

Chapter Thirteen

Frazzled, I put the ring in my pocket and took Omenita home, and once I saw that she was safely inside, I pulled from the curb and guided the truck back onto the street. And as I drove, I cursed myself inwardly, for now I felt lost and hollow and alone. A thousand times I started to turn back, but for some inexplicable reason, I did that which to me seemed impossible; I continued onward, in spite of the powerful forces summoning me back to undo the moment we had just lived. Yes, we had done this dance before, but somehow this seemed different. And the thought that this could be permanent tugged at my heart and twisted my mind in such a way that the simple act of breathing seemed too painful to bear.

I am a man. I told myself this over and over. And as a man, I had to find the strength to stand for that which was right. But with each mile I put between us, I felt my resolve weaken and my doubt rise until I was not sure that the principle for which I had stood was worth the price I might have to pay. And as I wrestled with the decision, I felt the pain from the shame of my weakness boring into my soul and piercing my consciousness until the tears that I had been fighting broke free, and in spite of my best effort, I felt myself crying.

I parked the truck next to the house, but I did not get out.

Instead, I remained there crouched over the wheel, trying to collect myself, for now I was in a free fall and my tattered emotions were such that I was not sure that I could stand, and if I could I was not sure that my legs, weak and fatigued, could carry me from where I was to where I needed to be. And if they could, I was not sure that my pained eyes would not betray me and reveal to those inside my weakened state, rendering me further shame for I was convinced that the conduct I was displaying would be perceived as that of a child and not that of a man.

I took a deep breath and dried my eyes and stepped from the truck. And though the wind was blowing and the temperature had dropped, I did not feel cold, rather I felt warm and moist and numb. I crossed the yard and mounted the steps, and I did not knock, for the lights were on and it was still early, and in all likelihood the door was not locked. I twisted the knob and pushed. The door swung in and I stepped inside. Daddy was sitting on the sofa; Mama was next to him.

"Back so soon?" Daddy asked me.

"Yes, sir," I said. My voice was low, my head was hung.

"Everything aw right?" he wanted to know.

I shook my head. I felt my eyes water.

"What's wrong, son?" Daddy asked, sitting erect. I opened my mouth to speak, but no words came. I felt my lips tremble. And I fought to stay the tears and quail my lips for though I could cry I would not cry, not here, not now, not in front of them.

"Son," Daddy said. "What is it?"

He raised to his feet and stood before me.

"She gave me the ring back."

Daddy looked at me, stunned.

"What happened?" he asked. And when he did I felt a hollow sensation where my heart had been. It was vast, it was empty, it was hot.

"I don't want to talk about it," I said.

Mama had been concerned, but when she heard what I said, I saw her relax, then I heard her say: "Good riddance."

And when she said it, I looked at her, and I felt rise in me an anger that until that moment I had not known.

"I love her, Mama," I said. "Can't you understand that?"

"Well obviously she don't love you," Mama said.

"Audrey," Daddy said. "That's enough."

"I'll be in my room," I said.

"Son," I heard Daddy call to me, but I did not stop and I would not stop, for now I needed to be alone in my room where I could lie and ponder these emotions, which at the moment I neither welcomed nor understood. I could hear him behind me when I entered my room and though he did not call to me again, I knew that he would enter. And I also knew that he would not pry and he would respect my feelings and my desires because to him, I was his son, but I was no longer a boy. No, I was a man; as much as he and much as Grandpa Luke, as much as anyone.

"You aw right, son?"

I was lying on my stomach.

"Not really," I said.

"You want to talk about it?"

"Don't know if I did the right thing," I said.

"I'm sure you did what you felt was right."

"Maybe I ought go back over there."

"No," Daddy said. "She left you, you didn't leave her. Run behind her now, you'll be running behind her the rest of your life. You got to wait her out. She left . . . she the one got to come back."

"What if she don't?" I asked.

"If she love you, she'll come to her senses. If she don't, she won't."

"What am I gon' do then?" I asked.

"Pick again," he said.

I looked away and I wanted to cry, but I knew that I would not. At least not while Daddy was present.

"Got to put your mind on something else for a while. It'll all work out. You a good man. Omenita know that. She just trying you, that's all. . . . Just got to stand your ground 'til this thing blow over."

"Yes, sir," I said.

I felt Daddy's hand on my shoulder.

"You had your dinner?"

"Yes, sir," I said.

"You need anything?"

For an answer, I shook my head.

"Well, I'll get out your way then."

I felt the spring give as Daddy pressed against the bed to stand, and when he was upright, he looked at me and smiled. "See you in the morning," he said.

"Okay, Daddy," I said. "See you in the morning."

Chapter Fourteen

The night passed and though I did not sleep sound, I did sleep, and when I awoke to the warm yellow rays of the risen December sun falling tenderly upon my face through the partially opened blinds, I was instantly relieved, for it had seemed that night would never end, and I was glad when I heard Mama scurrying about and thankful for the work that awaited me at the diner, for I could not bear the thought of being home all day, thinking about Omenita, pondering what she was doing—wondering if she would call.

I dressed and went into the kitchen. Daddy was sitting at the table eating breakfast and Mama was standing over the stove, cooking. Both of them were already dressed. Daddy was wearing his long-sleeve gray khaki shirt and a pair of gray khaki pants and Mama had on a long white dress that she wore to work and an old plain apron about her waist and a plain white rag covering her head. I spoke and sat down, and as I sat there, staring at my food—grits and eggs, bacon and biscuits—I asked myself again if I was doing the right thing or should I give in and call Omenita and make things right before this thing between us got out of hand. And at that moment, I hated myself, for I was weak in a way that I had not realized. No, I would not call . . . I could not call . . .

I was contemplating this when I heard Daddy's voice rise above the quietness.

"You aw right, son?" he asked me.

I looked up; he was looking at me.

"I'm aw right," I said. And when I did, I heard Mama sigh. And I looked toward the stove and Mama had turned toward the table and was looking in my direction and I could tell by her expression that she was perturbed, quite perturbed.

"Well, I hope you ain't gon' mope around all day," she said, "because I suspect that's just what that gal want you to do." She paused and I saw her turn back toward the stove and place a slice of bacon into the cast-iron skillet. I heard the hot grease sizzle, then pop. "Just don't make no sense," she mumbled. "Running behind a crazy girl like Omenita."

I looked at Daddy and I saw him shake his head. Frustrated, I raised my fork and took a small bite of scrambled eggs, and as I chewed I saw Mama looking at me and when I did, I looked away. I did not want to talk to her about Omenita, and I wanted her to know that I didn't. She remained quiet, but I could still feel her angry eyes on me. Behind me, I heard footsteps on the floor. I turned and looked; Grandpa Luke was standing in the doorway. He had on a plaid red-and-black shirt and a pair of well-worn overalls.

"How y'all making out this morning?" he asked. He sounded like he was still very, very tired and I didn't imagine he had slept too well.

"Good morning, Papa," Daddy said.

"How you feeling, Grandpa Luke?" I asked him.

"Oh, I guess I'll do," he said.

"Want some breakfast?" Mama asked.

"Naw. Just think I'll get myself a cup of coffee," he said.

I saw him move to the cupboard and remove a cup.

"Here you go, Papa," Daddy said. "You can sit here."

"Keep your seat," Grandpa Luke said. I saw him pour some coffee in his cup then turn toward the door. "I ain't staying," he said. "Still got a couple of things to do in my room yet."

"What kind of things?" Daddy asked.

"Just got to put a few things away," he said. "That's all."

"I can do that," Mama said. "Soon as I get off from work. You ain't got to worry with that. You ain't got to worry with that at all."

I saw Daddy look at Mama, then at Grandpa Luke.

"Papa, you ain't packing, are you?"

"Packing," Mama said.

"As a matter of fact," Grandpa Luke said. "I am."

"Then, you still thinking about leaving?" Daddy asked.

"Leaving!" Mama said. "What's all this talk about leaving?"

"Just time to go back home," Grandpa Luke said.

I saw Mama look at him, confused. And I looked at Grandpa Luke and thought how lucky he was to have had a love like Grandma. And how much he must miss her. And how eager he must be to return home to be close to her. And how sad he must be feeling after losing her.

"But this is your home," Mama told him.

"No, baby," Grandpa Luke said. "This your home."

"Did we offend you?" Mama asked. " 'Cause Lawd know we didn't mean to."

"No, child," Grandpa Luke said. "Just something there I need, I can't get here."

I saw Mama frown and I knew she did not understand for I had not understood—not in the woods when I first had heard him speak—but now I did. And since I did, I knew he could not stay . . . not here . . . not separated from the woman that he loved. Yes, I understood. I understood completely.

"What?" she asked him.

"Lucille," Grandpa Luke told her.

"Mama Lu!" Mama said. I saw her look at Daddy, but he was not looking at her; he was looking at Grandpa Luke.

"When you wanting to go?" he asked.

"Well," Grandpa Luke said, "I was hoping you could drop me off on your way to work this morning, if you got time."

Mama was standing behind Grandpa Luke. I saw her look at Daddy and shake her head no. I saw Daddy look at her, then lift the cup of coffee sitting before him and take a sip. "I got time," he said. "If that's what you want."

"It's what I want," Grandpa Luke said.

Outside, a horn blew and instinct made Mama turn toward the

door and look. And though she could not see, she knew it was Miss Alberto, the woman she rode to work with. I saw her look at Daddy and shake her head again. And I knew she was trying to tell him not to take Grandpa Luke away, but to keep him here until she got back and perhaps she would be able to talk him out of doing that which to her made no sense. I saw Daddy shrug, signaling his surrender. Grandpa Luke had made up his mind and as far as Daddy was concerned, it was out of his hands. He would do as Grandpa Luke wished, like it or not.

Miss Alberto blew the horn a second time, and I saw Mama remove her apron and grab her coat and purse from atop the deep freezer.

"Better go," she said. "Sound like Alberto in a mighty big hurry this morning."

Daddy took another sip of coffee, then spoke to her over the rim of his cup.

"Need me to bring anything back from town?" he asked.

"You can fill my prescription from the drugstore," she said, "if you don't mind."

"I don't mind," he said.

I saw Mama turn to leave.

"Y'all be good," she said.

"Bye, Mama," I said.

"Bye, son," she said.

"Have a good day," Grandpa Luke said.

"You do the same." She paused and looked at Grandpa Luke. "Will I see you when I get back?" she asked.

"Maybe tomorrow," he said. "Thank I'm gon' sleep in my own bed tonight."

She left, and Daddy dropped Grandpa Luke off by his house then the two of us went to work. When we got there, Jake and Reuben were already there; they were sitting in the kitchen at the table drinking coffee waiting for the diner to open and our shift to begin. I looked at them, but I did not really see them; my mind had again strayed to Omenita. I had seen her car in her yard when we passed, and the sight of it had spurned in me the desire to glimpse her face or hear her voice and that's what I was thinking when they spoke to Daddy and that's why I didn't hear them when they spoke to me.

"Ain't you gon' speak, son?" I heard Daddy say.

"Sir?" I said.

"Jake and Reuben," he said. "They spoke to you."

I looked toward the table, both Jake and Reuben were looking at me.

"Morning," I said.

"Morning," they both said in unison.

I looked at Jake and at Reuben, then looked away.

"Beautiful morning, huh, boss man," Jake said to Daddy.

"Yeah," Daddy said. "If I must say so myself."

"Want a cup of coffee?" Reuben asked Daddy.

"Had a cup 'fo I left home," Daddy said. "But thank you anyway."

"What about you, little boss man?" Reuben asked me. "You drank coffee?"

I heard him, yet I didn't hear him. I wasn't listening; I was looking out the back door toward the highway.

"Son!" Daddy called to me. Instantly, my head snapped around.

"Yeah, Daddy," I said.

"Ain't you gon' answer Reuben."

I looked at Reuben, confused.

"Want some coffee?" he repeated.

"No, thank you," I said.

I saw Jake looking at me strangely.

"Little boss man," he said, "you aw right?"

"Yes, sir," I said.

And instantly, I looked away for I was not interested in talking to him or Reuben or anyone. I raised my eyes and I looked at the big clock high on the wall. It was a quarter 'til seven. The diner would open any minute now and I wanted to get to work and occupy my mind with something other than thoughts of Omenita, for I was convinced that at this very moment she was not spending her time thinking of me. But of what was she thinking? And why had it been so easy for her to give up on that for which I had been convinced we both longed? Was it because of her certainty that I was not a man of resolve and that I would succumb to her? If not today, then tomorrow. And if not tomorrow, then next week. But, no, I would not succumb, I would occupy myself until time revealed to me our fate. And whatever it should be, I would accept it, once and for all. If not for her, then for me. For I was a man. Yes, I was a man.

I turned my face toward the door and I saw Tommy, the short-order cook, poke his head through and speak, then I heard the bell on the front door jingle and I heard the sound of feet on the diner floor and I smiled for from the sound of things it appeared as if once again we were in for a busy day. And before long, I found myself standing before the sink and my hands were submerged in the warm suds and the doors were swinging in and out and the grill was sizzling and Jake was talking and my mind was on my work and though my heart was still numb I was not sad, for there was no time to think and as I reveled in the work, I only hoped that the pace of things would last long enough to help me through the day. And though I liked the pace, I was not anxious for this day to pass, for after work, the only thing awaiting me was time.

Chapter Fifteen

At twelve, I headed to the drugstore to fill Mama's prescription. It was lunchtime and I was not hungry and I did not feel like sitting around the kitchen with Daddy and Jake and Reuben. I was okay as long as I was occupied, but when things slowed, my mind began to wander and I began to feel the strain of my situation with Omenita. And when that feeling came, there was in me an intense desire to move about and find something to occupy my mind.

I didn't leave through the front door; instead I exited the diner through the rear door just off the kitchen and made my way through the short alley and across the narrow intersection that separated the diner from downtown. And once across, I mounted the steps and followed the walk around the corner and along the shops that lined both sides of the street. And as I ambled along, I could not help but notice the long line of cars that seemingly stretched from one end of town to the other and the hordes of people that filled the walkways on either side of Main Street. And as I looked about, I figured that all of this activity was due in part to the hour and in part to the proximity of the holidays. And in spite of the activity and the hordes of people surrounding me, somehow, I still felt alone . . . terribly alone.

The drugstore was located near the center of the street, and though it was a place where many of the townsfolk congregated (mostly whites) and consumed sodas and milkshakes or ate ice cream and hamburgers, I never went there except to fill a prescription or to purchase some other type of over-the-counter medication. In fact, I had never sat at that counter, not once in my twenty years of life. Nor had I ever seen any other black person there. I'm sure they had, it's just that I had never witnessed it.

I pulled the door open and was headed back to the pharmacy counter when I heard a voice ring out.

"Fancy meeting you here."

I had been in a daze but when I heard the voice I turned and looked. Danielle was sitting at the counter on a bar stool next to a young white girl, drinking a cup of coffee. I smiled, but I did not speak. I was uncomfortable. The place was packed to capacity with white folks, and it seemed that every one of them was looking at me.

"I'm not accustomed to being kept waiting," she said. Her tone was playful.

"Sorry," I said. And though I did not look about, I could feel the eyes of the others on me . . . wide . . . white . . . curious. "Been kind of busy." I wanted to keep walking but I did not 'less she think me rude.

I raised my eyes and looked about. Yes, they were all looking at me. Suddenly, the place seemed quiet—too quiet. I started to leave but she stopped me.

"How's work?"

"Fine," I said. "As a matter of fact, I'm at lunch now. And I need to pick up a prescription for Mama."

"Not serious, I hope."

"No," I said. "Just blood pressure, I think."

There was silence.

"Good seeing you," I said. I turned toward the back.

"Wait," she said. "I just had an idea."

I looked but did not speak.

"What about right now?"

"Excuse me," I said.

"Lunch," she said.

I didn't answer.

"You are on break, aren't you?"

I tried to think of a lie, but shock had rendered my brain mute. I looked at her then nodded.

"Good," she said. "How long is your break?"

I looked about, uncomfortable. Why was she doing this? Why?

"An hour," I said.

I saw her push away from the counter.

"That settles it," she said. "Lunch it is."

"The prescription," I said.

"There's no line," she said. "Should only take a couple minutes."

"But—"

"But nothing," she said. "Now, I insist."

"Okay," I said.

Now I was sorry that I had come in here and I wanted nothing now but to leave and put some distance between me and those eyes staring out at me. I made my way back to the counter and as I walked I kept my eyes straight ahead and I hoped that she would not follow me, and I secretly prayed that in the few minutes it took the pharmacist to fill the prescription, I could think of some way to beg off from this thing that I did not want to do. When I made it to the counter, I glanced back and I saw that she had taken her seat at the counter and resumed her conversation with the young lady sitting next to her. Only now, she was not facing the counter. She was sitting on the stool facing the girl and looking toward me. Our eyes met and she smiled, and I quickly looked away, and when I did I saw Mr. John, the pharmacist, staring at me from the little desk behind the counter.

"May I help you?" he asked. I heard the springs on the old swivel chair squeak as he pushed back from the desk and turned toward me.

"Yes, sir," I said. "I need to fill a prescription."

I ran my hand deep into my pocket and retrieved the prescription, and I stretched forth my hand. But Mr. John did not move. Instead, he stared at me for a moment before standing and I knew he was letting me know that he did not approve of the way Danielle and I were talking. And after he was sure that I understood, I saw him place the palms of his hands flat against the arms of the chair. I heard him grunt, then I saw him push to his feet. And once erect, he paused a moment to gather himself before shuffling the short distance from his old desk to the counter. This was his store and he had been operating it for almost fifty years but he was old (he was in his late sixties) and his health was failing. And as a result, he now only worked a few hours a day, two or three days a week. Other than that, his oldest son, Eldridge, a pharmacist as well, ran the place.

I saw him pick up the prescription and look it over, then slowly move back behind the shelves, and once he had filled it, I paid him and made my way back up front. And as I did, I saw Danielle slide off the stool and step away from the counter. And at that moment, I wished that I had not come here. And I wished that she was not standing there. And I wished these people were not staring at me. For if I had not, then I would not have to deal with her or lunch or her father ever again. I looked at my watch and was somewhat disappointed that only a couple of minutes had passed. *Oh, what am I going to do?* I said to myself. *Oh God, what?* I walked on and when I was but a few feet from her, she stopped me.

"Ready, Maurice?" she asked, then smiled.

I nodded but did not speak.

"Where would you like to go?"

No place, I told myself. But, I could not say that to her. And at that moment, I hated her for putting me in such an awkward position.

"Wherever you'd like," I said.

I looked at the door then behind me. I saw a man rise and walked toward us. And as he passed, he looked at me and I quickly looked away. I did not want this . . . I did not want this at all.

"Let's see," she said. "I've been craving catfish lately." She paused and looked at me. "Do you like catfish?"

I nodded.

"Then catfish it is," she said. "Is that okay with you?"

"It's okay," I said.

I followed her out of the store and onto the landing and as she walked, I looked at her. Yes, she was a pretty girl. I would guess about five foot seven or five foot eight. She had long blond hair that stopped midway down her back. Her eyes were a soft shade of blue. Her ruby-red lips were round and full, forming a dainty baby doll mouth inside of which were the whitest teeth I had ever seen. Outside, she stopped and looked about.

"Where's your car?" she asked.

I looked at her, then back toward the diner.

"At the diner," I said.

"Mine is right here," she said, pointing. Her car was parked just beyond the landing in front of the drugstore. "If you like," she said, "we can take it."

I hesitated, wondering if that was the right thing to do.

No, I heard a voice deep within me say. How would I explain riding all over town with a white girl. A rich white girl at that. No, that would not be wise.

"No thanks," I said. "I'll meet you there. I need to stop at the diner."

"You sure?" she asked. "I don't mind driving."

"I'm sure," I said. "But thanks anyway." I turned to leave, then paused. She had not said where we were going. Oh, I should have decided, lest she take me someplace I had rather not go. "By the way," I said, "where are we going?"

"Oh, I'm sorry," she said, smiling. "I didn't say, did I? You must forgive me. Sometimes I can be such a ninny."

She looked at me, but I remained silent.

"The Catfish Cabin," she said. "Do you know how to get there?"

"Yes," I said. "I know."

"So I take it you've eaten there before?"

"No," I said, then shook my head. "I haven't."

"Are you serious?" she asked.

"I'm serious."

"Really?"

"Really," I said.

"Well brace yourself," she said. "You're in for a real treat. It's just the best catfish in the whole state of Louisiana."

I headed back to the diner and as I did, I saw her climb into her car and head west on Main Street toward the restaurant, and I stood there in the cold and I watched her car move farther and farther away until it disappeared into the horizon. And all about me the streets and walkways were still filled with people. And I stood there a moment longer taking them in. Then I wandered into the diner and explained the situation to Daddy, then borrowed the truck and a few dollars, and headed out to meet her. As I drove, I was anxious to get this done and over with. She was a nice girl and all, but my mind was on Omenita and our unstable situation. I pulled into the restaurant's lot and parked the truck just east of the building.

Chapter Sixteen

The Catfish Cabin was a beautiful little restaurant located just outside of the city limits. And when I got there Danielle had already selected a table and I was happy to see that it was near the back in a section of the room that afforded us privacy. I made my way to the table and took my seat and I faced the large beautiful aquarium with its beautiful aquatic fish. And between me and the aquarium was Danielle. And she was sitting quietly reading the menu, but when I sat down, she looked up at me and smiled.

"Nice, hunh?" she said.

And when she did I was still looking around, but when I heard her voice, I lowered my eyes and looked at her. And it was quiet in the room, and I felt strange sitting there with her for I could not remember the last time I sat across from a lady, in such an intimate setting and that lady was not Omenita. And never, in my twenty years of life had I sat in such a setting with a white girl. I turned my face from her and looked about. And though no one was looking at me, I knew they could see me, and I knew that they had seen me long before I entered the building and long before I had sat down across from her. They had seen me, of this I was sure. And because I knew this, I could not shake the feeling that I was being watched. And the fact that I felt this way made me uneasy and I had a wild impulse to rise and walk out for I wanted to end this thing and leave this place and go outside where I could breathe.

I nodded, then smiled. I wanted to answer her, but I could not. I was too nervous and because I was nervous my thick tongue would not work. I picked up the menu and began looking through it. And while my eyes were averted I heard her speak to me again.

"Order whatever you like," she said. "It's on me."

I lowered the menu and looked at her.

"I can't let you do that," I said.

I saw her expression change, and I was afraid that I had offended her.

"But I insist," I heard her say.

"That's not necessary," I said.

And I saw her eyes on me again.

"But I want to," she said.

"No," I said. "I can't let you pay for me. I just can't."

She looked away, then looked back. I saw her blue eyes become sad. And at that moment, I thought, *my God, she's going to cry.*

"You're really hurting my feelings," she said.

I paused, stunned.

"I don't mean to," I said.

"I know you don't," she said. And I could hear her struggling to maintain control of her voice. "I'm just being silly."

"No," I said.

"Yes," she said. "I am, but it's just that I really appreciate what you did for me yesterday."

"But that was nothing," I said again.

"Well, it meant a lot to me," she said. "I was in a difficult position and you went out of your way to accommodate me."

"I guess," I said.

"No," she said. "Really. That was so incredibly nice. And I would really like to do something nice for you. After all, one good turn deserves another, right?"

"I guess," I said again.

She sniffled, then smiled.

"Besides," she said, "I was thinking, let me do this for you now and when you get to be this big, hotshot lawyer, you can take me out on the town. I mean chartered plane, limousine, fancy restaurant, the whole nine yards. Deal."

She smiled again and I smiled back.

"Like you said," I said, "one good turn deserves another."

"Well that settles that," she said.

And no sooner had the words passed from her lips than the waiter appeared and I looked up at him, and he was young and white, and in his left hand was a small pad and in his right was a pencil. He looked at Danielle, then at me, then back to Danielle.

"Afternoon, Miss Davenport," he said.

"Good afternoon, Joe," she spoke to him.

He looked at me again.

"How are you, sir?"

"Fine," I said, then averted my eyes.

"How's your mother?" Danielle asked him.

"She's fine," he said.

"When you see her again please say hello for me."

"I will," he said.

There was silence, then he looked at Danielle. ·

"Ready to order?" he asked.

"I think so," she said.

She looked at me. I nodded, then she turned back toward the waiter.

"We're ready," she said.

"Alright," he said "What will it be?"

"I'll have the catfish," she said.

I saw him write her order on the little pad, then look up.

"Would you like the fries or hush puppies with that?"

"Hush puppies," she said.

"Anything to drink?"

"Iced tea," she said, "if you have it."

"We have it," he said. Then he looked at me. "And you, sir?"

"I'll have the same," I said.

He marked his pad then paused.

"Iced tea as well?"

"No," I said. "I'll have a Coke."

"Okay, sir," he said. "A Coke it is."

He turned to leave and there was in me this strange feeling that he, too, like all the rest had been evaluating me. And like the others, he was angered and incensed by my presence with her. Yes, she was a girl of this new South, but not him, and not them. I could feel it. I took a quick glance around and I could see them, young and old, male and female, sitting tall and important under the warm, yellow glow of the dim restaurant lights and yet I sensed an uneasiness among them. An uneasiness, not at my presence, for that was a condition to which they had long ago become accustomed. But their uneasiness was with the two of us sitting here together. And because of their uneasiness, I felt uneasy. No, guilty. And I wanted to scream: "We are not together. I have a woman . . . a beautiful black woman." Or did I? I was contemplating that when I heard a voice, soft and sweet, rise above the dull muddle of people talking.

"I spoke to Father," she said.

I turned my face toward her, and she was looking at me again.

"You did?" I said, somewhat shocked.

"Yes," she said. "And he was so pleased to hear of your decision."

"Really!" I said, louder than intended.

"Oh, God, yes," she said, smiling. "He's so proud of you."

I smiled, but did not speak, and I did not speak because I thought her words strange for he neither knew me nor I him.

"He would like to talk to you as soon as possible," she said. "If that's alright with you."

"It's alright," I said.

And though I said it, I was not comfortable with the prospect of conversing with the judge. In fact, I would rather not, but under the circumstances I felt obligated.

"Can you meet with him on Sunday?"

"Sunday!" I said. I thought this strange.

"Yes," she said. "He's out of town until then. But he would love to have you over as soon as he returns."

"You mean at your house?"

"Yes," she said. "He's extremely anxious to speak with you. I can't remember when I've seen him so excited."

I looked at her again, then looked away.

"What time?" I asked.

"Would three be okay?"

"Three is fine," I said.

"Fantastic," she said, and when she did I laughed.

"What?" she asked.

"Nothing," I commented.

"Really," she said. "What?"

"Nothing," I replied.

"Liar," she said, then smiled.

"It's just that you say that a lot."

"What?"

"That word."

"What word?"

"Fantastic."

"Really!"

"Really," I said.

She was quiet.

"I'm sorry," I said. "I shouldn't have laughed."

"No, it's okay," she said. "I'll work on that."

"Why?" I said. "It's you."

"It makes me sound like a ninny."

"No," I said. "It doesn't."

"Then why did you laugh?"

"I shouldn't have," I said.

"But you did."

"I'm just being silly," I replied.

"If you say so," she said, "but I must admit, when I look at you I don't see silly."

I paused and looked at her.

"What do you see?" I asked. She had opened a door and I was curious as to what lay on the other side.

"I don't know," she said. "Maybe shyness."

There was silence.

"You are shy, aren't you?"

"No," I said. "Just quiet."

"And considerate," she said.

"I guess," I said.

"Well, it's very becoming."

"It's just me," I said.

"And modest."

"I'm not trying to be," I said.

"And polite."

"Stop it," I said. "Please."

She smiled. "And charming."

I looked at her, but I did not speak.

"Quiet, charming, polite. Yes, you're going to make a fine attorney."

"Well, I don't know about all that," I said.

"Well, I do," she said. "Trust me. I do."

"Good that somebody knows," I mumbled, "because I'm definitely having some serious doubts."

"Why?" she asked.

"Difficult not to."

"I don't understand what you mean," she said.

"A boy like me," I said. "From a place like this."

"And?" she said.

"And!" I said.

"Yes," she said. "What's your point?"

"Well, do you know any other attorneys like me?" I asked.

"As a matter of fact I do," she said.

"Who?" I asked, stunned.

"Well, not exactly like you," she said. "But Maurice, I come from a long line of lawyers. And over the years, I have learned that there's something about the good ones. They have 'it.' Now, I'm not exactly sure what 'it' is. But, whatever it is, you have it . . . I mean it," she said. "You have a presence about you that is simply uncanny. I noticed it the first time we met."

"Really?" I said.

"Yes, really! I mean it. You're going to make a fine attorney."

"I don't know," I said. "But, thanks for saying so."

"I'm serious," she said. "You'll do fine."

"I suppose," I said.

"You'll feel better after you speak to Father," she said.

I paused and looked at her.

"Why is Judge Davenport so anxious to help me?" I asked.

"Why?" she said.

"Yes," I said. "Why?"

"Are you serious?"

"Yes," I said. "I am."

"Maurice, you're practically family."

"Family," I said. I looked at her strangely. "How you figure?"

"Maurice!" She called my name again.

"What?" I said, dumfounded.

"Are you serious?" she asked again.

"Yes," I said. "I'm serious."

"We share the same mother, silly."

"What!" I said, then chuckled.

"That's right," she said. "My brotha." And she emphasized the word *brotha*. And when she did I laughed. I didn't mean to, but when she said that I could not help but laugh. I brought my hands to my eyes.

"Really," she said. "All jokes aside. I admire Mother Audrey so much."

"Admire," I said.

"Yes," she said. "Does that surprise you?"

"Kind of," I said.

"Why?" she asked.

"She's your maid," I said.

"Well, I don't see her that way," she said. "She's much more than that to us. She's a very special human being and an integral part of our family. We love her."

I looked at her, astonished.

"Is that hard for you to believe?"

"Never thought about it," I said.

"Well, we do," she said. "She's my second mother. And I love her with all my heart."

"*Love* is a mighty strong word," I said.

"Maybe so," she said, "but it's how I feel, and that's why Mother and Father were so excited when I told them that you were going to law school. Of course, they were happy for you, but they were even happier for Mother Audrey. They know how much she loves you. And how hard she has worked to have your life be meaningful. She talks about you all the time."

"So they don't think it's crazy?" I said. "A boy like me . . . with parents like mine . . . talking about being a lawyer."

"Heavens no! Father thinks it's great. As a matter of fact, he has so many thoughts he would like to share with you. For example, did you know that there has never been an African-American attorney in this entire parish?"

"Do you mean in Brownsville?" I asked.

"No," she said. "The entire parish."

"No," I said. "I didn't know that."

"Neither did I," she said, "until Father informed me."

"Wow!" I said.

"That's why father feels it is so important for African-American men from the parish to go into the legal profession. Especially men of character such as yourself who have been raised not only to believe in a strong work ethic, but who also understand the importance of spending a significant portion of their lives thinking of others. And when I told him that you wanted to be a defense attorney, he thought that was absolutely wonderful and he said that you would make a fine attorney . . . a fine one indeed."

"Really!"

"Oh, he's absolutely convinced."

"Hope he's right," I said.

"Oh, I know he's right," she said. "There's no doubt about it."

The waiter returned with our food and placed it on our table before us and when he was done, I lifted my fork and cut a small piece of fish and brought it to my mouth. And as I did, I leaned back in my chair and looked around. And I had just begun to chew when my eyes strayed toward the door and in that instant my jaws locked and I watched in disbelief as I saw Omenita walk into the room. And as I watched her, my heart sank for she was not alone—she was with a man. And he was adorned in an expensive suit and an elegant tie and he was carrying himself in such a manner that led me to conclude that he was someone of importance. Of that I was sure. But who was he? I strained my eyes and looked. No, I had never seen him before. I lowered my head for a moment. I did not want her to see me. Then, when she was seated, I looked at him again. She was smiling and gazing upon him with eyes that I had believed were reserved only for me.

Then I realized that I had seen him before. He was older now and a little heavier and a number of years had passed, but it was him, the only other man whom she had ever loved besides me. Her former boyfriend . . . Gerald.

Chapter Seventeen

Under the dim light of the flickering bulb, I saw him take Omenita's hand in his own and instantly I felt my pounding heart stop and I felt my eyes widen and I looked at them and for a brief moment, vague panic made me lean forward in my seat and stare. And I could feel myself drifting to a place of which I was unfamiliar and I felt myself giving in to a strange force beckoning me to rise and go to her and confront her, and I tried to will myself calm and I told myself to breathe and even in the telling, I could feel the rage mounting and I was just about to rise when I heard the soft, far-away whisper of Danielle's voice calling my name. I heard her, yet I did not hear her for both my gaze and my attention was fixated on Omenita, and though I wanted to respond to that which I had heard, I could not for now there had engulfed me a haze so thick and so dense that I felt myself in a trance, hypnotized by that which I was seeing and numbed by that which I was feeling.

"Maurice," she summoned me again.

I heard the soft echo of her voice penetrate my consciousness and I felt my lips part and my mouth open.

"Yes," I said.

"What is it?" she asked.

I glanced at her, then back toward the table. Suddenly, a

thought occurred to me. Maybe Gerald was the reason Omenita had been so cavalier. Maybe she was involved with him. Out of the corner of my eye, I saw Danielle's head slowly turn toward them and when her eyes rested upon the strange faces sitting just beyond us, I saw her squint and slowly turn her head back toward me.

"Do you know them?" she asked.

I nodded, but I did not speak. She looked at them again, then back at me.

"Who are they?"

I looked at her, and I could feel my heart racing.

"She's my lady," I said, then quickly looked away. And at that moment, there was silence. And I knew Danielle was confused. And I wanted to explain. But I could not. Suddenly, I felt myself engulfed by a wave of sadness so intense that I feared at any minute the floodgates would give way and I would weep. I saw her look at the table again, then back at me.

"Didn't know you were involved," she replied.

"I am," I commented. Then it was quiet again.

Out of the corner of my eye, I saw her glance at them again, then back at me. Then, I saw her forehead wrinkle and I knew she was trying to figure out what was going on and why my mood had suddenly changed. I turned back toward Omenita. And though I was no longer looking at Danielle I could feel her looking at me.

"Maurice," she said gently. I heard her and yet I did not hear her. "Maurice!" she called to me again. The tone of her voice startled me and I quickly turned toward her and looked.

"Hunh?" I said.

She paused, staring.

"Is something the matter?"

"No," I said.

"You sure?"

"Yes," I said. "I'm sure."

She paused again.

"You seem a little distracted," she said.

"Wonder what she's doing here with him?" I mumbled. I saw her look at them, then shake her head and shrug.

"Who knows?" she said. "Could be any number of reasons."

"Well, I'm going to find out," I said.

I pushed away from the table but the sound of her voice stopped me.

"No," she said.

I paused and looked at her.

"You'll just make a scene," she explained.

"I don't care," I said.

"Well, you should," she said. "You have your future to think about. If you want to be a lawyer in this town, you can't go around getting into public confrontations. Besides, things might not be as they appear."

"What else could this be?"

"It could be anything."

"Like what?" I asked.

"I don't know," she said again.

"Well, I'm going to find out."

"No," she said. "Not here . . . not now."

"Well," I said, then hesitated, "what do you propose I do?"

"Wait until they leave," she counseled. "Talk to her outside."

"I can't sit here and watch them."

"Then let's leave."

"They'll see us," I said.

She paused and looked about.

"We can leave through the back."

She motioned for the waiter and we lingered until he came, then she paid for our meal and he escorted us out through what I assumed to be a fire exit. When we were outside, I thanked her for lunch and apologized for the situation, and I turned toward my truck but the sound of her voice stopped me.

"Do you mind if I wait with you?" she asked.

I turned and looked at her. "You don't have to," I said.

"I know," she said. "But I would like to."

"Why?" I asked. "This doesn't concern you."

"I'm afraid you're going to do something stupid."

"I'm just going to talk to her," I said. "That's all."

"I would still prefer to wait with you, if it's alright."

I was quiet, thinking. I wanted to be alone. But how could I get rid of her without hurting her feelings?

"We can wait in my car," she said. "I'll keep you company until she comes out. And when she does, I'll leave . . . I promise. I just don't want anything to happen to you. That's all."

"Alright," I said.

We went to her car and I sat slouched upon the passenger's seat for what seemed an eternity staring headlong at the closed restaurant door. And as I waited, I felt mount in me an anger so hot and so vile, I feared at any moment, I would tear from the car and storm into the building and confront them in a manner commiserate with the warring emotions raging inside my tormented soul. So this was what it had come to. I looked at the closed door again, and as I did, my whirling emotions overtook me. Suddenly, I reached for the door handle and was readying myself to get out when I saw the restaurant door swing open. Stunned, I fell back against the seat and watched the two of them stroll out together. Her hand was nestled in his and upon her face was a smile, and I could not let my eyes move beyond them.

"It may not be as it appears." I heard Danielle's voice cut through the stillness.

"But what if it is?" I said.

There was a brief silence then Danielle spoke again.

"We should leave," she said.

"No," I said. "I need to talk to her."

"Not now," she said. "Not like this. Please . . . let's just go."

"I can't," I said. "I have to talk to her and I have to talk to her right now."

I pushed the door open and got out. I took a few hurried steps, then I called to her. From a distance, I saw her whirl and look in my direction, and as she stood statuelike watching me make my way across the lot, she still held on to Gerald's hand. Behind me, Danielle called to me again and I heard the sound of her shrill excited voice float to me across the vast open space. I heard her but I wasn't listening. My focus was on Omenita and this man holding her hand. I continued moving forward at a quick pace and when I was close, I stopped before them. I saw Omenita gaze at me. She seemed startled. She seemed vexed.

"We need to talk," I told her.

"There's nothing to talk about," she said in a huff.

"You call this nothing," I said.

"I got to go, Maurice." She turned to leave and I grabbed her arm, then she pulled away again. "No," she said. "I mean it . . . I got to go."

Out of the corner of my eye, I saw Gerald step forward.

"Hey, man," he said. "Why don't you let her be?"

"And why don't you mind your own business?" I said.

"Omenita is my business."

I turned and faced him directly.

"What's that supposed to mean?" I said.

He remained quiet and I looked at Omenita but she wasn't looking at me. She was looking off in the direction of her car.

"What is this?" I asked her.

She glanced at me briefly, then looked away.

"I got to go," she said again.

"Wait," I said.

"Man, why don't you just leave her alone?"

"And why don't you get out of my face?" I said.

"Come on, Gerald," Omenita said, "Let's go."

"No," I said. "We need to talk."

"Say, man," Gerald said, stepping toward me. "You heard the lady."

"Back up off me," I said.

"Stop it!" Omenita said. "Both of you, stop it!"

I paused and looked at her. Beyond us I could see a small group congregating near the restaurant door. They were looking in our direction.

"What is this anyway?" I asked. "And why are you here with him?"

"What right you got asking me that?"

She was incensed by the question. I could see it in her face.

"What right!" I said.

"Yeah," she said, her voice elevated. "What right?"

I looked beyond her. A few more people had exited the restaurant. A lone white man had separated from the group and I was sure that he was trying to hear what we were saying.

"Omenita," I said, "how can you ask me that?"

"I'm leaving," she said.

"No," I said. I grabbed her arm again. "Not before we talk." She tried to pull away but I wouldn't let her. I saw the white man move a little closer, then stop. I felt Omenita struggling. I tightened my grip. I didn't want her to leave.

"Maurice!" She said, through clenched teeth. "I mean it! Let me go!"

"No," I said. "Not before we talk."

"Turn her loose," Gerald demanded.

I felt Omenita pull harder and I squeezed even tighter.

"Turn her loose," Gerald said again. "Turn her loose before I bust a cap in your crazy ass."

In the distance, I heard a woman scream. Then I heard feet scampering across the asphalt parking lot. I turned and looked. Gerald had a gun and the barrel was pointed at my head.

"Call the police," I heard someone shout. "Call the police."

I saw the white man remove a cell phone. Then I saw the others hurry back into the restaurant.

Chapter Eighteen

In the chaos of the moment, I stood frozen and unsure of what to do next. And then above the haze of my uncertainty, I heard the familiar sound of Omenita's voice cutting angrily through the madness.

"Gerald!" she screamed forcefully, "what's wrong with you? Put that goddamn thing up before somebody gets hurt!"

I saw Gerald look at her, then back at me.

"Not until this bastard turns you loose," he said.

I hesitated, looking for a moment to rush him. I saw an empty beer bottle on the ground behind him. Yes, when he looked away, I would grab the bottle and even the odds. I was looking at the bottle when I heard Omenita's voice again.

"Goddammit, Maurice! Do what he say!"

I released my grip and eased my hand away, and when I did, Omenita stepped to the side. But Gerald did not lower the gun. Instead, he kept it pointed at me—no, not at me, at my head.

"Why don't you put that gun down," I said, "and come at me like a man?"

"And why don't you step aside?" he said. "So me and the lady can leave."

"I need to talk to her," I said.

"How many times she have to tell you? She don't want to talk to you."

There was silence, and for a moment I stared at him without a thought or an image in my mind. There was just the pain of seeing Omenita standing next to him and hearing him speak for her against me. I looked at the bottle again. Oh, if I could just grab it and swing it with all my might and blot him out, then find the words with which I could utter to make her mine again. I was contemplating the bottle when I heard footsteps on the pavement behind me. I turned and I saw Danielle walking toward me; her eyes were wide, her gait accelerated, her demeanor alarmed. Oh, I did not need this. Not here. Not now.

I turned back toward Gerald and Omenita. And just as I thought they were no longer watching me; they were watching her. God! My whole world was crashing right here before my very eyes. I looked at the bottle again. But before I could move, I felt Danielle grab my arm and pull.

"Come on," she said. "Let's go."

"Not before I talk to Omenita," I said.

"Not here," Danielle said. "Not like this."

I saw Omenita look at Danielle.

"And who in the hell you suppose to be?" she asked.

"Ain't no need to talk to her like that," I said.

"What!" Omenita said.

"It's okay," Danielle said, "Let's just go."

I saw Omenita frown. "Y'all together?" she asked.

I didn't comment, neither did Danielle.

"Well ain't this a bitch?" I heard Omenita say.

"Why don't you watch your mouth?" I said.

"And why don't you go on about your business?" Gerald said. "She don't want to be bothered with you."

"Was I talking to you?" I asked.

I looked at him; he had dropped the gun next to his side and I considered rushing him, but I did not. He was too far away, and it was too dangerous.

"Maurice," Danielle said, "you don't need this."

"Don't need what?" Omenita said.

"This," Danielle said.

"You mean me?" Omenita said. "You trying to rag on me?"

"Miss, I don't even know you," Danielle said.

"And let's just keep it that way," Omenita said.

"This is crazy," Danielle said.

In the distance, I heard a siren wail. I turned and looked. I saw a police car whip into the parking lot and sped toward us. And I saw the white man with the cell phone extend his hand and point in our direction, and when he did, I thought about leaving. But fear rendered me immobile. I looked at Gerald and I saw him reach back and tuck the gun in the waist of his pants. The squad car pulled up next to us and stopped. The door swung open and an officer stepped out.

"What's going on, here?" he asked.

I looked at the officer. He was a big man. I would guess he was six foot two or six foot three, and close to two hundred forty pounds. He appeared to be in his mid-to-late thirties. He was clean shaven and his short blond hair was neatly cropped and partially hidden under his policeman's hat. He was dressed in the standard blue uniform of his office, only now he was wearing a heavy blue jacket and a pair of thick black gloves.

"Nothing, officer," I said.

He looked at me, confused.

"Who called the police?"

"I did," the white man with the cell phone told him. I turned and looked at him. He was a short, stocky fellow with long, stringy hair. I had never seen him before.

"What's the problem?" the officer asked.

"Those two," he said pointing at us, "were causing a disturbance."

"Hello, Jeff," Danielle interrupted before the stranger could continue. I saw the officer look at Danielle, then frown.

"Miss Davenport?" he said.

Danielle smiled and the officer removed his hat.

"Afternoon, ma'am," he said, then nodded.

She nodded, then smiled again.

"How's the judge?" the officer asked her.

"He's fine," she said.

"And your mother?"

"She's fine as well."

"Please tell them I send my best."

"I will," she said.

I saw the officer look at us, then back at her.

"Well," he said, "what's going on here?"

He was speaking to Danielle, but I answered.

"Just a misunderstanding," I said.

The officer turned his head and looked at me.

"And who are you?" he asked.

"He's a friend of the family," Danielle answered for me.

"Your family?" the officer asked, confused.

"Yes," Danielle said. "He's Miss Audrey's son."

The stranger glanced at me then at the officer.

"Well, he sure wasn't acting very friendly a minute ago," he said.

"Now there's no need to blow this thing out of proportion," Danielle said. "This was just a little disagreement between friends. Pure and simple."

"A misunderstanding," the officer said.

"Yes," she said. "Nothing more."

I saw the officer smile and nod, then place his hat back atop his head. For him the matter was settled. He started to turn away but before he could the stranger spoke again.

"He had a gun," the stranger said. "Does that sound like a little misunderstanding to you?"

The officer looked at the stranger, wide-eyed.

"Who had a gun?"

"Him," the stranger said, pointing at Gerald.

The officer turned toward Gerald and their eyes met.

"Move against the car!" The officer issued an order.

Gerald complied and when he did, the officer eased forward.

"Face the vehicle and place your hands on the hood."

"Yes, sir," Gerald said coyly then did as he was told.

"Where's the weapon?" the officer asked.

"In my pants," Gerald told him.

The officer eased the gun from Gerald's waist, then removed the clip and place the gun on the ground.

"Any more weapons on you?" he asked.

"No, sir," Gerald said, still smiling. "That's it."

"You know it's illegal to carry a concealed weapon in this state, don't you?" the officer asked.

"I have a permit," Gerald said.

"You from around here?" the officer asked.

"Grew up here," he said. "I live in Texas now. Dallas, Texas."

"Why are you carrying a weapon?"

"Because of my job."

"And what do you do?"

"I'm head of security."

"For who?"

"The mayor."

"You're a police officer?"

"That's right."

"Why didn't you say so?"

"You didn't ask," he said.

"Did you draw this weapon?"

"Yes, I did."

"Why?"

"Just protecting the young lady," he said.

"What lady?" the officer asked.

"Her," Gerald said, pointing to Omenita. "He attacked her."

"He's lying," I said.

I saw the officer look at her.

"Ma'am, are you hurt?"

Omenita began to cry but didn't answer.

"Did he attack you?" the officer asked.

"My God, Jeff," Danielle said. "He didn't attack her. She's his girlfriend."

"Ex-girlfriend," Omenita said.

I looked at Omenita hard.

"There's no need for this," Danielle said. "No need at all."

"I don't care if he is an officer," the stranger said. "He shouldn't be brandishing a gun in public. Someone could get hurt. My God, man, there were a bunch of innocent people out here."

"Tell me what you saw," the officer said.

"Well, I was standing over by the restaurant when I saw this man here." He paused and pointed at me. "Grab that young lady by the arm."

"Wait a minute," I said. "I—"

"Let him finish," the officer said.

"And I saw that man over there—" he paused and pointed at Gerald—"pull a gun and that's when I called the police."

I saw the officer look at Gerald, then at Omenita.

"Ma'am, did he touch you?"

She nodded but did not speak.

"Do you want to press charges?"

"Charges!" I said.

"That's right," he said. "Charges."

He waited, but she didn't say anything.

"This is ridiculous," Danielle said. "He didn't attack her."

"I'm sorry, Miss Davenport," the officer said, "but I have two witnesses here who say that he did."

"They're lying," I said again.

"I just want him to leave me alone," Omenita said.

"What about him?" I asked, looking at Gerald. "Officer or not, he doesn't have the right to go around pulling guns on innocent people."

"Shouldn't of attacked her," Gerald said.

"I didn't attack her," I said. "And you know it."

"Both of you need to be quiet," the officer said.

"I just want to go back to work," Omenita said, raising her gloved hands to her face and gently dabbing her tearing eyes.

"Omenita," I said. "Baby, we need to talk."

"You need to leave me alone," she said.

I saw Gerald look at the officer.

"See," he said. "He's still harassing her."

"I don't know what this is all about," the officer said, "but it needs to end right here. Does everybody understand that?"

"I just want to go back to work," Omenita said again.

"Go ahead," the officer said.

"Me too," Gerald said.

"You all together?"

"Yes, sir," he said "We are."

Gerald turned to leave, then stopped.

"May I have my weapon?"

The officer handed him the gun.

"Now, I don't want any more trouble out of you," he said. "You hear?"

"Yes, sir," Gerald said. "I hear you."

"I watched the two of them walk away. And when I saw Omenita get into the car with Gerald, I felt my heart sink.

"That goes for you too," the officer said.

"Yes, sir," I said.

He turned to Danielle.

"I'll be seeing you, Miss Davenport."

"Thank you, Jeff," she said. "Take care of yourself."

"Yes, ma'am," he said. "I will."

I watched him climb into his car and drive away. I was still watching the car when I heard Danielle speaking to me.

"Are you going to be okay?" Danielle asked me.

"I'll be alright," I said.

"Are you sure?" she asked.

"I'm sure," I said.

She paused a moment, and I saw her looking toward her car.

"Well," she said softly, "I'll see you on Sunday."

"Okay," I said. "See you Sunday."

And when she was gone, I climbed into the truck and I drove back to the diner. And when I walked in, Daddy and the crew were at their stations working. I looked at the clock. I was late . . . only a few minutes, but late nonetheless. I looked at Daddy and he looked at me.

"Sorry," I said.

"Ain't had no trouble, hunh?"

"A little," I said.

"Nothing serious, I hope."

I shook my head and went to work.

Chapter Nineteen

I sank my hands into the warm, soapy water. Behind me, I could hear the dishes clanging and the soft, steady murmur of chattering voices emanating deep from within the diner. And in the distance, I heard Daddy tell Jake that we should finish a little early today, and inside I secretly hoped that this was true, for try as I may, I could not shake the image of Omenita climbing into the car with Gerald, and as I thought of the two of them together, it occurred to me that if I did not talk to her now there was the very real possibility that I could lose her forever.

And because the thought of that reality was too painful to bear, I worked steadily until it was time to go home and not once did I speak of her or of what had happened or of what I was feeling. Nor did I allow my mind to stray to the fragile spot of my innermost fears, instead, I told myself that I would remain optimistic until day's end and then I would go to her and make her understand that which in my heart I knew she must have also known— I loved her and she loved me, and whatever terrible thing had brought us to this wretched point, we could work it out and make it right and move forward with our lives together.

I was more than ready to leave when I heard Daddy yell, "quitting time!" I had not known this thing that happened today would happen and because I had not expected it, I could feel myself falling apart inside. Yes, I had made a terrible mistake, and I could not help but worry that I had overplayed my hand and as a result Omenita had done that which I had not believed she would ever do. Move on.

I put my things away and followed my father out to the truck, and as we walked, I could feel the frigid air about my ears and I thought how nice it would be to snuggle with Omenita under a cozy blanket and the thought of the two of us together caused my spiraling emotions to sink even deeper, for in my heart, I knew that under the circumstances that was highly unlikely.

There was a tune on the radio. An old school tune with which I was unfamiliar. It was soft and soothing, and though it was not my kind of music, I was thankful for it nonetheless for it filled the quietness between Daddy and me, and for a brief moment it lulled my senses and eased my mind, and as I began to relax, I found myself looking up the road, far up the road, and that is precisely what I was doing when I heard my father speak.

"Silas called in today," he said.

"Yes, sir," I said, acknowledging that I had heard him.

"Said he'd like to come in tomorrow and finish out the week."

"Guess he's feeling better," I said.

"Some, I reckon. But probably just need the time more than anything else. After all he does have a family to feed."

"Yes, sir," I said. "I understand."

"Had hoped you could be with us at least until Monday."

"That's alright," I said, and I turned my head and looked at him, and when I did, he looked at me and smiled.

"You did a good job for us," he said. "Everybody up there talking about what a good worker you are. And how well you handle yourself. I'm real proud of you, son. But, then I reckon you know that."

"Yes, sir," I said. "I do."

"You turned out to be a fine man," he said. "A fine man indeed."

"Thank you," I said.

"I mean it, son. You're a good man. Always remember that."

"Yes, sir," I said. "I will."

Then it was quiet again, and I could feel the rugged truck

slowly plowing along, and I could see the vast countryside with the long row of houses just off the highway tucked neatly behind the railroad tracks, and I followed the tracks with my eyes, and out of the corner of my eye I could see Daddy, and he, too, was looking beyond the railroad tracks toward the houses. And I knew he was thinking about Grandpa Luke, and how he was getting along, and how he didn't really want him living by himself. But I wasn't thinking about that. I was thinking about Omenita and that man she was with, and what I should do. Maybe I had lost her, and if I had, it was all my fault. I should never have pushed her. I should have never taken that stupid ring back. Why had I done that? Why?

Daddy pulled into the yard and I bound out and followed him up the steps. He pulled the door open and we went inside. Mama had been in the kitchen, cooking. But when she heard the door open and close, she walked into the living room. She stopped when she saw us, but she did not look at Daddy, instead, she kept her eyes focused on me. Even when she spoke to Daddy, she only glanced away briefly then quickly fixed her gaze back on me.

"Something smell good," Daddy said.

Mama glanced at him briefly.

"It's on the table," she said, then quickly fixed her gaze back on me.

I moved forward to speak.

"Hi, Mama," I said.

She frowned. "Mister, don't you 'Hi, Mama' me, you hear?"

I looked at her as if I didn't know what she was talking about. Then I frowned and shrugged.

"What!" I said.

"What!" she said. "Boy, don't play with me."

"Audrey," I heard Daddy say, "what's this all about?"

"Ask your son," Mama said. "Let him tell you."

"Tell me what?" Daddy asked, and I could see that he was tired. I looked at him for a moment, then averted my eyes.

"Nothing," I said.

"Nothing!" Mama said sarcastically.

She paused and waited for me to respond, but I remained quiet. I saw Daddy walk to his recliner and sit down. Only, he did

not sit all of the way back on the chair. Instead, he sat on the edge
and rested his elbows on the arms. He was tired. Dead tired. And
I wished Mama would drop this and let Daddy eat and go lie
down.

"Were you down at the Catfish Cabin?"

"Yes, ma'am," I said.

There was a calendar of famous African-American leaders on
the wall behind her. I did not look at her, rather I looked at the
calendar, focusing on the faces while hoping that she would soon
tire of this conversation and let me go.

"Did you have some trouble?" she asked me.

"It wasn't nothing," I said, hoping to end this.

"Nothing!" she said.

"No, ma'am," I said.

Then I was quiet again.

"Well, that's not the way it was told to me," she said. "That's not
the way it was told to me at all."

She paused and looked at me, but I remained quiet.

"Somebody called Miss Hattie on one of them cell phones,"
she said. "You have any idea what they told her?"

"No, ma'am," I said. "I don't."

"They told her that her child was out at the Catfish Cabin with
some black folks and it looked like it was going to be trouble. Big
trouble. You know anything about that, mister?"

"It wasn't nothing," I said again.

"Was the police involved?"

"Yes, ma'am," I said.

"Was a gun involved?"

"Yes, ma'am," I said again.

"Well," she said. "That sound like something to me."

I looked at the calendar again and I heard the springs in the recliner squeak and I knew Daddy was shifting in the chair so that
he could get a better look at me. Marcus Garvey's picture was on
the calendar. He was wearing a purple hat with a big yellow
plume, and a purple jacket with shiny gold buttons. There was a
red, black, and green medal affixed to his jacket just above his
heart. And there was a brown leather strap running diagonally

across his chest. I was looking at his picture when I heard Daddy speaking to me.

"Son," he said, "what's this all about?"

"It's not as bad as it sounds," I said.

"You care to explain it?" Daddy asked.

"Ain't much to explain," I said. "Me and Danielle were at the restaurant eating, and Omenita and her ex-boyfriend, Gerald, showed up."

"Together!" Mama said, interrupting me.

"Yes, ma'am," I said. "Together."

"Sweet Jesus," Mama said. "Sweet Jesus in Heaven. Well, I knew something like this was gon' happen," she said. "I just knew it. That girl ain't no count. She ain't no count at all. She just like her mama. That child Sue all over."

"Who is Gerald?" Daddy asked.

"His last name Carter," I said. "Gerald Carter."

"Carter," Daddy said, still confused.

"Alvin Carter's oldest boy," Mama said. "By his first marriage."

"That boy they use to call Monday?"

"That's him," Mama said.

I waited for Daddy to say more but when he didn't, I continued. "They sat down not too far from us, and I told Danielle that I was going to go over and see what was going on. And she told me not to. She said she thought it was a bad idea and that I was just going to create a scene."

"But you didn't listen," Mama said, "did you?"

"I listened," I said.

I saw Daddy gazing at me.

"So you didn't talk to them?" He asked.

"Not then," I said. "I waited outside and when she came out I tried to talk to her then."

"Where was Gerald?" Daddy asked.

"He was with her," I said.

"My Lord!" Mama said, then shook her head.

"And where was Danielle?" Daddy asked.

"She was still in the car."

"And that's where you should have been," Mama said. "Didn't

your daddy tell you not to go running behind that gal? Didn't he?"

"I wasn't running behind her," I said. " I just wanted to talk to her."

"Talk," Mama said. "Talk about what?"

"Us," I said.

"Good Lord!" Mama said again.

"It just bothered me," I said.

"What bothered you, son?" Daddy asked.

"Seeing them together," I said.

"That's why she did it," Mama said. "Goodness gracious, Maurice, that's the oldest trick in the book. Don't you know that?"

"Audrey!" Daddy said.

"Well it is."

"I just wanted to talk," I said.

"But she didn't want to," Daddy said.

"No, sir," I said. "She tried to walk away."

"And you should have let her," Mama said.

"Mama, I love her," I said.

"What about the gun?" Daddy asked.

"Gerald pulled it."

"He pulled a gun on you?"

"Yes, sir," I said. "When I wouldn't let Omenita go."

"What did the police say?"

"He said Gerald and me need to stay away from each other."

"And so do you and Omenita," Mama said.

"I can't," I said.

"You can," Mama said. "And you will."

"Daddy, I need to talk to her."

"Son, I think that's a bad idea," Daddy said, "but it's up to you."

"Can I use the truck?"

"Where's Gerald?"

"I don't know," I said.

"I don't want you getting into nothing, you hear?"

"I won't," I said.

"I mean it, son," he said. "Trouble easy to get into but it's hard to get out."

Chapter Twenty

Iheld my face straight ahead and guided the truck lumberingly through the streets just outside Omenita's neighborhood. It was a little after five and though the traffic on the main highway had lightened considerably, the narrow neighborhood streets were still busy with playing children and a few tired pedestrians trying to make it home after a hard day's work. I came to Jade Avenue. And once I was near Omenita's house, I pulled to the side of the road and stopped. And as I did, I could not escape the fact that I was still haunted by questions that I could not answer. And because I could not answer them I was ill at ease and confused. Why was Gerald back here? And why had Omenita gone out with him? Perhaps there was an explanation. But for the life of me, I could not come up with one.

Outside, I jumped the small drainage ditch and made my way toward the house. And when I was on the porch, I paused briefly before knocking. I was beginning to stress again. She was home. Her car was parked next to the house. But what would I say? What could I say? I took a deep breath, then raised my hand and knocked. The door opened and I saw Omenita staring at me through the half-opened door. Instantly, her eyes narrowed.

"What do you want?" she snapped.

"To talk," I said.

"I don't want to talk to you," she said.

She tried to push the door shut but I lunged forward and caught it with my hand. Incensed, I stared back at her.

"Why are you acting like this?" I asked.

"Why don't you quit bothering me?"

"Don't mean to bother you," I said. "Just need to talk. That's all."

"There's nothing to talk about."

"May I come in?" I asked her. "It's cold out here."

"No," she said, and when she did, she stepped out onto the stoop and pulled the door shut. I tried to look past her but she blocked my view.

"Why are you acting like this?" I asked her again.

She didn't answer. Then suddenly it dawned on me.

"He's here," I said, "isn't he?"

I stepped toward the door and she stepped in front of me.

"Maurice," she said, "I don't want any trouble. You hear?"

Why was she protecting him? I felt myself becoming angrier.

"What is he doing at your house?"

"Keep your voice down," she said. "I'm warning you."

"Answer my question," I said.

"I mean it, Maurice."

"Why are you doing this?"

"You made your choice," she said, "and now I've made mine."

"What choice?" I asked her.

"It's over," she said. "That's what choice."

"You don't mean that," I said.

"Don't I?" she said, then paused. "Look! Gerald asked me to go away with him."

"What!" I said.

"Keep your voice down," she said again. "I mean it."

"Omenita," I said, "what is this all about?"

"He's going back to Texas on Sunday," she said. "And I'm going with him."

"You can't be serious."

"Can't I?" she said, then paused and looked at me.

"Why are you doing this to me?" I asked.

"I'm not doing anything to you," she said.

"I thought you loved me."

"I do love you," she said, "but I love me too."

"What's that suppose to mean?"

"It's always been about you, Maurice. Well, as of now, I'm gon' do what's best for me. I waited, Maurice. Just like I said I would. But you went back on your word. And now I don't trust you anymore."

"Why are you acting like this?" I asked.

"That's right," she said, "go ahead and blame everything on me."

"I'm not blaming you," I said. "I just want to give us a better life. Why can't you see that? Why?"

"Maurice, stop it," she said.

"I don't understand," I said.

"I got to go," she said.

"But—"

"But nothing," she said.

"Don't be like this."

"I got to go," she said again.

"Just like that?"

"Just like that," she said.

"I can't believe this," I said.

"Well, Maurice, what do you want me to do?"

"Talk to me," I said.

"I'm tired of talking," she said.

"Do you love him?" I asked.

"That's none of your business."

"Do you love him?" I asked her again. "Do you love him like you love me?"

"I got to go," she said. She turned to leave. But I stopped her.

"Why are you doing this to us?"

"Me!" she said. "You're blaming me!"

"You're the one walking away," I said. "Aren't you?"

"What choice do I have?"

"You could stand by me," I said.

"And you could keep your word," she said.

"Don't be like this," I said.

"Maurice, I'm leaving."

"No," I said. "Wait."

"For what?" she asked.

"I don't want to lose you."

"It's too late," she said. "You already have."

"Don't say that," I said. "Please, don't say that."

"I've made up my mind," she said. "I'm going to Texas with Gerald."

"Why are you doing this?" I asked.

"I need to get on with my life," she said. "That's why."

"But you don't even know him," I said. "This doesn't make sense. It doesn't make sense at all."

"I do know him," she said.

"How could you?" I asked. "He's been in Texas all of this time."

"We have a history," she said, "or have you forgotten?"

"That was a long time ago," I said.

"Hasn't been that long," she said.

"Hasn't it?" I asked.

"I'm not going to argue with you, Maurice."

"People change. That's all I'm saying. Over the years people change."

"He hasn't changed," she said.

"How do you know?"

"He came back for me, didn't he?"

"Why are you doing this?"

"I need to move on," she said again.

"This doesn't make any sense," I said.

"I'm going back inside."

She turned to leave but I stopped her.

"Do you still love him?" I asked her.

"I don't know," she said.

"You don't know?"

"Maybe."

"Maybe," I said.

"Look," she said. "I don't know what I feel."

"But you do feel something?"

"Yes," she said. "I feel something."

"I thought you loved me," I said again.

"I do love you," she said.

"Then I don't understand this," I said.

"Maurice, I can't wait for you," she said. "Not anymore. And that's all there is to it. Why can't you understand that?"

"Don't do this," I said. I reached into my pocket and removed the ring then I extended it to her. "Please, take the ring back," I begged her. "Please."

"No," she said. "I can't."

"Please," I said. "Please."

"No."

"Why not?" I asked her.

"I can't wait three more years to be your wife," she said. "I just can't. Now, I have to go. He's in there and I'm being rude."

She turned to go back inside.

"Omenita!"

"No," she said. "I can't and I won't." I saw her grab the door-knob and just as she was about to turn it, I spoke again.

"You won't have to," I said.

She hesitated and looked back at me.

"What?"

"I won't go," I said.

"You won't go where?"

"To law school," I said. "I won't go. We can get married just like we planned. Just don't go away with him. Baby, please don't go."

"How do I know you're telling me the truth?"

"I am," I said. "I swear."

"So, you're ready to marry me?"

"Yes," I said.

"When?"

"As soon as I graduate."

"No," she said. "I don't want to wait."

"But—"

"I want to do it now."

"Now!"

"Yes," she said. "As soon as we can get a license."

"But—"

"It's either now or never."

"You don't mean that."

"Yes," she said. "I do."

"If I agree, will you take the ring back?"

"Yes, I'll take it back."

"And you'll tell him to leave?"

"I'll tell him to leave."

"Right now?" I asked.

"Right now," she said.

I paused again.

"Exactly how soon is soon?" I asked her.

"Thursday," she said. "We can get the license on Monday. Then we'll have to wait seventy-two hours before the justice of the peace will marry us."

"Are you sure about that?"

"I'm sure," she said.

"Okay," I said.

"Okay," she said, then extended her hand. I placed the ring on her finger and watched her push the door open and disappear inside the house.

Chapter Twenty-one

Ireached the truck and I had done no more than climbed behind the wheel when I saw the door open again and I watched
Omenita and Gerald step out onto the porch. I smiled because I
figured she had brought him outside to ask him to leave and with
that this problem between us was now over.

My parents' home was only a couple of miles away. And when I
made it home, Daddy was sitting in the living room watching the
news. I approached his chair and he spoke first.

"Hi, son."

"Hi, Daddy," I said, then paused and looked about. "Where's
Mama?"

"In the kitchen," he said. "Why?"

"I need to talk to y'all," I said. "If y'all not too busy."

I saw him lean forward, then rise to his feet.

"Ain't too busy," he said. "Let me get her for you."

Daddy went into the kitchen, and I sat on the sofa and waited.
When they returned, I stood and asked them to sit down. Daddy
sat in his recliner and Mama sat on the sofa. She seemed agitated
that I had gone to see Omenita again. I looked at her briefly, then
at Daddy.

"Well, I talked to her," I said.

"How did it go?" Daddy asked.

"We decided to get married."

"Married!" I heard Mama say.

I looked at her. Her eyes were hard, angry.

"Yes, ma'am," I said. "This coming Thursday."

"My Lord . . . my Lord," she said.

I saw Daddy lean forward in his chair.

"Son," he called to me, and I could hear the concern in his voice, "I thought you two were having problems."

"We were," I said, "but we worked them out."

"What about this other fella?"

"What about him?" I asked.

"Did y'all talk about him?"

"Yes, sir," I said.

"And?"

"Well, he was over there," I said.

"What?" Mama said again.

I saw Daddy looking at me and I knew he wanted an explanation.

I felt my eyes water.

"She was going to go away with him," I said.

"Is that what she told you?"

"Yes, sir," I said.

"So you asked her to marry you?" Mama said.

"I couldn't let that happen," I said. I felt my voice quiver.

"That girl making a fool out of you."

"No, ma'am," I said. "She's not."

"She getting you to do just what she want."

"This was my decision," I said.

"That's what you think," Mama said.

"What about school?" Daddy asked.

"I'm not going," I said.

"What!" Mama said. She had been sitting but now she rose to her feet.

"I'm not going," I said again.

"Guess that's your decision too," she said.

"Yes, ma'am," I said. "It is."

"So let me get this straight," Mama said. "You gon' give up your education for that piece of trash?"

"Don't talk about her like that," I said.

"And don't you raise your voice to me."

I looked at her hard.

"Son."

"Sir."

"Thought you had already decided."

"Yes, sir," I said. "I had."

"What happened?"

"Nothing," I said. "I just changed my mind."

"Just like that?" he said.

"Yes, sir," I said.

"Thought your education was important to you," he said.

"It is," I said. "But so is Omenita. Besides, I have an education. Or have y'all forgotten I graduate in May?"

"You have a degree," Mama said. "That gal about to educate you."

"She's not like that," I said.

"Son," Daddy said, "marriage is a serious step."

"I know," I said.

"No," Mama said. "You just think you know."

"I know," I said again.

"Down the line," Daddy said. "Don't you think you might resent her for making you change your plans and give up on your dreams?"

"No, sir," I said. "I don't."

"But how do you know you won't?"

"I just know."

"But how?"

"This was my decision," I said. "Nobody forced it on me."

"Hunh!" Mama said. "That's what you think."

"No," I said. "I know."

"You sure?" Daddy asked.

"Sir?"

"That this is your decision."

"Yes, sir," I said. "I'm sure."

"Son," Daddy said, "if this other fella wasn't in the picture, would you still be getting married instead of going to school?"

"I don't know," I said.

"Then how can you be sure that this is your decision?"

"It's my decision," I said.

"But how can you be sure?"

I didn't answer.

"You're giving up a lot," Daddy said. "You realize that, don't you?"

"Yes, sir," I said. "I do."

"Is she worth it?"

"Yes, sir," I said. "She is to me. I love her. I love her with all my heart."

"What if you don't feel that way tomorrow?"

"I will," I said.

"But what if you don't?"

"I'll just have to deal with it," I said.

"And you willing to do that?"

"Yes, sir," I said. "I am."

"You're sure?"

"Yes, sir," I said. "We can have a good life together. I know we can."

"Okay," Daddy said. "If that's what you want."

"Okay!" Mama said. "What do you mean okay?"

"Audrey, it's his life," Daddy said. "And he gon' have to live it his own way."

I saw Mama frown angrily.

"What that boy know about life?" she asked.

"I'm not a boy," I said. "I'm a man."

"No," Mama said. "You a schoolboy and that gal the teacher. And I suspect she about to teach you a lesson you ain't soon to forget."

"It's not like that," I said.

"It's not," Mama said.

"No, ma'am," I said. "It's not."

"Boy, that gal don't respect you," Mama said.

"Yes, she does," I said.

"How can she," Mama said, "when you let her walk all over you?"

"That's not true."

"It is true," Mama said. "And you better hear me when I tell you that gal ain't never gon' respect a man what's weak. And she ain't never gon' love a man she don't respect. And honey, you can't get no respect without a backbone."

"Audrey!" Daddy said.

"She loves me," I said.

"No," Mama said. "She educating you."

"She's not like that," I said again.

"Y'all have a round," Mama said. "And then her ex-boyfriend show up. Don't you think that's a little strange?"

"Just a coincidence," I said.

"And don't you think it's strange," Mama said, "that she gon' up and leave with somebody she ain't seen in years?"

"They have a history," I said.

"That's what she told you?"

I nodded. "Yes, ma'am," I said. "It is."

"Did you ask her what kind of history?"

I paused, then squinted. I did not understand the question. "Ma'am?" I asked, confused.

"Ancient history or recent history?"

Suddenly, I understood.

"She's not like that," I said.

"Ain't she?" Mama said.

"No," I said. "She's not."

"Did you ask her?"

"No, ma'am. I didn't."

"Why not?"

I paused again. "I don't know," I said.

"You don't know?"

"No, ma'am," I said." I don't."

"Don't you think it's important?"

"I don't know," I said.

"You don't know!" Mama said. "Gal running around on you and you don't know if it's important."

"She's not running around," I said.

"How do you know?" Mama asked.

"I just know."

"Could be she making a fool out of you," Mama said.

"I don't think so," I said.

"History," Mama mumbled. "She got a history alright."

"What's that supposed to mean?" I asked.

"You want to know her," Mama said. "Study her mama."

"Audrey," I heard Daddy say, "now that's enough."

"It's true, Nathaniel, and you know it," Mama said. "That gal just like Sue when Sue was her age."

"She's going to be my wife," I said.

"She gon' be the death of you," Mama said. "She done already killed your dreams. What's next?"

"I've made my decision," I said as firmly as I could. "And I don't want to talk about it anymore."

"You gon' talk about it some more," she said, nullifying my decision.

I looked at her and shook my head.

"No, Mama," I said. "I'm not."

"What about Mr. John?" Mama said.

"What about him?" I asked, frowning.

"Ain't you supposed to talk to him?"

"Yes, ma'am," I said. "That was the plan."

"Good," she said. "Maybe he can talk some sense into you. Lord knows I can't."

"I'm going to cancel," I said.

"What?" she said angrily.

"Ain't no sense wasting Mr. John's time," I said. "I've made up my mind. And there's nothing he or anyone else can say to change it."

"You gon' talk to him," she said. "You told him you was gon' talk to him and that's what you gon' do."

"Why?" I asked her. "I've made up my mind."

"Because I said so. That's why."

"No, Audrey," Daddy said, breaking his silence. "That's up to him. It's his choice, not ours."

"Then I'll cancel," I said.

Mama looked at me hard after I said that. I could see that she didn't like my decision. She didn't like it at all.

"Well you gon' do it yourself," she said. "You gon' march right over there and tell him face-to-face that you backing out on your word."

"Fine," I said. "I'll go first thing tomorrow morning."

"He won't be home in the morning," Mama said.

"Well, I'll tell Danielle," I said, "and she can tell him."

There was silence and I saw Mama shaking her head. "This don't make no sense," Mama said.

"Audrey," Daddy said, "that's enough."

"Well it don't," she said. "Why in the world that boy want to up and throw his life away over a gal like that is beside me."

"Well, it's his life," Daddy said. "He got to live it his own way."

Chapter Twenty-two

It was ten minutes 'til eight, and I was exhausted and ready for bed. I said good night to my parents and went to my room. The curtains on my bedroom window were open and I could see the fading light of the moon cast upon my bed. I removed my shoes and pants, and in the stillness, I lay contemplatively upon my back, and the heaviness about my heart had subsided, and my spirit was light, and my heart was warm and for the first time in days I was happy. And no, I was not afraid nor was I worried. And my parents' concerns were not my concerns, and their reservations were not my reservations. And I was glad that I had gone to Omenita and I was glad that she had said yes, and I was glad that she would be my wife. And I felt complete now, and for the first time in days, I knew that I could close my eyes and sleep. And my sleep would be restful and my dreams would be peaceful, and my thoughts would be happy ones of us and the beautiful life we would share together.

In the nearby room, I could hear my folks talking and I knew they were not pleased but I did not care. Soon Omenita and I would move far away from this town. And once we did, her spirit, too, would be light, and her heart glad, and with us would reside the love and joy that up until now she had been afraid to allow herself to feel. And we would be happy together. And I would love her and cherish her for the rest of my life. And my love would make her strong. And her fears would subside. And her insecurities would dissipate. And she would see that I was not her father and she was not her mother and their love was not ours.

My window was cracked and I could feel the cool air seeping inside and I felt my face and my hands grow cold. I closed the window and pulled back the covers, and as I slid between the sheets, I heard Daddy say that he was going to go check on Grandpa Luke, then I heard the door open and shut, and I heard Mama's feet on the old, wooden floor moving toward the kitchen.

Then I dozed off and I must have slept sound for I neither heard nor saw anything until I heard Mama knock on my bedroom door. The sound startled me and I sat up in the middle of the bed and I could see the early morning light seeping through the curtains, and I was not aware of where the night had gone or when Daddy had returned. And neither was I aware of when Mama had gone to bed or when she had risen. And I smiled because for the first time in a long while, I had slept through the night, and my mind was fresh and my spirit was light and it was Saturday and not only was I free to spend the day with Omenita, but I was eager to see her and hold her in my arms and talk of our life together. And that is what I was thinking when I heard Mama's voice again.

"Maurice," she said. I saw the door creep open and she poked her head through. "You up?"

"What time is it?" I asked, looking around drowsily.

"Little bit before seven," she told me.

I sat up and looked about confused. "Is something the matter?" I asked her.

"I need to talk to you," she said, "before I go to work."

"Talk," I said, "about what?"

"You planning on seeing that gal today?" she asked.

"Her name is Omenita," I said.

"Don't get smart with me, mister."

"I'm not getting smart," I said. "I would just appreciate it if you would call her by her name. That's all."

"You gon' see her or not?" Mama asked.

"I'm gon' see her," I said.

"Well, I don't want her in this house while me and your daddy at work," she said. "You hear?"

"Yes, ma'am," I said. "I hear."

I sat up against the headboard and Mama sat on the edge of my bed. I could hear Daddy moving around in the other room.

"You still planning on going through with this?"

"Yes, ma'am," I said. "Why?"

"I just don't think you thought this thing through," she said. "I don't think you've thought it through at all."

"I have thought it through," I said.

"You have?"

"Yes, ma'am," I said. "I have."

She stared at me for a moment.

"Where y'all planning on living?" she asked.

"Ma'am?" I replied. Her question had caught me off guard.

"After y'all marry," she said. "Where y'all planning on living?"

"I don't know," I said, then shook my head.

"You don't know?"

"Wherever I find a job," I said.

She looked straight in my eyes for a moment, then asked, "And where do you figure that's gon' be?"

"I don't know," I said.

"You don't know."

"I'll figure it out after I finish school."

"You still figure you gon' finish?" she asked me, and I could hear the skepticism in her voice.

"I graduate in May," I said.

"Well I hope so," she said. "Be a shame to get this close and let that gal get in your way."

"I'm going to graduate," I said.

"Well, I hope so," she said again.

"I will," I said. "Count on it."

I saw Mama pause and look away as if she was thinking, but I knew she wasn't. She was just giving me time to ponder what she had just said.

"Y'all gon' start a family?" she asked.

"Hadn't talked about it," I said.

"Hadn't talked about children?"

"Not yet," I said.

"When you plan on talking about it?"

"I don't know," I said.

"You don't know?"

"We'll work it out," I said.

She paused again, and I knew she was trying to make me feel uncomfortable. I felt myself fidgeting; I felt myself looking away.

"She going back to Baton Rouge or she gon' stay here?"

"Here," I said, then sighed.

"She said that?" Mama asked, the tone of her voice indicating doubt.

"No, ma'am," I said, "but she will."

"How do you know?" she asked, pressing me for an explanation.

"I just know," I said.

"But you hadn't talked about it?"

"No, ma'am," I said. "Not yet."

"Why not?"

"Just hadn't," I said.

Mama was silent again and I knew she was trying to make me feel uncomfortable again.

"Well," she finally said, "when a woman marry, she usually want her own nest and she usually expects her man to provide it."

I didn't say anything.

"She gon' keep working?"

"Yes, ma'am," I said.

"She said that?"

"No, ma'am," I said.

"Then how do you know?"

"She will," I said. "At least until we get on our feet."

"And how long you figure that's gon' be?" she asked.

"I don't know," I said. "Why?"

"Hope you ain't depending on her working too long," Mama said. " 'Cause she don't seem like the kind of girl that'll work steady when she don't have to."

"She'll work," I said.

"What if she won't?"

"Then I'll take care of her."

I heard Mama chuckle.

"What's so funny?" I asked.

"You gon' take care of her?"

"Yes, ma'am," I said. "I am."

I saw Mama shake her head. "That'll be the day," she mumbled.

"Why do you say that?" I asked.

"That gal just like her mama."

"And what is that supposed to mean?"

"She like living in the fast lane."

"She's not like that," I said.

"Ain't she?"

"No, ma'am," I said. "Not at all."

"I been watching her," Mama said. "That gal stay in the road. If she ain't ripping and running and wasting money on that little ole car she got, then she wasting it in them ole stores. Gal been on that job almost two years now and I bet she ain't got two nickles to rub together."

"She's not like that," I said.

"Oh, I think she is."

"I don't," I said.

"Well, I'd advise you to make sure," Mama said, "before you tie a knot with your tongue you can't tear loose with your teeth."

"I don't see her that way," I said. "I don't see her that way at all."

"I know you don't," Mama said. " 'Cause you looking at her with your heart and not with your eyes. And by the time you do see her, you'll be tangled up with a house full of children and a box full of bills."

"Mama, on Thursday I'm going to marry her," I said, "and there's nothing you or anyone else can say to change that. Nothing at all."

"Well, I don't approve of it," Mama said. "I don't approve of it one bit."

"Sorry you feel that way."

"Mark my words," she said. "Before this is all said and done, you gon' regret the day you laid eyes on that gal."

"I don't want to discuss this anymore," I said.

"Maurice," Mama said, "I swear, the way you act sometimes I think that gal done worked roots on you."

"That's not it," I said. "That's not it at all."

"Well, I sho wish you would explain it to me."

"It's simple," I said. "She's all I've ever wanted."

"Then you don't want much."

"I'm not going to talk about this anymore," I said.

I heard Mama sigh again. Hard this time.

"Well, you need to get up and get a move on."

"A move on," I said. "Why?"

"Your daddy waiting on you."

"For what?" I asked, confused. "I'm not working today."

"He wants you to drop him off."

"I don't understand," I said.

"He said you can keep the truck," she explained. "In case you need to do some running around. Now come on," she said. "Get a move on."

"Yes, ma'am," I said.

She turned to leave, then stopped. "I meant it," she said. "I don't want that gal in this house while me and Nathaniel ain't here either."

"Why?" I asked.

"Because I said so! That's why!"

She waited for me to respond, but I remained quiet.

"And don't get too far out of pocket," she said, "because I'm gon' need you to pick me up from work today."

"Yes, ma'am," I said.

"I get off at one," she said. "You can talk to Danielle then."

"Yes, ma'am," I said. "I will."

"And Maurice."

"Ma'am?"

"Don't be late."

Chapter Twenty-three

I dropped Daddy off at the diner, then I returned home, and after I had taken a bath and gotten a bite to eat, I drove to Omenita's house to talk to her about our marriage plans. When I knocked on the front door, I had not expected her to answer, and I was pleasantly surprised when the door swung open and I saw her standing before me in her housecoat and slippers. I smiled at her, and in turn, she smiled back at me.

"Is it alright if I come in?"

"Of course it is," she said.

She stepped aside and I walked through and when I did, she immediately closed the door behind me. I looked around. The house was extremely quiet.

"Hope I didn't come by too early," I said.

"You didn't," she said. "Everybody's up."

We made our way to the sofa and she sat down first, then I sat next to her. And when I did, I looked around the room. There was a bedroom pillow propped against the far arm of the sofa and there was a book lying face down on the end table closest to the pillow and I figured she had been lying on the sofa reading before I knocked. I glanced at the book then at her.

"Well," I said.

"Well, what?"

"Did you tell him?"

She tilted her head and looked at me with narrowed eyes.

"Who?"

"Gerald," I said.

"I told him," she said, then looked away. I waited for her to say more but when she did not, I spoke again.

"Well, what did he say?"

"He didn't say anything."

She looked down at the floor and I stared at the side of her face. Suddenly, I was concerned again.

"Is he gone?" I asked her

"Not yet," she said.

"Why not?"

"I don't know," she said.

"Well, when is he leaving?"

"Sunday, I guess."

"You guess," I said. "You don't know."

"No," she said. "Not really."

"Well, I don't want you talking to him anymore," I said. I waited. She didn't say anything. "Omenita!"

"I heard you," she said.

"I'm serious," I said.

"I already told you I wouldn't," she said.

"When?" I asked. "When did you tell me that?"

"When I agreed to be your wife."

There was a moment of silence and I saw her looking down at the floor again, and I leaned back against the sofa and stared toward the window seeing the soft rays of early sunlight seeping just beneath the curtains. I was still staring at the curtains when I heard her voice again.

"Did you tell your folks?" she asked me.

"I told them," I said.

She paused a moment then resumed.

"And what did Miss Audrey have to say?" I hesitated, and in that moment of hesitation she answered for me. "Let me guess," she said. "She tried to talk you out of it?"

"Something like that," I said.

"I should have known," she said, and as she spoke, I could hear the disappointment in her voice. I watched her rise and go to the window, then pull the curtains open and stare out into the streets. I moved behind her and put my arm around her. She turned to me, and I looked into her eyes.

"It doesn't matter," I said.

"It matters to me."

"It shouldn't," I said.

"Well, it does."

I looked at her, and her eyes began to water. I pulled her to me and she gently laid her head on my shoulder.

"Don't cry," I said. "Please don't cry."

"I want to be your wife," she said, "but I can't take Miss Audrey."

"You won't have to," I said.

She lifted her head and looked at me, and I could see in her eyes that she wanted to believe me—no, she needed to believe me. I brought my hands up to her face and tenderly dried her eyes with the tips of my fingers.

"Are you sure?" she asked, her voice breaking slightly.

"I'm sure," I said.

"I don't want to get married if you're not sure."

"I'm sure," I said again.

"It's either me or her," she said.

"I know," I said.

"And if it's me—"

"It is you," I interrupted her.

"Well, I don't want her interfering in our life."

"She won't," I said.

"You promise?"

"I promise."

I saw her looking out the window again and she was looking well past the highway and far beyond the railroad tracks, and I knew she wasn't thinking about what she was seeing. She was thinking about us. She was thinking about our future.

"And I don't want to live with her."

"We won't," I said.

"And I don't what to live with my folks."

"We won't."

"And I don't want to live in this town."

"We won't," I said.

"I mean it. I want to get away from this place. As far away as we can."

"We will," I said.

"You promise?"

"I promise," I said.

She laid her head on my shoulder again and began to cry. I put my arm around her and tried to comfort her.

"I love you," I said.

"I know," she said. "And I love you too."

She looked up at me again, and I leaned over to kiss her and just as I did her mother entered the room.

"Miss Jones," I said.

"Good morning, Maurice." She came to me, and I hugged her, then kissed her on the jaw, and she immediately looked at me and smiled.

"Omenita told me the good news," she said.

"Yes, ma'am," I said. "We were just talking about it."

"Well, I'm so happy for the two of you," she said. "You're a fine young man, and Omenita is lucky to have you."

"Thank you," I said.

"You two should have such a fine life," she said. "Provided you stick together and don't let nothing come between you."

"Yes, ma'am," I said.

I saw her look at Omenita. "That goes for you too, missy."

"I know, Mama," Omenita said. "I know."

They looked at each other for a moment then Miss Jones turned her attention back to me.

"How are your folks?" she asked me.

"They're okay," I said.

"Guess they're excited about the news."

I smiled but didn't answer.

"When you see them again, please tell them that I said hello."

"Yes, ma'am," I said. "I will."

"And tell Audrey I said we gon' have to get together soon."

"Yes, ma'am," I said. "I'll tell her."

She left the room again and I directed my attention to Omenita.

She had turned toward the window again and was staring out into the empty streets. I put my arms around her waist and gently kissed her on the back of her neck.

"Why didn't you tell her?"

"Tell her what?" I asked.

She turned and looked at me.

"How your folks really feel?"

"For what?" I asked.

She didn't answer. Instead, I saw her eyes cloud as if she was going to cry again. I sighed and I felt myself becoming frustrated.

"I just don't see the point," I said

I waited, but she remained quiet.

"Does your daddy know?" I asked.

"Not that I know of," she said.

"You didn't tell him?"

"No," she said.

"Why not?"

"I didn't want to."

"Why?" I asked.

She hesitated for a moment and I could see that she was pondering the question. Then she shrugged her shoulders and shook her head.

"I just didn't."

"Well," I said. "He is your father. And he does have a right to know."

"He has no rights with me," she said.

"Maybe your mom told him," I said.

"She didn't."

"How do you know?"

"I told her not to."

"Why?" I asked.

I waited but she did not respond.

"Is he home?" I asked.

"Ought to be out back," she said, "tinkering with that old truck."

"In this weather?" I asked.

"He probably don't feel it," she said. "By now, I don't imagine he feel anything."

"Well, I think I should go out there."

"That's up to you," she said.

"He has a right to know," I said.

"It's up to you," she said again.

"Then I'm going to go talk to him," I said. "It's only right."

"Suit yourself."

I went outside and made my way behind the house. Mr. Jones was standing before his old Ford truck. The hood was propped up and the top half of his body was bent underneath it. There was a bottle of white port sitting atop the cab. It was half empty. I approached the truck then stopped.

"Mr. Jones," I said.

"Yeah," he said. He was in the middle of something and did not stop. I waited a moment thinking he might come out but when he didn't I spoke again.

"Like to talk to you," I said. "If you have a minute."

He raised up and looked back at me.

"About what?" he asked.

"Your daughter," I said.

He paused. Then I saw him take the bottle from atop the truck.

"You want a drank?"

"No, sir," I said.

"Well, I believe I do," he said. He took a drink, then placed it back. I saw him look toward the house, then back at me. "What about her?" he asked.

"Last night we decided to go on and get married."

"Is that a fact?"

"Yes, sir," I said.

He looked at me and his jaundiced eyes were bloodshot and his large pear-shaped head seemed unsteady.

"She did, hunh?"

"Yes, sir," I said. "She did."

"Thought she was going to Texas with that other boy."

"That was just a little misunderstanding," I said.

"A misunderstanding?"

"Yes, sir," I said.

He looked at me then down at his tool box.

"Hand me that wrench yonder."

"Yes, sir," I said.

I retrieved the wrench and passed it to him. I saw him duck back underneath the hood. Then I heard him banging, and as I waited, a breeze stirred and I felt the cold wind on my ears, and I raised the collar of my coat until it was covering my ears, then I dug my hands deep into my pockets and hunched my shoulders against the cold. He banged a moment more then stopped.

"Think my battery done give out," he said.

I didn't answer him.

He poked his head out and looked in my direction.

"You know anything about cars?"

"No, sir," I said. "Not much."

"It's the battery," he said. "Then again it could be the cable."

I remained quiet.

"Get in there and hit the switch for me."

"Yes, sir," I said.

I climbed in and turned the switch. I heard a click, then I heard him banging with the wrench again.

"Try her again."

I heard a click and I heard him yell "that's good." I climbed out and when I did, I saw him remove the bottle and unscrew the top, then take another drink.

"Yep," he said. "It's the battery."

I listened without responding.

"Guess I'd better take her in."

"Yes, sir," I said.

"She probably got a dead cell."

"Yes, sir," I said again.

He took another drink from the bottle and placed it back on top of the hood. Then he removed the wrench and began disconnecting the cable.

"Would like to know if it's alright with you," I said.

I waited. He didn't say anything. Then I heard him curse.

"Goddamn bolt," he said.

He eased from beneath the hood and looked about.

"Hand me that Crescent wrench," he said.

I handed him the wrench and he ducked back beneath the hood. I heard him grunt and I saw the bolt give. Then I heard the wrench strike the metal frame, and when it did, I heard him curse again. I believed he hit his hand. I waited a moment, then I spoke again.

"Well, sir?" I said.

"Well, what?" he asked me.

"Is it alright with you?" I asked.

"Is what alright with me?"

"Me marrying your daughter?"

"Well that's between you and her," he said. Then I saw him looking at the battery again.

"Yes, sir," I said. "I understand that. And as I said earlier she has already said yes. But I guess I would just like to know what you think."

"Well it's fine with me," he said. "She grown."

"Yes, sir," I said.

I paused and waited for him to say more but he didn't and I could tell he was still thinking about the battery.

"And I also want you to know that I plan to do right by her," I said.

"Well, I suspect she gon' see to that," he said.

"Yes, sir," I said. "I suspect she will."

He removed the cable and lifted the battery from the car, then set it on the frame, and when he was satisfied that it was stable, he looked at me again.

"Y'all done set the day?"

"Yes, sir," I said. "Thursday."

"Well, we ain't got much money," he said. "Don't reckon we'll be able to help much with no wedding."

"Yes, sir," I said, and when I did, I saw his body wobble a bit and he quickly leaned against the truck for support, and I sensed the alcohol was making him drunk. "We'll probably just go before the justice of the peace."

"Well, that's probably best," he said.

"Yes, sir," I said.

"You say Thursday, hunh?"

"Yes, sir," I said.

"Up at the courthouse?"

"Yes, sir," I said.

"What time?"

"We don't know yet," I said.

"Well, y'all just let me know," he said. "And I'll see if I can take off work."

"Yes, sir," I said. "We will."

Chapter Twenty-four

I followed Mr. Jones back into the house. When we got there, Omenita had changed clothes and was sitting on the sofa reading a magazine, and Miss Jones was standing next to the recliner combing her hair. Her purse was on the floor next to her and her coat was draped across the back of the chair. From the looks of things she was on her way out. They both looked up when we entered the room. Miss Jones spoke first.

"Made it back, hunh," she said to me.

"Yes, ma'am," I said.

I closed the door, then I joined Omenita on the sofa. Mr. Jones, visibly tipsy from the liquor, continued, and I watched him stagger across the floor and stop just before his wife. From where I sat, I could not see his face because his back was to us, but I could see his large, powerful hand gripping the back of the recliner as he braced himself steady. I saw him look at the coat and then at her.

"You going somewhere?" he asked.

"To get my hair done," she said. "Why?"

"I need some money," he said.

Instantly, I heard Omenita sigh, then I saw her wave her hands at her mother and when her mother looked at her, I saw Omenita shake her head no. Her mother looked at her then back at her husband.

"For what?" she asked.

"Battery shot," he said. "Got to buy a new one."

"And how much is that gon' cost?"

Mr. Jones hesitated before answering.

"Ought to be able to get one pretty cheap at Wal-Mart," he finally said.

"What you call cheap?" she asked.

He paused again. "Oh, forty or fifty dollars." Miss Jones looked at Omenita trying to figure an answer, but before she could Mr. Jones spoke again. "Goddammit, Sue!" he said. "You gon' have to hurry up. My ride be here any minute."

"Alright," she said. "Let me look in my purse. I don't even know if I got fifty dollars."

I heard Omenita sigh again. "What ride?" she asked. "Who gon' take you?"

I saw Mr. Jones look at her. He seemed unsteady.

"Byrd," he said.

"Byrd!" Omenita said.

"That's right," he said. "Byrd."

"You ain't got no business riding around with that wine head," she said.

"How else I'm gon' get there?" he asked.

"I'll go get the battery," Omenita said.

"Naw," her father said. "You got company."

"He can come with me."

I saw her daddy sway then brace himself against the wall. "Ain't no need in that," he said.

"I don't mind," she said.

"Ain't no need," he said again.

"You just want to go across the river," Omenita said. "That's all."

"And what if I do?" he said. "What's it to you?"

"Can't you go one weekend without getting drunk?"

"Omenita!" I heard Miss Jones say.

"Omenita, nothing," she said. "Look at him, Mama. He can't

hardly stand up as it is." Omenita rose and extended her hand toward her mother. "Give me the money," she said. "I'll go."

"Sit down!" her father said. "And mind yourself."

"Don't tell me to sit down," she said. "I'm grown."

"Omenita!" Miss Jones called to her again. "Don't speak to your father like that. What's done got into you?"

"Mama, please," Omenita said. "I'm begging you. Please don't give him any money. Please," she said. Suddenly her voice began to shake.

"Omenita," Miss Jones said, "why you carrying on so? You got company. Why you carrying on so?"

"Don't give it to him," she repeated herself. "I'll go get the battery."

I saw Miss Jones open her purse and remove the money.

"Mama, please," she said. "He just gon' drink it up."

"Omenita, now that's enough," Miss Jones said. She removed the money and handed it to her husband. "I mean it."

Omenita looked at her and frowned. "This don't make no goddamn sense," she said. "No goddamn sense at all."

"Well, he has to have his truck," Miss Jones said. "And if it need a battery, it need a battery. And batteries ain't free."

"He's lying," Omenita said, "and you know it."

"Battery is dead," he said. He paused and looked at me. "Ain't it, son?"

"Yes, sir," I said. "It's dead."

Outside, a horn blew.

"That's Byrd," he said. "I got to go."

"Me too," Miss Jones said. "Before I'm late for my appointment."

They left and Omenita started crying. "Why you taking up for him?" she snapped at me.

"I'm not," I said.

"Yes, you are!"

"The battery was dead," I said.

"How do you know?"

"I tried to help him start the truck," I said. "It was dead."

"So," she said.

I looked at her, confused.

"How do you know he didn't run it down on purpose?" she asked.

"What?" I asked.

"How do you know he ain't just pretending it's dead? How do you know he ain't gon' take that battery to town and charge it up, then take the rest of that money and go across the river and get sloppy drunk? How do you know?"

"I don't know," I said.

"That's right," she said. "You don't know."

"I already said that," I said.

"Then why are you taking up for him?"

"This is crazy," I said.

"Who you calling crazy?"

"Nobody," I said.

"Oh, now I ain't nobody," she said.

"Omenita, I don't want to fight with you."

"Could of fooled me," she said.

"Look, I'm sorry. Okay?"

"Why can't he just do the right thing?" she said, ignoring my attempt to apologize.

"Maybe he is," I said. "Give him a chance."

"Why are you taking up for him?"

"I'm not," I said.

"You are!" she snapped at me.

"Why are you angry at me?" I asked.

"Because you're just like him," she said.

"I'm nothing like him."

"Yes, you are," she said. "Everything has to be your way."

"How can you say that?"

"It's not gon' be like that with us," she said. "You hear?"

"Like what?"

"You walking all over me."

"Walking over you?" I said. "When have I ever tried to walk over you?"

"I can't take this anymore," she said.

"Can't take what?" I asked her, but she didn't answer. Instead, she turned and looked near the chair where her mother had stood.

"Why did she have to give him that money?" she asked. "Why?"

"He asked for it," I said. "What was she supposed to do?"

"She could have said no, couldn't she?"

I remained quiet.

"I take it you don't agree."

She paused and waited. But I still did not speak.

"Maybe you think this is his house," she said, "and in his house what he say goes. Maybe that's it, hunh?"

"I didn't say that," I responded. "You did."

"But you were thinking it," she said. "Weren't you?"

"I don't want to argue with you," I said.

"It's not gon' be like that with us," she said again. "You hear? I'll be your wife, but I won't let you walk over me."

"Why are you doing this?" I asked.

"I know what you're thinking," she said. "Once we get married things gon' be different. Maybe you gon' lay down the law. Put me in my place. Make me toe the line. Maybe that's what you're thinking."

"Why are you doing this?" I said again. "Why are you doing this and we're getting married in a few days?"

"I'm tired of this," she said.

Suddenly, she turned her back and began to cry. I went to her and placed my arms around her and pulled her to me.

"I would never disrespect you," I said. "You know that."

"I'm tired," she said again.

"I love you," I said. "More than I have ever loved anyone or anything in my entire life. I would never disrespect you," I said. "Never."

"I wish I was away from this place," she said. "Far, far away."

"Let's talk about something else," I said. "Something pleasant."

"I hate him," she said. "I know I'm not supposed to. And I know it's wrong. But I do. I hate him."

"No, you don't," I said.

"I do," she said.

"Let's just go somewhere," I said. "I have the truck. We can take a ride."

"I know what's going to happen," she said.

"It's no point in thinking about that," I said. "Come on. Get your coat and let's just go."

"He gon' go get something to drink," she said. "Just like he always do."

"Come on, baby," I said. "Let's go."

"And then when he's good and drunk, he's gon' go downtown hooping and hollering and raising hell until the police lock him up. And when they lock him up he gon' call here begging and crying for Mama to come get him out. And she gon' make me go with her. Just like she always do. And when we get there all them white folks gon' be looking at us like we something less than human. And we just have to sit there and take it. I hate him," she said. "And I hate Mama for letting him do this to us."

She began to cry again. I tried to console her.

"It's going to be alright," I said. "Try not to think about all that. Try to think about us. Try to think about the future."

"Make love to me," she whispered.

"What?" I said.

"Make love to me," she whispered again.

"Here?" I asked.

"Yes," she said. "Here."

"Now?" I said.

"Yes," she said. "Right now."

"Are you sure?" I asked.

"I'm sure," she said.

I looked around.

"Where are your brothers?" I asked. "Where is your sister?"

"They're gone," she said.

"Gone where?" I asked.

"Russell Jr. and Eric are playing in a basketball tournament. They won't be back until tonight; Lauren is spending the weekend with Aunt Jena."

I paused, thinking.

"Make love to me," she said again. "Please, make love to me."

I leaned over and kissed her tenderly. She smiled, then took me by the hand and slowly led me to her bedroom.

Chapter Twenty-five

I felt her hands on my legs moving back and forth gently, slowly. And I heard her whisper again, "Make love to me." I moved closer to her. And she undid my buckle and I unzipped my pants, and I felt my desire mount and I wanted to slow the moment, for we were alone, and we had time, and the moment was right.

There was a peace between us now. And I was not her father, nor she her mother. And there was no thought of things given up or things lost. And there was no fear or trepidation, for all of that was far from me now.

I felt my pants sliding down my thighs and over my knees. And I felt the weight of her body on top of me. And I closed my eyes, and I felt her lips about my ear, and I heard the soft, sensuous sounds of her bated breath. And I felt the motion of her hips. And I felt myself becoming excited. And I wanted to slow the moment, and enjoy the nakedness of her body against the nakedness of mine. And I undid her bra and removed her panties. And I felt the fullness of her breasts against my naked chest. And I ran my hand down the small of her back and over her firm, naked bottom. And I felt her moving again. And I heard her moan, and I heard her whisper, "Please make love to me."

And at that moment, the smoothness of her skin and the slow roll of her hips bested me, and I felt patience give way to desire,

and suddenly I was inside of her, and I wished that it was
night, and I wished the lights were low, and I wished the music
was soft, and I wished that we were alone in a room overlooking
the beach, and I wished that this was our wedding night, and that
she was my wife, and that we were joyously celebrating all that
would come, and bidding a final farewell to all that had been.

I heard the springs on the bed creaking. And I was aware that
we were in her parents' house. And that this act with which we
were engaged was forbidden here. And the fact that it was forbidden excited me even more. And I closed my eyes. And she was
straddling me. And I could feel the heat of her flesh against
mine, and I could feel the gentle sway of her hips keeping time
with the sway of mine. And I could see the brownness of her eyes
and the fullness of her lips, and the moment between us became
more intense, and I felt her body tighten, and I felt her head on
my shoulder, and I felt her hands gripping the sheets, and I
heard her breath become shorter; I heard her moans become
louder. And I felt the pressure of her knees pressing into the mattress. And I gave into the moment, and I heard myself moan. And
in that instance, I felt lucky to have a chance with her again and I
felt happy that this moment was a good moment, and not just for
me but also for her.

It had been a long time since I'd felt this way. Not since the
night before I left for school and we made love in the backseat of
her car. And for some reason, I thought of that moment. The two
of us, completely naked, in the backseat of her car, on a starlit
night, in the middle of Mr. Hadnot's sweet potato field. And
there was no one out there to hear us, except the squirrels and
the racoons and the wild coyotes. And the love was long and loud,
and hot and passionate.

I dug my fingers into the small of her back. And I felt my heart
accelerate, and I felt the weight of her body on top of me as my
body rose and fell. And try as I may, I could not control my
breathing. She moaned again and the passion in her voice excited me. And I pressed harder against her body. And at that moment, I knew she was the one. I had thought so many times
before. But not until this moment had I truly known. It was
strange to me, but at this moment, there was a magic in her

touch—a magic which heretofore I had never felt before. And instantly, I wanted to possess it, and make it mine. And not just for today, but forever.

She sat upright and tilted her head back. And I felt rising in me a force that I could not contain. It was gentle at first, then I felt the intensity rise, and I felt my blood burn hot. And I heard her moan again. Then a feeling came over me. One which I could not control. And I felt the moment accelerate, and I heard the bedsprings creaking, and I felt my hips shudder, and I heard her moan again, and I felt her body tense. And I felt the pressure of her hips against mine. And I was happy for this moment. For in this moment, all doubts ceased. And for the first time, in a long while, things were clear in my head. There were no more questions and no more doubt. She was the one. And in that moment of truth, I felt burst forth from me every ounce of passion that I felt for her. And instantly, I felt her body quake and I felt her hands tremble. Then I felt her collapse forward, exhausted.

I closed my eyes and laid the palms of my hands on her warm, naked butt. And her presence at this moment pleased me. And I felt her move her mouth close to my ear and I felt the warmth of panting breath gently touching the side of my face. And though my eyes were still closed, I could sense the parting of her lips just before she whispered, "I love you."

Her words made me smile, and I opened my eyes and turned my face toward hers. Then our eyes met, and I whispered back, "I love you too."

I kissed her again, then she laid her head back on my chest and we laid there for a while, quietly holding each other. And the sheet was over us now, and the only light in the room was the tiny rays of sun seeping through the tiny crack at the seams of the curtain, and we had repositioned our bodies. Now, she was lying next to me, and my arm was about her waist, and her right leg was draped across my midriff, and though I was no longer inside of her, I felt just as close to her as I had only moments ago. I felt her body shift again, and I pulled her even closer.

"Promise me it will always be like this," she said.

"I promise," I said.

"I mean it," she said. "I don't ever want things to change."

"They won't," I said.

She looked up at the ceiling and started to cry again.

"I don't respect him," she said. "I don't respect him at all."

"Who?" I asked.

"My father," she said.

"I'm sure he's doing the best he can," I said.

"Well that's just not good enough."

"It'll all be behind us soon," I said.

"Promise," she said.

"I promise," I said.

She buried her face into my chest and sobbed. I held her tight. We both closed our eyes and went to sleep.

Chapter Twenty-six

I heard a strange sound outside and I opened my eyes and looked about. Omenita was still asleep but when I moved, her eyes opened and she looked at me and smiled, and I smiled back at her. And instantly, I felt my heart flutter. Yes, I was in her bed and she was in my arms and the door was shut and the world was locked out and there was nothing else on this entire planet that I craved and there was no other place I wanted to be. I felt the bed give and I saw her fidget, then turn her face toward me, and I could see that her eyes were still foggy and that she was somewhat disoriented.

"What is it?" she asked me.

"I heard something," I told her.

And when I did, she snuggled closer against me, and I felt the warmth of her naked body pressed tight against mine, and I draped my arm around her, and the side of her face was against my chest, and the crown of her head was beneath my chin, and I could smell the faint fragrance of her perfume. Intoxicated by her scent, I gently kissed the top of her head, then I lifted my hand and slowly ran my fingers back and forth along the small of her back. She purred softly and then she relaxed, and I could tell that this moment was nice for her, and I was happy about that, and I did not want it to end. I wanted to stay here with her, tucked beneath the warm, cozy covers away from the problems and confusion that had become my life, but I knew that I could not for they were waiting on me. And I had to face them, and their questions, and their concerns.

I heard the sound again. This time, she heard it too.

"It's just a cat," she whispered.

"Are you sure?" I asked her.

She did not answer immediately and I remained very still listening again for the odd sound, which I was sure I had not heard before. The fact that the sound unnerved me amused her. She lifted her head and I saw her smile.

"I'm positive," she said. "He lives underneath the house. I imagine he's just trying to stay warm." She paused again, then tilted her head. "I know you're not afraid of a little pussycat, are you?"

"Of course not," I said.

Now my mind tells me that this is not so. And there is a part of me that fears that we are no longer alone, and I am unnerved by the fact that I am naked with her in her folks' house. Yet, in a strange way, the thought that someone may be out there titillated me. I closed my eyes again, and she curled against me, and I held her for a moment, then I looked up at the ceiling. Suddenly panic swept me.

"What time is it?" I said.

I saw her raise her arm and look.

"Twelve-thirty," she said. "Why?"

I removed my arm and sat up. Inside my head I could hear the imaginary ticking of an invisible clock. We had slept away the morning and now I would surely be late.

"I got to get up," I said.

"Why?" she said. "What's wrong?"

I swung my legs over the edge of the bed and grabbed my pants.

"I have to go," I said.

"Go," she said. "Go where?"

"To pick up Mama," I said.

"What!" she said, then rose to her feet quickly. I could see that she was upset. I looked at her. I didn't want to argue. Not now. Not after this.

"I told her I would be there by one," I said.

"Then why did you come over here?" she asked me. There was a robe on the back of a chair. She removed it and hastily draped it around her naked body.

"To see you," I said.

"I don't believe this," she said.

"I'll be back," I said. "As soon as I take Mama home."

"Thought she rode home with some lady."

"Not on Saturday," I said.

"I don't believe this," she said again.

"I'm sorry," I said, "but what do you want me to do?"

"Be a man," she said.

"I am a man."

"Then stay here with me," she said.

"I can't," I said.

"Why?"

"I told you. I have to go pick up Mama."

"Go on, then," she said. "Go on to your mama."

"Why do you do this?" I asked.

"Do what?"

"Act this way?"

"What way?" she said, then squinted as if she did not know what I was talking about.

"Like I'm the worst person in the world."

"Just wish you'd grow a backbone," she said. "That's all. I'm getting tired of dating a boy. It sure would be nice to date a man."

"I am a man," I said again.

"Then start acting like it."

"What's that supposed to mean?"

"Figure it out," she said.

"Why don't you tell me," I said. "You seem to know everything."

"Why did you come over here?" she asked again, "if your mama wasn't gon' let you stay."

"It ain't like that," I said. "And you know it."

"Oh," she said.

"Omenita, what do you want me to do?" I asked. "Let Mama walk home in the cold?"

"Go get your mama," she said, "but just remember this. After you say I do, the only person you gon' be going to get is me."

"Please," I said.

"I'm serious, Maurice. Come Thursday, you gon' start being my man and you gon' stop being your mama's boy."

"I'm nobody's boy," I said.

She looked at me hard. "Just remember what I said."

"Fine," I said. "I'll see you later."

"I'm going to be busy later," she said.

"Fine," I said again. "Then, I'll see you tomorrow."

"Fine," she said.

Chapter Twenty-seven

I dressed quickly and hastily drove the short distance to Miss Hattie's house, and I had no more than guided the truck under the carport when I saw Mama pull the kitchen door open. I parked the truck a short distance from the door and though I did not look at her directly, I could feel her eyes on me. Yes, I was late, and she wanted to let me know that she did not appreciate me keeping everybody waiting. I stepped from the truck and walked toward her, and when I was close, I stopped and looked at her. She continued to gaze at me, and I dropped my eyes. Then, and only then, did she speak.

"Where you been?" she asked me.

"Nowhere," I mumbled.

She looked at me hard, but I did not say anything else. There was no need to. I was sure she knew where I had been, and I was equally sure that she knew why I was late. A gust of wind swept us, and she pulled her sweater tight and folded her arms across her chest.

"Come on," she said. "Folks waiting on you."

I followed her through the kitchen and down the hallway to the parlor. Miss Hattie, dressed in a blue pantsuit, was sitting in a chair next to the fireplace drinking a cup of tea. And Danielle, dressed in a pair of plaid wool slacks and a white pullover sweater was sitting on the sofa Indian-style. There were two Italian-style sofas in the room, both facing each other, and both separated by a cocktail table. Danielle sat on the sofa facing the large bay window. That way, she could see Miss Hattie, as well as see outside. She had been thumbing through a magazine, but when we entered the room she looked up. They both did.

I spoke to Miss Hattie first, then to Danielle, and after we had exchanged pleasantries, Mama directed me to my seat, then she excused herself saying that she had a couple of things to take care of before going home. From the sofa facing the hall, I watched Mama leave, then I looked around. It was a stunning room. There were expensive paintings and a vaulted ceiling and hardwood floors and antique furniture and a stunning grand piano that was perfectly positioned before a large bay window that overlooked a magnificent flower garden. Only it was late December, and the flowers were bloomless, although there was an unusual amount of greenery for this time of year, which I would assume was due to the fact that it had been an unusually long, warm winter. I was admiring the room, when it occurred to me that they were both watching me. Suddenly, I felt the need to say something.

"I apologize for keeping you waiting," I said.

"Oh, that's okay," Danielle said. "Mother and I were just chatting."

There was a small serving tray on the cocktail table. I saw Miss Hattie look at the tray, then back at me.

"Care for a cup of tea?" she asked me.

"No, ma'am," I said politely.

"We have coffee," Danielle said, "or hot chocolate if you like."

"No, thank you," I said. "I'm fine."

I looked away then I heard Miss Hattie's voice again. "Audrey told us the news," she said. I saw her pause, then smile. "We're sure proud of you." She paused again. "You couldn't have chosen a finer field had you tried. The legal profession has been good to this family, and I'm sure it will be good to you as well. The judge has big plans for you," she said. "Really big plans."

"That's what I wanted to talk to you about," I said.

"Well, you should probably talk to the judge," she said. "He'll be home tomorrow afternoon."

I was quiet. I saw Danielle looking at me, concerned.

"Is there a problem?" she asked me.

"Just a little change in plans," I said. "That's all."

"What kind of change?" she pressed me.

I hesitated a moment, searching for the right words to answer her.

"I've decided to go in a different direction," I said.

"I don't understand," she said.

I was uncomfortable, and I did not know why, for this was my decision, not theirs. Then it dawned on me. There was a reason for my anxiety. I was concerned that they were going to judge me just as Mama had. Well, if they did, so be it.

"I'm not going to law school," I said.

Danielle turned and looked at me sharply.

"Why?" she said. "What happened?"

"Is it your scholarship?" Miss Hattie asked. "If so, perhaps the judge can help. Perhaps he could speak to someone for you."

"No, ma'am," I said. "It's nothing like that."

They paused, waiting.

"Then what?" Danielle asked.

"I've decided to get married," I said.

I saw Danielle's eyes widened. "Married!" she exclaimed.

"Yes," I said. "Married."

Miss Hattie frowned.

"Aren't you a little young for marriage?"

"No, ma'am," I said. "I'll be twenty-one in a few months."

"Well, can't you do both?" she asked.

Suddenly, I heard the sound of Mama's voice floating in from the hallway.

"No, Miss Hattie," she said. "That gal made him choose."

I turned and looked. Mama had returned and was standing in the doorway. I looked at her hard to let her know that I did not appreciate her unsolicited comment.

"Well, is she pregnant?" Miss Hattie asked.

"Oh, God no! Miss Hattie," Mama said. "It's nothing like that."

Suddenly, I felt myself becoming incensed.

"You should speak to Father," Danielle said.

"There's no need," I said. "I've made up my mind."

"He won't listen," Mama said. "God knows I've tried."

I swallowed hard and gazed at her. Why was she doing this? Why here? Why now? Why in front of them. Why?

"Well, do I know the intended?" Miss Hattie asked Mama.

"You know her," Mama said. "She's Russell Jones's oldest daughter."

"Russell Jones, the pipe fitter?"

"Yes, ma'am," Mama said. "That's him. One and the same."

Danielle looked at me, stunned.

"You need to speak to Father," she said again.

I didn't answer her.

"Well, have you set the date?" Miss Hattie asked me.

"Yes, ma'am," I said. "Thursday."

"This Thursday?"

"Yes, ma'am," I said again.

"Why so soon?" she asked.

"Well, that was my question," Mama said, "but to this day, I still haven't got a satisfactory answer."

"We've just decided it's time," I said.

"Then I guess congratulations are in order," Miss Hattie said.

"Or condolences," Mama mumbled.

There was a moment of silence and I rose to my feet. I had a strong desire to leave. I felt angry—no, I felt violated.

"Well, I don't want to take up any more of your time," I said as politely as I could. "Please tell Judge Davenport that I'm thankful for all of his help." I looked at Mama. "Are you ready?" I asked her.

"Not quite," she said. "I need to speak to Miss Hattie for a minute."

"I'll be in the truck," I said.

I turned to leave. Danielle stopped me.

"I'll walk you out," she said, then she rose and followed me out of the room, and when we were in the kitchen she stopped and looked at me.

"Are you okay?" she asked.

"I'm fine," I said.

"You seem a little upset."

"I'm alright," I said.

"Well," she said, "I must admit, I'm a little surprised by what just happened in there. A few days ago you seemed so certain about law school."

"I was," I said.

"Well, what happened?"

"I chose love over law," I said. "That's all."

"That's all!" she said, then smiled faintly.

"You think I'm crazy?" I said. "Don't you?"

"No," she said. "I respect your choice."

"But you are disappointed."

"No," she said. "Not really."

"Not even a little?" I said.

"Well," she said, "maybe just a little."

"At least you're being honest," I said.

"And you're being true to your feelings," she said. "I definitely respect that."

"Wow!" I said. "Thanks."

"Now, don't get me wrong," she said. "I still say you would make a fine attorney. And this community is the worse for your decision, but I am happy for you. Law is a beautiful thing, but you do have to love it."

"I do," I said.

"But just not as much as you love her?"

"No," I said. "I don't think so."

"And she's definitely against law school?"

"Totally," I said.

"Forever or just for now?"

"I don't know," I said.

"May I ask you a personal question?"

"Sure," I said.

"Is she your first love?"

"Yes," I said. "Why?"

"Oh, I was just curious."

I nodded, but remained quiet. She paused a moment, then asked a related question.

"Is she your only love?"

I squinted. Her question was confusing.

"What do you mean?"

"Have you ever dated anyone else?"

"No," I said. "I haven't."

"But, she has?"

"Yes," I said. "One other person."

"The guy at the restaurant?"

"Yeah," I said. "The guy at the restaurant."

"He was her first love?"

"That's right," I said.

"Well," she said. "What happened?"

"Excuse me?" I said.

"Between them."

"Omenita and him?" I asked.

"Yes," she said. "I don't understand."

"It's kind of a long story," I said. "But the long and short of it is, his mom and dad got divorced. And when they did, his mom moved to Texas and she took him with her. And that's where he's been until now."

"So, when he left, they broke up?"

"Yeah," I said.

"And then you started seeing her."

"About a month or two later."

"How old were you?"

"I was in the eleventh grade," I said.

"And you've been with her ever since?"

"Yeah," I said. "Going on six years."

"And during that time have you ever dated anyone else?"

"No," I said.

"Not even while you were away at school?"

"No," I said.

"Really?" she said.

"Really."

"Did you ever think about it?"

"No," I said. "I didn't."

"Are you serious?" she asked, and I could tell she did not believe me.

"I'm serious," I said.

"Let me get this straight," she said. "You were at LSU. With all of those beautiful southern belles. And you never even thought about it?"

"Never thought about it," I said.

"Wow!" she said. "That's amazing."

"I love her," I said. "I always have and I imagine I always will."

"Unbelievable," she said.

"You have to remember," I said. "I majored in engineering."

"And?" she said.

"Well, when I wasn't in class, I was in the lab, and when I wasn't in the lab I was working some odd job trying to help my parents pay for school. I just didn't have the time nor did I have the interest. I have always been serious about engineering. Plus, there just aren't that many black girls at LSU."

"And?" she said again.

I hesitated a moment, then it dawned on me what she was asking me.

"No offense to anyone," I said, "but that's just not a road that I've ever wanted to travel."

"None taken," she said.

"Besides," I said, "my heart has always belonged to Omenita. And it always will. Going away to school didn't change that."

"Well, she's a lucky girl."

"Thank you," I said.

"And I wish you two the best."

"I appreciate that."

"But I still think you should speak to Father."

"No," I said, "I've made my choice. I don't see any reason to waste your father's time. I know he's a busy man, but I do appreciate your interest."

"Well, alright," she said, "but if you change your mind, please let me know."

"Okay," I said. "I will."

I saw her look back toward the parlor.

"Mother Audrey sure seems angry."

"She doesn't like my decision," I said. "She doesn't like it at all."

"I sensed that," she said.

"And, to be perfectly honest, she doesn't like Omenita."

"I sensed that as well."

There was silence.

"Are you sure that she's the one?" Danielle asked.

"I'm positive," I said.

"You're giving up a lot," she said.

"I know."

"Is she worth it?"

"She is to me," I said.

There was a moment of silence then she spoke again.

"What about your cousin?"

"I don't know," I said, then I paused and sighed heavily. "I just don't know."

"Well, I thought that one of the primary reasons you wanted to go to law school was to eventually help him," she said.

"Yes," I said. "It was. I guess I'll just have to find another way."

"Perhaps Father could help," she said.

"Do you think he would?"

"I don't see why not."

"Really."

"Yes," she said. "I'll speak to him."

"Thanks," I said.

"You're welcome," she said, then paused and looked back toward the parlor. "I better go back in there," she said.

"Okay," I said. "See you later."

"See you later," she said.

She turned and walked back toward the parlor and I went out to the truck, started the engine, and waited for Mama.

Chapter Twenty-eight

From behind the wheel, I watched Mama amble out of the house and climb into the truck beside me. And as soon as she was inside, I backed from beneath the carport and guided the truck down the driveway out into the street. From the corner of my eye, I saw Mama sitting with her hands resting across her lap and her eyes looking straight ahead. And though I was not looking at her directly, I could tell that she was perturbed no doubt at me, but perhaps even more so at the way things had gone at the Davenports. Her anger made no sense to me. For I had informed her of my decision, and like it or not, that decision had not changed; nor would it change. Omenita would be my wife—there was no doubt about that.

And so, I retreated to that quiet place within myself, and drove on, guiding the truck along the road toward the busy intersection just west of the Davenports' house. And as I did, I regretted nothing about my situation except for the way my mother was behaving toward me and the woman I loved. Her behavior concerned me, for I sensed that it was causing to rise in me certain feelings of resentment that I feared threatened to tear apart the beautiful relationship that she and I had forged over the course of our lives. I stopped at the intersection and Mama broke her silence.

"Talked to Miss Hattie," she said.

I remained quiet.

"I think you making a big mistake not talking to Mr. John," she said. "He was wanting to talk to you about a job in his old firm. When you finished law school of course."

She waited. I remained quiet.

"Ain't you got nothing to say?" she asked me.

I did not look at her, but I could feel her eyes on the side of my face.

"I just wish you wouldn't tell Miss Hattie my business," I said, still looking far up the road. "She doesn't have anything to do with this. None of them do."

"They just trying to help you," Mama said. "God knows you need it."

"I've made up my mind," I said. "Like it or not, I'm going to marry Omenita, and there is nothing anyone can do or say to change my mind."

"I don't understand you," Mama said. "I don't understand it at all."

"Nothing to understand," I said. "I love her and I'm going to marry her."

"Love," Mama mumbled.

"Yes, ma'am," I said. "Love."

"One of these days you gon' find out what love is," she said. "And when you do, you gon' realize that this ain't it."

"Mama, please," I said, "could we just talk about something else?"

"What you want to talk about?" she asked. "The weather?"

"Anything," I said. "Anything but this."

"You hardheaded," Mama said. "And mark my words. That's gon' be your downfall. You just wait and see."

I didn't say anything.

"You don't have to say nothing," she said, "but one of these days you gon' remember this conversation. And when you do, you gon' wish to God almighty you had listened."

"I am listening," I said. "I just don't agree with you."

"You don't, huh?"

"No, ma'am," I said. "I don't."

"What if you wrong?" she said. "You ever thought about that?"

"I'm not," I said.

"But what if you are?"

"Then I'll live with it," I said.

"That's your answer," she said. "You'll live with it."

"Yes, ma'am," I said. "That's my answer."

I heard Mama sigh. Then I saw her look far up the road.

"Hope you know what you doing," she said.

"I know," I said.

"Naw, you don't," she said, "because if you did you wouldn't do it."

"I'm not afraid to marry Omenita," I said, "but I am afraid not to."

"Look to me like you afraid of the wrong thing," Mama said. "Ought to be afraid of losing out on a chance to further your education. That's what you ought to be afraid of. And if that gal cared anything about you, she'd be afraid of that too."

"She cares," I said.

"Sho' got a funny way of showing it."

"You just don't understand," I said.

"You right," Mama said. "I don't."

"I love her," I said again, "and that's all there is to it."

"That's it," Mama said. "That's your explanation."

"Yes, ma'am," I said. "That's it."

"Well you need to think about what you doing. You need to think about it long and hard."

"I have thought about it," I said.

"Well, then you need to think some more."

"There's nothing else to think about," I said. "She makes me happy. And that's what's important to me."

"Maybe right now," Mama said. "But what about down the road?"

"I'll see what's down the road when I get there," I said.

"Might be too late to see by then," she said.

"I don't want to talk about this anymore."

"Not talking about it won't make it go away."

"I've made up my mind," I said.

I heard Mama sigh again.

"That girl gon' ruin your life."

"Well, it's my life," I said.

"Now you getting smart with me," she said. "I guess that's what that gal teaching you, how to get smart with your mama."

"I'm not getting smart," I said. "I'm just telling you how I feel."

"How you feel or how she feel?" Mama said.

"She doesn't have anything to do with this," I said.

"You ain't never acted this way before."

"I'm just tired of this," I said. "That's all."

"Ought to be tired of her. She the one mistreating you. Not me."

"She's not mistreating me," I said.

"Well if she ain't mistreating you, I guess I don't know what mistreating is."

"She's a good person," I said. "And if you would just take the time to know her, you would see that."

I paused and waited. Mama remained quiet.

"Mama, Omenita's just scared," I said. "That's all. Her life has been hard and full of disappointments. And she's just scared."

"That's just an excuse. Life's hard for everybody."

"Harder for some than for others," I said.

"That's just an excuse," Mama said again.

"I've made up my mind," I said. "Why won't you accept that?"

"Because I can't accept her."

"Well if you can't accept her," I said, "I guess you can't accept me."

"What you mean I can't accept you?" Mama said. "You my child. What you mean I can't accept you?"

"I'm nobody's child," I said. "I'm a grown man."

"One of these days that gal gon' show you who she is," Mama said. "And when she does, you accept that, you hear?"

"I know who she is," I said emphatically.

"No," Mama said. "You know who you want her to be."

"I don't want to talk about this anymore," I said.

"You just remember what I told you," Mama said. "She gon' show you who she is, and when she do, you just be man enough to accept it."

"Mama, please," I said again. "I don't want to talk about this anymore."

"You don't need to talk," Mama said. "You just need to listen."

"I am listening," I said.

"Naw," Mama said, shaking her head. You hear me. But you ain't listening."

"Maybe you're right, Mama," I said. "And if you are, I guess it's about time."

"And what's that supposed to mean?"

She looked at me and I could see that she was becoming angry.

"Just that ever since I was a kid you've been telling me what to do. And all of my life, I've listened. But not this time," I said. "Now, I don't know what you got against Omenita, and right now, I don't care. This is my life. And I'm telling you I'm going to marry her."

"Then God help you," Mama said.

I didn't say anything. I clutched the wheel and stared at the highway.

"Never thought I see the day you'd talk to me like this."

"I don't mean any disrespect," I said, "but this is how I feel."

"Feeling or no feeling," Mama said. "That gal's wrong for you."

"I don't think so," I said.

"Well, I know so."

I turned and I looked at her.

"Mama," I said, "please accept this! Please!"

"I can't," she said.

"Why not?"

"I just can't accept a girl like that. Not in this family."

"A girl like what?"

"Like her."

I felt myself becoming angry. "She's going to be my wife," I said.

"I can't accept her."

"Can't or won't?" I asked her.

"Won't," she said. "I won't accept her." She paused. "I just wish she would've left town with that boy then all of this would have been over."

I turned my head, stunned.

"You'd wish for that?" I said. "Knowing how I feel about her?"

"Everybody would have been better off," Mama said.

"Not me," I said. "And I think you know that."

"She not right for you," Mama said again.

"Mama, who are you to judge her?"

"I'm your mother," she said.

"But you're not God."

"I never said I was."

"Then why are you acting like it?"

"Since when have you talked like this to me?" Mama asked me. "You the parent now? You the parent and I'm the child?"

"I just want you to respect my wife."

"The way you respecting me?"

"You're not being fair to her," I said.

"That girl's not right for you," Mama said.

"Well, that's for me to decide," I said. "Not you."

"Since when have you talked to me like this?" Mama repeated her question.

"I'm just getting tired of you telling me what to do," I said.

"And I'm getting tired of you sassing me," she said.

"Well, if that's the way you feel," I said, "then maybe it's time for me to get my things and go," I said.

"That's up to you," Mama said.

I slowed the truck and turned off the road into the driveway. I heard the seashells beneath the wheels as I pulled next to the house and stopped.

"I'll pack my things," I said.

I got out and went inside and gathered my things. When I emerged from my room, I heard Mama moving about in the kitchen. I went to the door. She was at the sink. Her back was to me.

"Tell Daddy that his truck will be at Grandpa Luke's."

"Uh-hunh," she said.

I turned and left.

Chapter Twenty-nine

At Grandpa Luke's house, I removed the luggage from the truck and placed it on the step then knocked on the door.

"Who is it?" Grandpa Luke yelled.

"It's me, Grandpa Luke," I said. "Maurice."

"Just a minute," he said.

I heard his feet moving on the floor. Then I heard the chains on the door rattle. The door swung open and I saw Grandpa Luke look at me, then at the luggage, then back at me.

"Me and Mama had words," I said.

"Words!" he said.

"Yes, sir," I said. "Harsh words."

He looked at the luggage again then back at me.

"She put you out?"

"No, sir," I said. "I left."

He pulled the door open wider and stepped aside.

"Well, come on in out the cold," he said.

I put the luggage inside and closed the door and followed Grandpa Luke to the living room. There was a fire in the fireplace and I went to the fire and warmed my hands, then turned back toward Grandpa Luke. His pipe was on the stand next to the sofa. He lit it, took a long puff, then sat in the recliner.

"Is this about your lady friend?"

"Yes, sir," I said.

I looked at the fire a moment, then back at him.

"I don't mean to bother you with this, Grandpa Luke," I said, "but I was wondering if I could stay here for a few days."

"You always welcome here," he said. "You know that."

"Are you sure you don't mind?" I said. "I don't want to intrude."

"Don't be silly," he said. "I got plenty room. Put your things in that room back yonder. You know where it is."

I gathered my luggage and placed it in the far bedroom, and when I was done, I returned to the living room. The television was on but Grandpa Luke wasn't watching it. He was sitting quietly next to the fire, smoking his pipe, and staring deep into the flickering flames. It had been a while since I had actually been in his house. In fact, I had not been inside since Grandma had passed. But as I looked around, I could see that very little had changed. The small living room was exactly as it had always been. The sofa was still on the wall next to the door. Grandpa Luke's recliner was still next to the fireplace. Grandma's sewing basket was still in the far corner next to the television. And the same three or four potted plants were sitting exactly where Grandma had placed them.

I crossed the room and sat on the sofa. Grandpa Luke had put the tree up, and it, too, had been placed before the window in the precise spot it had always been. I looked at the tree a moment, then at Grandpa Luke.

"It looks nice," I said.

"Did the best I could," he said. "Of course, I ain't had much experience decorating trees and such. That was always your grandma's department."

"I guess Grandma really loved this time of year, huh?"

"Loved life in general," he said. "She was a good woman." I saw him looking at the tree again. "A real good woman."

I looked at the tree a moment more then back at Grandpa Luke. He was sitting in his recliner, but he was no longer looking at the tree, instead he was gently rocking back and forth staring in the direction of the television. But he wasn't looking at the television. He was contemplating something. What, I do not know.

"You ain't working today?" he asked me.

"No, sir," I said. "Silas came back today. Daddy gave him his job back."

I paused and looked at Grandpa Luke. He was staring deep into the fire. I began fidgeting with my hands, and after a moment of silence, I spoke again. "Omenita and I set a date," I said. "We're getting married this Thursday by the justice of the peace."

"Is that what you and your mama had a round over?" he asked.

"Yes, sir," I said, then waited for him to say something else, but when he said nothing, I continued. "Mama just won't accept Omenita," I said. "And if she won't accept Omenita then I don't reckon she can accept me either."

"That's what you told her?" he asked me.

"Yes, sir," I said. "It is."

"Hadn't never known you to sass your mama."

"Didn't think I was sassing her," I said.

"Kind of sound that way to me."

"Then I guess you think I was wrong."

"Don't matter what I think," Grandpa Luke said. "What do you think?"

"I don't know what I think," I said.

"Well, I guess you gon' have to figure it out for yourself," he said.

He lifted the pipe to his mouth again and took another puff. I watched the little rings of smoke rise into the air, then disappear. I looked at him, but he was no longer looking at me. He was looking into the fire again.

"I don't know what she wants from me," I said.

"Maybe she want you to think about your future."

"Omenita is my future," I said. "I've explained that to her."

"Thought the law was your future."

"I'm going to be an engineer," I said. "That's what I went to school for."

"Guess I understood that to be one of the things you went for," Grandpa Luke said. "But not the only thing. I thought you had your mind set on going to law school."

"I can go later," I said.

"Ain't your scholarship for now?"

"Yes, sir," I said.

"Then what's all this talk about later?"

"I had to make a choice," I said.

"Between the girl and school?"

"Yes, sir."

"And you chose the girl?"

"I love Omenita," I said. "And I have the right to marry her if I so choose. Right now, Mama don't want to see that, but she's going to have to because Omenita and I are getting married. And there's no doubt about that."

"Maybe your mama see more than you give her credit for," he said. "Her eyes old. And they done seen a whole lot more of this world than you and that girl of yours put together."

"Grandpa, you think she's right?" I said. "Don't you?"

"Ain't for me to say," he said.

"Mama just don't like Omenita," I said, "and that's all there is to it."

"Is that what you think?"

"Some way or another, she's got it in her mind that Omenita is standing between me and where I'm trying to go."

"Is she?"

"No," I said. "Not really."

"You don't sound too sure of yourself."

"I'm sure," I said.

"You better be," Grandpa Luke said. "Marriage is a serious thing."

"That's what Daddy said."

"Well, he telling you right."

"I love her, Grandpa Luke," I said.

"Why?"

"Sir?"

"Why do you love her?"

"I don't know," I said. "I just do."

"That's your answer?" he said.

"Yes, sir," I said. "I don't know what else to tell you."

"Well, I hope you think of something," he said. " 'Cause it's been my experience that when hard times come, folks who couldn't tell you why they should get together, usually can't figure out why they should stay together." I saw him look into the fire again. "And believe me, son, sho' as there is a tomorrow, hard times is coming. And you and that girl of yours can count on that."

"We'll be alright," I said.

He had been looking in the fire. Now, he looked directly at me.

"What kind of wife will she be to you?" he asked. "What kind of mother will she be to your children? What kind of in-law will she be to your folks?"

I didn't answer. I couldn't.

"Love is just a word," Grandpa Luke said. "The way folks live is what give it meaning. You understand that, don't you, son?"

"Yes, sir, Grandpa Luke," I said. "I understand."

"Maybe your mama don't think you do."

"I'm a man, Grandpa Luke. Mama still thinks of me as a boy. I'm a man, and I'm old enough to make my own choices."

"Age don't make you a man," Grandpa Luke said. "And a man ain't defined by his ability to make choices. He's defined by the choices he make. And there ain't no greater choice that a man will ever make than the woman he choose to spend his life with. And if he lucky, when it's all said and done, he can look back and say that the woman he chose wasn't just his wife but she was also his friend."

He paused. And all of sudden his face changed. And I saw him look away. But before he did I could see that his eyes had begun to water, and I thought he was going to cry. But he did not. Instead, he just stared into the fire. And I knew he was thinking of Grandma. And I wanted to say something, but I did not know what to say. Suddenly, he looked up again.

"Son, I'm a old geezer now. And maybe a lot of things done passed me by, but when I was young, a man used to find a woman he could build a life with then he married her. And love came later. But now days, folks marry for love and let life come later. Seem to me like they got it backward." He paused and stared deep into my eyes. "Will she stand by you, son?" he asked. "Come hell or high water. Will she stand by you?"

"I believe she will," I said.

"Well," he said, "that's what's important."

I saw him looking deep into the fire again.

"This Thursday, huh?"

"Yes, sir," I said.

Suddenly, I saw him smile.

"The twenty-third."

"Yes, sir," I said again.

"The day before Christmas Eve."

I frowned.

"I hadn't realized that," I said.

I saw Grandpa Luke smile again.

"Ain't nothing nicer than a Christmas wedding," he said.

"It's not going to be much of a wedding," I said.

He didn't respond. Instead, he paused and stared into the fire again.

"Your grandma and me eloped," he said.

"I didn't know that," I said.

"It was right about this time of the year too."

"Is that right?" I said.

"We went to the preacher's house just before daybreak on Christmas Eve. He married us right there in his living room. Just me, your grandma, the preacher, and his wife."

"I didn't know that," I said again.

"That was fifty years ago."

"And you and Grandma stayed together all that time?"

"Yes, we did," he said, and there was a far-away look in his eyes. "We had our trials and tribulations, but with the help of the good Lord, we made it."

"Grandpa Luke," I said. "Do you think I'm doing the right thing?"

"Can't tell you who to marry and who not to," he said. "You the one gon' have to live with her. But I can tell you this: If a woman loves you, she'll honor you. And if you love her, you'll do the same."

I was silent. He paused and looked at me.

"You had your dinner?" he asked.

"No, sir," I said. "Not yet."

"Well, come on," he said. "Let's eat."

Chapter Thirty

After we finished eating, Grandpa Luke and I put the dishes away, and when that was done, I excused myself, then went into the back room, stretched across the bed, and fell asleep. I must have slept for at least two or three hours, for I was unaware of anything until I heard the sound of the door creaking open and I saw Daddy pop his head through and look.

"Hi, Daddy," I said. I tried to read his face, but I could not.

"Hi, son," he said. "Didn't mean to wake you."

"That's okay," I said. "I was about to get up. Just felt like taking a little nap."

"Mind if I come in?"

"No, sir," I said. "I don't mind."

I sat upright and he entered the room and sat on the bed next to me. He was still wearing his work clothes, so I assumed he had not gone home but instead had come straight to Grandpa Luke's house. It had been a long week and he looked tired.

"I guess Mama told you what happened," I said.

"She did," he said.

"I'm sorry," I said.

"No need to be," he said. "These things happen."

"Guess she's pretty upset with me," I said.

"Not you," he said. "The situation."

"Well, I guess I did say some things to her that I shouldn't have said. I guess I was just a little angry. I didn't really mean 'em."

"In due time, I'm sure you'll make it right."

"Yes, sir," I said. "I will."

"Well, that's all I ask," he said. "She is your mother. And you must always remember that. Son, she did something for you that no other woman can ever do. She gave you life. She's your mother," he said again. "Always honor her."

"I'll apologize for what I said. But not for what I'm doing."

"Fair enough," Daddy said.

In the other room, I could hear Grandpa Luke tinkering with the fireplace and I assumed the fire was getting low and he was putting on another piece of wood. I listened for him for a moment, then I spoke again.

"You been by the house?"

"No, not yet. Reuben dropped me off here. Your mama called the diner and said you said for me to come by and pick up the truck."

As he spoke he was not looking at me. The shades were up and he was looking at the large branches of an old oak tree moving back and forth in the cold, brisk wind.

"I'm sorry about all this," I said again.

"Ain't your fault," he said.

I looked at him.

"You think Mama will come?" I asked.

"To the wedding?" he asked me.

"Yes, sir," I said.

I saw Daddy shake his head.

"I don't know, son," he said. "I just don't know."

I saw him looking off again. And I knew he was thinking.

"I wish she would," I said.

"I'll see what I can do. But I can't promise anything."

"I know," I said. "I just wish that she would. That's all."

I rose from the bed and walked to the window, then looked out.

"Can I ask you a favor?" I asked.

"Sure, son," he said. "What?"

I turned and looked at him.

"Will you stand with me?" I asked.

He looked at me. And I realized he had not understood.

"Be my best man," I said.

He smiled.

"Of course, I will," he said. "I'd be honored."

"It won't be anything fancy," I said. "Just me and Omenita, a few family members, and the justice of the peace."

"That doesn't matter," he said. "What matters is the vow you take. Not where you take 'em. And not how you take 'em."

"Yes, sir," I said, then I looked away.

"What is it, son?" he asked me.

"Just thinking about Mama," I said.

He rose and walked next to me.

"Son," he said, placing his hand on my shoulder, "don't worry about your mama. She'll come around in time."

"I hope so," I said.

"She will," he said. "Now, she may never agree with your choice. But in time she will respect you for having had the courage to make it. You're a man. And you've cut the apron strings. And that's always hard on parents, especially on mothers."

"So, you're alright with this?"

"If you are," he said.

"I am," I said. "I love her."

"Then I love her too."

I paused and stared at the ceiling.

"I can't believe I'm getting married," I said.

Daddy smiled.

"I'm happy for you, son," he said. "Real happy." He paused and looked away, emotional. "I've thought about this day for a long time. And I had a lot of things prepared to say to you when it came. But now that it's here, I can't think of any of 'em."

"Well," I said, "I wish you could."

Daddy took a deep breath then looked me in the eye.

"Always pay your bills."

"Yes, sir," I said.

"If you give a man your word, keep it."

"Yes, sir," I said.

"Raise your sons to be men and your daughters to be ladies."

"Yes, sir," I said.

"Teach them to give respect to others and demand respect for themselves."

"Yes, sir," I said.

"Remember to tell your wife you love her. Women need to hear that."

"Yes, sir," I said.

"Never forget why you married her."

"Yes, sir," I said.

"And always remember that you're my son."

"Yes, sir," I said. "I will."

"I love you, son," he said. "And I'm proud of you." His eyes became moist. "Real proud of you."

"I love you, too, Daddy."

We hugged each other for a long time. Then he pulled away.

"Well," he said, "I better go. I'm sure your mama got supper waiting."

"Yes, sir," I said. "See you Thursday."

"See you Thursday."

I handed him the keys, then I heard him say good-bye to Grandpa Luke. Then I heard the front door open, then close, and he was gone.

Chapter Thirty-one

On Sunday, Omenita and I spent the entire day together. I apologized for having left her, and she apologized for getting so upset, and we agreed to put it behind us and get on with the business of preparing for our impending nuptials. And so, that afternoon, we drove to Monroe and purchased our wedding bands. Then on Monday, we applied for our marriage license. On Tuesday, we met with Mr. Bailey, the justice of the peace, and he gave us final confirmation that he would marry us on Thursday, at twelve o'clock in his office. And today, which was Wednesday, we had lunch together in town, and afterward we bid each other good-bye, and she went back to work, and I went back to Grandpa Luke's house.

When I got there, I saw that Grandpa Luke and his camera were missing. I briefly looked around outside for him and when I could not find him, I went back inside, took a seat in the recliner next to the fire, and clicked on the televison. I wasn't worried about him. I just figured he had gone for a walk, and though I did not know where, I suspected he had gone to the cemetery to visit grandma again. Their wedding anniversary was approaching and I sensed that he needed to be close to her.

I was still sitting by the fire, watching the television when I heard someone pull into the yard and stop next to the front porch. Then I heard a car door open and close, and then I heard the dry leaves in the yard crunching, and I went to the door and pulled it open to see who was out there, and to my surprise, I saw Danielle standing on the stoop, clutching a small purse.

"Hi," she said, and though she was wearing a heavy coat and gloves, I could tell by the way she was standing that she was still cold.

"Hi," I said.

"Do you have a minute?"

"Of course," I said. "Please come in."

She entered the house and sat on the sofa near the door, and I sat in Grandpa Luke's recliner next to the fireplace. She sat for a moment, and when she was warm, she removed her coat and draped it across the arm of the sofa. I looked at her, trying to figure out how she knew I was here and wondering what in the world she wanted.

"Can I get you anything?"

"No, thank you," she said, and when she looked at me I could see that the side of her face was red from the weather.

"Well, what can I do for you?"

She sighed deeply, as if what she had to say was difficult.

"I wanted to talk to you about Mother Audrey."

I frowned, then looked at her.

"What about her?" I asked.

"She's hurting," she said. "She's hurting really bad."

"I'm hurting too," I said.

"Can't you work this out?" she asked.

"I'm getting married," I said. "And she can't handle it."

"She's your mother," Danielle said.

"But I'm not her boy anymore," I said. "I'm my own man."

"Yes," she said. "I understand, but does that mean you have to hurt her?"

"No," I said, "but it does mean that I have to live my own life. And she has to accept that."

"And are you willing to live your life without her?"

"If I have to," I said.

"You won't be happy," she said.

"I'll try."

"It's not going to work."

"I think it will," I said.

"It's just not possible."

"Why do you say that?" I asked her.

"Because Mother Audrey won't be happy."

I shook my head.

"I can't worry about that," I said.

"But you will," she said. "And you know you will."

"I don't think so," I said.

"I know so," she said.

"You do?"

"Yes," she said. "I do."

"And how is that?"

"Because of something Thomas Paine once said."

"And what is that?" I asked her.

"No man can be happy surrounded by those whose happiness he has destroyed."

"He said that?"

"Yes, he did," she said. "And I believe he was right. Especially as it pertains to you and your mother. I've known Mother Audrey all of my life. And all she has ever talked about is you. And from the short time that I have known you, I can see how special you are. And how special your relationship is with her. And you should never allow anything to change that. Because if it does, she won't be happy and neither will you. Now, if Omenita is the one—"

"She is the one," I said abruptly.

"Then help Mother Audrey see it."

"I can't," I said.

"Why not?"

"Because I can't even make her see me."

"I don't understand."

"I'm a man," I said, "but she won't acknowledge that. And until she acknowledges who I am, she will never be able to acknowledge how I feel."

"She loves you," Danielle said. "She loves you more than life itself."

"And I love her."

"Then talk to her."

"And say what?"

"Tell her that you love her."

"She knows that."

"Tell her anyway."

"And what will that do?"

"Give you a nice point from which to begin."

"No," I said. "This is something that she has to work out for herself."

"I think you have to work it out together."

"I disagree."

"Well, will you at least consider it?"

"I'll consider it," I said.

She smiled, then glanced at her watch.

"Well, I know you probably have a lot to do," she said, "so I won't take up much more of your time. But, in spite of everything, I know that Thursday is a very special day for you. And because it is, I want to give you something. A wedding present of sorts."

"You don't have to," I said.

"I know," I said, "but I want to."

I saw her open her purse and remove a small present. Then she stood and handed it to me.

"No," I said. "That's not necessary."

"Please," she said. "I want you to have it."

I looked at the gift then at her.

"What is it?" I asked.

"Open it and see."

"Now?" I said.

"Yes," she said. "Now."

I placed the gift in my lap and gently removed the wrapping. Inside, I saw a rather crude-looking drawing encased in a frame. I gazed at the drawing, then smiled.

"What is it?" I asked her.

"It's a map."

"A map," I said.

She nodded.

"I don't understand," I said.

"Well, this is probably the most precious thing that I have ever owned in my entire life."

I looked at the drawing again, then frowned.

"This!" I said.

"Yes," she said. "And I want you to have it."

"Thanks," I said, then looked at it again, still confused.

"It was given to me by your mother."

"My mother!" I said.

"Yes," she said."When I was thirteen years old."

"Why?" I asked, my curiosity piqued.

"Because she knew I needed it."

"I don't understand," I said.

"Well, let me explain," she said. "When I was thirteen years old, my folks sent me back East to finishing school. In the long run, that turned out to be one of the best things that ever happened to me. I learned things at that school that I still utilize today. And I met my best friend there, as well as any number of other wonderful people. And in hindsight, I am so thankful that I had an opportunity to go there. But the night before I left was the absolute worst night of my life. For much of the evening, I sat in my room and I cried, and I cried, and I cried.

"Well, I guess Mother Audrey heard me. And she came in and sat at my little desk and took out a piece of paper and drew this map. Then she folded it and put it in my purse. Then she looked at me and said, 'there is no need to cry and there is no need to be afraid. You go on up there and if things get too bad this is the way home. And as long as you know the way home, there is nothing in this world to worry about.' "

She paused and I looked at the paper again

"And I will have you know, that for the first full week at that school, I carried this little map with me everywhere I went. And just having it seemed to ease my mind and give me peace. Well, it has served its purpose for me. Now I want you to have it. And I want you to look at it. And when the time is right, I want you to use it to find your way back home. Mother Audrey loves you. And she needs you. And seeing this gulf between the two of you is breaking my heart."

She turned her back and I could tell that she was crying.

"Thank you," I said, then I stood and hugged her. "This is really sweet of you," I said, then I released her.

She nodded, then dabbed at her eyes with the tips of her fingers.

"I'm sorry," she said.

"Don't be," I said.

"I hope you and Mother Audrey can work this out."

"We will," I said.

I saw her look toward the door.

"Well, I better go," she said.

"Okay," I said. "Thanks for coming."

She retrieved her coat from the sofa then turned and faced me.

"Oh, by the way, I spoke to Father. He's going to have someone look into your cousin's case."

"Thank you," I said.

"You're welcome," she said. "I just hope they can help."

"May I ask you a question?" I said.

"Sure," she said.

"Why are you doing all of this?"

I saw her smile. "I told you," she said, "We're practically family."

"You must think I'm terrible," I said.

"To the contrary," she said. "I think you're fantastic."

Suddenly I laughed and so did she.

"I think you're fantastic, too."

"For a white girl?" she said jokingly.

"No," I said, "for any girl."

"Well thank you," she said. "That's a very nice thing to say." She put her coat and scarf back on and turned to leave then stopped. "Best of luck to you and your new bride."

I walked her to the door. Then I watched her climb into her car and drive away.

Chapter Thirty-two

I took the tiny map into my room and placed it on the nightstand, then I laid across the bed and cried. And though there was in me an overwhelming desire to go to my mother, I consciously fought to keep that desire at bay, for deep inside of me, I realized that to act on such a feeling would be nothing short of engaging in an exercise of futility. For as it stood, I could not tell my mother that I would not marry Omenita nor could my mother tell me that she would accept Omenita as my wife. Thus, I had to choose between the woman who gave me life and the woman I would give my life to. And that choice, however right I knew it to be, still pained me. And now, more than ever, that pain seemed too much to bear. And so, I did all that I knew to do, I cried. And I cried not out of any fear of the future, but I cried because I loved my mother, and I knew that my mother loved me. And I cried because I was a man, and as such, I had to leave that which had been safe and comfortable and embark upon that which, though exciting, was laced with uncertainty. And I cried because I loved Omenita and tomorrow all of this would end and she would be my wife. And I cried because my daddy had cried, and my granddaddy had cried, and my mama had cried.

Through the open window, I could see the large branches of the huge oak tree swaying majestically in the cold, stiff wind. And

I could see the dark gray clouds lingering in the dull, overcast sky. And I could see the thin layer of ice floating atop the water barrel that Grandpa Luke had placed out back under the eave of the old storage shed. But in spite of the cold weather, and in spite of the fact that I had no transportation, there was in me a sudden impulse to go see Omenita.

So, I rose from the bed and put on my coat and gloves and went into the living room. Grandpa Luke had returned and was sitting in front of the fire watching the evening news. I spoke to him and bid him good-bye then I stepped out onto the porch. Instantly, the cold wind hit me, and I dug my hands deep into my pockets, and I hunched my shoulders and walked out of the yard toward the railroad tracks. And once I reached the tracks, I walked between the rails, measuring my stride against the length of the cross ties. And as I walked, I looked around. On the west side of the track, for a quarter of a mile or so, I could see acres and acres of barren cotton fields. The fields had been recently harvested and the huge trailers of cotton had been dumped at the end of the fields and covered with a tarpaulin in lieu of being transported to the gin.

Along the east side of the track, I could see Highway 17. And beyond Highway 17 I could see the long row of wood-frame houses all neatly aligned, one after the other, and all perfectly following the contours of the highway. I followed the track, passing one house after another, until finally, jutting out from beyond the huge oak tree, I saw the familiar sight of my parents' house. I slowed and stole a glimpse of the house. Daddy's truck was in the yard, and the curtains were open, and the lights were on, and I had a strong desire to climb from atop the tracks and leap the drainage ditch, and cross the highway and enter the house. I had not seen my mother in days, and there was in me a strong desire to see her but an even stronger desire to live my life.

And so, I turned from the house and I looked far up the tracks. And I could hear the steady sound of automobile tires passing on the asphalt highway. And my mind drifted to Omenita, and no sooner had it done so than I heard my mother's voice calling to me from a time long past: "When she show you who she is be man enough to accept it." And I embraced that thought. For I was a man, and as a man, I would go to Omenita, and I would gaze upon her as I had not done before, and I would trust my eye and not my heart, and I would see whatever there was to see. For I was confident that I knew her and she knew me and that this love we shared was truly meant to be.

At Omenita's house, I crossed into her yard and climbed onto the steps. The blinds were opened and I could see that the television was on. I knocked on the door and immediately I heard the lone voice of a young male yell, "Who is it?"

"Maurice," I said.

The door opened and Omenita stood before me, smiling. She was still wearing the wool slacks and sweater that she had on earlier when we met with the justice of the peace.

"Hi, beautiful," I said.

She smiled again, then I saw her looking past me out toward the street.

"You walked over here?" she asked me.

"Every step," I said.

"In this weather?"

"It's not that bad," I said. "Once you get moving."

"Why didn't you call me?"

"I just felt like walking," I said.

She hesitated, then frowned.

"Is anything wrong?"

"No," I said. "I just wanted to see you."

"But you just saw me a few hours ago."

"Seems like days ago," I said.

She smiled, then blushed.

"Well come on in," she said, "and get a good look."

I came in and her mother, her sister, and her two brothers were sitting in the living room watching television. The two boys were sitting on the floor—the older one still eating his dinner, and the two women were sitting on the sofa. No one was sitting in the recliner. Come to think of it, in all the years I had been coming here, I had never seen anyone sit in that chair other than Mr. Jones.

I spoke to everyone then Omenita and I went into the kitchen and took a seat at the table. I sat with my back to the wall and she sat directly across from me. And I could tell from the clutter that they did not actually use the table for meals. Instead, it appeared to be utilized for additional storage space. On the far end were several aluminum pots and pans. Near the center was an assortment of bananas and oranges. They had been there for a while. Several of the bananas had begun to turn brown and one of the oranges had begun to mildew. A half-eaten chocolate cake was concealed under a plastic cake dish and sat near the fruit. On the end nearest us was a stack of mail and a pile of old coupons that someone had clipped. And just beyond the mail were several jars of canned figs. One was half empty and the other two had yet to be opened.

And other than the table there was no additional furniture in the moderate-size room. Only a white refrigerator, a gas stove, and a small microwave oven, which sat on the counter next to the window. The back door leading onto the rear porch was closed but through the rear window I could see the branches on the large fig tree closest to the house swaying in the wind. The temperature was dropping, and I was happy to be out of the weather and in the warm, cozy kitchen with the woman that I loved. I was looking around the room when I heard her voice calling to me.

"I'm glad you came," she said.

"So am I," I said.

She looked at me and smiled.

"Well," she said, "this time tomorrow, we'll be husband and wife."

"Yes," I said. "This time tomorrow."

"Are you happy?" she asked me.

I looked at her.

"Am I happy!" I said. "What kind of question is that? Woman, do you know how much I love you?"

She smiled again.

"No," she said. "Why don't you show me?"

I looked over my shoulder at the closed kitchen door. Then, I rose from my seat and went to her. She tilted her head back and I bent low and kissed her softly on the lips. She kissed me back then gently pulled away.

"You better not let my daddy catch you doing that."

"I ain't scared of your daddy," I said.

"Oh, is that a fact?"

"It must be a fact," I said, "because it sure ain't fiction."

"You talking mighty big," she said.

"Why shouldn't I? I practically got papers on you."

"Correction," she said. "We practically got papers on each other."

"And I wouldn't have it any other way," I said.

I kissed her again. Then I sat back at the kitchen table. "Do you know that there is nothing in this whole world that I would not do for you? And nothing that I would not give up."

"Yes," she said. "I know."

I paused and my face became serious. "Do you?" I asked her again.

"Yes," she said softly. "I do."

I looked at her again.

"I love you," I whispered.

"I love you too," she whispered back.

And when she did, I instantly looked into her eyes and searched her face for any sign that her words were a true indication of how she felt and not simply a response given without thought and offered without meaning. I needed to know that she loved me, and that she would stand by me as I had stood by her. And I needed to know that this woman whom I had loved since the first day I laid eyes on her would share a crumb with me. I continued to look deep into her eyes, for what I do not know. Suddenly, I saw her eyes soften, then water.

"I hope you mean that," I said.

"I do," she said. "I really, really do."

I smiled and leaned back, and I was about to rise again and move around the table and kiss her, this beautiful woman with whom I would spend the rest of my life when the kitchen door opened and Miss Jones walked through. She was carrying a glass and an empty plate, which she placed in the sink, then turned back toward us. I released Omenita's hands and looked at Miss Jones. She looked at us and smiled, and I could see that she was happy that we were together and that we had worked things out and that we would be husband and wife.

"Have you eaten dinner, Maurice?"

"No, ma'am," I said. "Not yet."

"Got some red beans and rice on the stove," she said, then paused. "Omenita, why don't you fix Maurice something to eat?"

I saw Omenita roll her eyes.

"I'm not hungry," I said.

"Are you sure?" Miss Jones said.

"Yes, ma'am," I said. "I'm sure."

"Okay," she said. "Then I'll leave you two alone."

She left and I looked at Omenita, then at the stove. There was a skillet and several pots of food sitting on the burners. I looked at the food a moment, then back at her. I had not eaten and the offer of food caused me to realize that I was indeed hungry. Omenita looked at me and frowned.

"What?"

"I am a little hungry," I said.

I heard her sigh.

"What?" I said.

"I see how you're looking at me," she said.

"How?" I asked.

"The same way he looks at her."

"Who?" I asked.

"I'll be your wife," she said, "but I won't be her."

"You won't be who?" I asked her.

She didn't answer. Instead, she rose to her feet, walked to the sink and pulled opened one of the doors to the cupboard. "Here's the plates," she said. "Then she pulled open a drawer. "Here's the forks." She pulled opened another door. "Here's the glasses. Food's on the stove. Drink's in the refrigerator. If you want a plate, fix it yourself."

Chapter Thirty-three

I dressed in the new suit that I had purchased and I drove to the courthouse to meet Omenita, and to my surprise she was there when I arrived, and she was wearing a full-length coat and a beautiful beige dress, and her hair was pulled back, and her neck was girded with pearls, and on her finger was the engagement ring, and on her face was a smile, and at that moment she looked more beautiful than I had ever seen her, and in spite of everything to me this still felt right.

I sat and watched her for a moment. She was standing in the parking lot near the little gazebo, and I knew she was waiting for me. And I knew that I should hurry, but for some reason I could not explain, I wanted to sit and gaze at her from afar, and as I did, I told myself that this was right, and she was the one, and that this was the happiest day of my life.

I was still gazing at her when she finally spied the truck. Instantly, I saw her smile, then wave, and I got out and went to her.

"You look wonderful," I said.

"So do you," she said.

I kissed her softly, and she kissed me back.

"I love you," I said.

"And I love you too."

We climbed the courthouse steps together, and she stood to my right, and our hands were clasped, and I felt myself trembling as I pulled open the door and stepped aside to allow her to enter. And just before I went into the building, I looked back toward the diner, and in the distance, I saw Daddy and Grandpa Luke coming up the sidewalk, and I knew that Daddy had dressed at the diner, and I was happy that it wasn't quite so cold out today, and I was happy that Grandpa Luke had come, and I was happy that Daddy had allowed me to use the truck, and I was happy that he had allowed me to drive here alone so that I could claim my bride like a man.

She entered the building, and I moved up beside her, and we clasped hands again, and there was no fear in me now. There was only peace and joy and serenity, and I knew that each of these emotions was deeply rooted in the reality that our day had finally come, as well as the reality that from this day forth we would abide in each other's love for as long as we both shall live. I felt her hand squeezing mine. And instantly, there was a surge inside of me, and there was the return of the yearning, which I had felt for her only a few days ago when I laid with her in her father's house. And suddenly, I was having trouble breathing, and I felt a tightness about my legs, and I feared that at any moment, my legs would give way and I would lose my ability to stand, then I told myself to calm down, to breathe slowly, to enjoy the moment, to take in all that it had to offer. And I looked around, and I reveled in the quietness of the moment, and the length of the long hallway, and the smells of the season, and the promise of the journey upon which Omenita and I were about to embark.

It was approaching noon. And most of the offices in the building were closed. And I assumed that Mr. Bailey had stepped out for an early lunch, since he had agreed to marry us at noon. And so, we stood outside his door waiting. Grandpa Luke and Daddy, Omenita and I, her mother and father, and her brothers and sister.

And as we stood outside the office door awaiting the arrival of the justice of the peace, I asked Grandpa Luke to offer a prayer for us. And as he did, we all held hands, and we bowed our heads, and he asked God to watch over Omenita and me, and he asked

Him to bless our love as He had blessed his and Grandma's. And in his hand, he had a Bible. And when he was done, I saw him remove his glasses from his pocket and place them on his face, and I saw him open the Bible to read a scripture, and his hands were trembling, and I knew he was thinking about Grandma, and I knew in his mind, he was young again, and I was him, and Omenita was her, and this was their day. And I thought to myself how special it must be to have loved someone as much as he had loved Grandma and to be loved by someone as much as Grandma had loved him. And I looked at Omenita, and I felt honored that she and I would begin our foray into holy matrimony so similar in time as Grandpa and Grandma had begun theirs. And as that thought resonated in me, I squeezed her hand even tighter, for inside of me this all served as further confirmation that this was right, and she was the one, and we were meant to be together.

A reverent moment passed, and when Grandpa had found the page for which he had been searching, I saw him slowly run his fingers across the words, then I saw him close his eyes and collect himself. And I was glad that he was here to share in this moment, and I was glad that he was here to give of himself, and I was glad that on this day, he, too, could honor Grandma. We waited for him to begin, and when he was ready, he raised his head and looked at Omenita and then he looked at me.

"When a man lives as long as I have, he realizes that there are just a few things that truly give life meaning." He paused a minute and I could hear his voice breaking. "There is art, if you have the eyes to see it. There is music, if you have the ears to hear it. There is laughter, if you have the spirit to release it. And most important of all, there is love, if you have the heart to receive it and the generosity to give it" He looked at us again. "I hope you two will always remember that."

"Yes, sir," we both said. "We will."

I saw Daddy smile and I saw Miss Jones slowly nod. Tears had formed in her eyes, and I hoped she was happy for us and not sad for herself.

"Almost fifty years ago," he said. "I got married. And as circumstances would have it, it was almost on this day exactly."

He paused again and looked far up the hall. And I knew he was thinking about Grandma. I could see it in his eyes and I could hear it in his voice. Daddy could see it too. I saw him reach over and place a hand on Grandpa Luke's shoulder. But Grandpa Luke did not look at him. He continued to look far up the hall. I was still holding Omenita's hand, and I slowly raised her hand to my mouth and kissed it. She smiled, and I lowered her hand. Then I heard Grandpa Luke's voice again.

"And before the preacher married us, he told us to love each other always." Grandpa Luke paused again to let his words sink in. "Then because we were so young, he said he wanted to make sure that we knew how to do just that." I saw Grandpa Luke fumbling with the Bible again. "So, he opened his Bible and by the light of a ole coal lamp, he read us a passage." For much of the time, Grandpa had been looking up the hall. But now he looked directly at us. "If it's alright," he said, "I would like to do the same for you. That is if you don't mind."

"We don't mind," I said.

Omenita didn't speak, but she did nod.

"Very well," Grandpa Luke said. He cleared his throat then began. And as he did, I could tell by his voice that he was in another place now, far, far away.

"Love is patient and kind . . . " Grandpa Luke was quiet a moment, and I could see that he was becoming emotional. "Love is not jealous or boastful . . ." His voice began to quiver. "It is not arrogant or rude . . ." He paused and collected himself. "Love does not insist on its own way . . ." Now he looked directly at me and I could feel my heart pounding in my throat. "It is not irritable or resentful . . ." I felt my eyes water. "It does not rejoice at wrong, but rejoices in right . . ." Now, his words came to me from some distant place, and in my mind I was no longer standing, but I was suspended in midair, dangling from a line I could not see. And my emotions were tattered, and my mind was whirling. And there was this feeling that at any moment I would fall, never to rise again. "Love bears all things, believes all things, hopes all things, endures all things. Love never ends."

He closed the Bible then looked at us. His eyes were moist.

"Love each other always," he said, "and don't forget to enjoy the journey because it's not as long as it seems. I'm a living witness. It's not as long as it seems."

And at that moment, I could not breathe, and I turned from them, and I walked toward the end of the hall and I fell against the wall, and I felt a huge dark cloud come over me, and I felt a wrenching in my heart and an emptiness in my stomach, and at that moment, I knew that which I had not wanted to accept. I loved Omenita, but she did not love me. Behind me I heard my father calling to me as if from some far-away place. And I watched him come next to me and stop. I could see the concern on his face.

"Are you all right, son?"

He looked directly at me and I tried to answer him, but no words came until I finally heard myself mumble. "It's over."

And I saw him grimace, still not understanding.

"Son," he said, bewildered, "I don't understand."

I did not answer immediately. Instead, I gazed out of the window and far beyond the streets. I told myself to be calm. "I'm sorry," I said, and again, my lips quivered and my eyes grew misty. "I can't go through with this. I just can't."

"No need to be sorry," Daddy said, and I felt his hand on my back. "That's your choice, son. You do what's best for you."

I turned and faced him.

"She doesn't love me," I said. "Not like Mama loves you; not like Grandma loved Grandpa Luke; not like a woman should love a man."

We were both quiet for a moment and I knew he was trying to find the words to console me. Then, suddenly, he gazed at me in a matter-of-fact way.

"Then you have to tell her," he said.

I looked over at the families then back at him.

"I love her," I said, then I paused, listening to the sound of my words and contemplating the reality of my situation, "but that's not enough. Is it?"

"I'm afraid not," Daddy said.

I looked out of the window again. I could feel my legs shaking.

"Son," Daddy said, "I know it may be hard to believe right now, but one day you will find someone who loves you as much as you love her. I can't tell you when, and I can't tell you where, but I promise, you will find her. And when you do, she will be as good to you as you are to her. And she will do it because she care about you and she wants you to be happy. So, you just have to go on with your life and keep your eyes open. And when you least expect it, you'll see her."

"Yes, sir," I said. And instantly I heard a voice emanating from deep within me: *Perhaps you already have.*

Then I turned my back to him and I kept it turned until Omenita came to me. And when she did, I told her, and she cried. Then I found myself on the highway driving, and I saw myself pulling into the driveway, and I heard myself ringing the doorbell, and I saw her standing before me.

"Maurice!" she said, surprised by my presence.

"Hi," I said. "Is Mama here?"

She smiled and instantly her eyes began to cloud.

"Yes," she said, and I knew she was happy that I had come. She was happy for me and she was happy for Mama. "Come in and I'll take you to her."

"Wait," I said.

She looked at me.

"I have something that belongs to you."

I reached into my jacket and removed the tiny map.

"No," she said. "I gave it to you."

"And now I'm giving it back," I said. "It has served its purpose, and I won't be needing it anymore."

I saw her looking beyond me toward the truck.

"How did things go?" she asked.

"I called it off," I told her.

"I'm sorry," she said. "I'm very, very sorry."

"Thanks," I said. My voice broke, and I looked away.

"Are you okay?" she asked.

"I think so," I said, and I lowered my eyes.

"Is there anything I can do?" she asked, and I could tell that she was sincere. I could hear it in her soft, gentle voice.

"You've already done it," I said.

I looked at her, and she smiled again. I smiled also.

"May I ask you a question?" I said.

"Of course," she said.

"Would you like to go out some time?"

Her eyes softened and she looked at me tenderly.

"Are you sure that's a road you want to travel?"

"No," I said, "I'm not sure, but I recently came to understand that it does not matter which road I travel as long as I know the way home."

"Sounds like you had a good teacher," she said.

"Good?" I said. "Try fantastic!"

"Okay," she said. "Looks like I'm going to have to find a new word."

"I don't care what word you find," I said, "as long as it's yes."

"I would be honored to go out with you," she said.

"Seriously," I said.

"Seriously," she said.

In the distance I saw Mama standing in the doorway. I went to her and when I was close I placed my head upon her bosom, and I felt her arms embrace me and instantly I felt her warm, salty tears. I saw her look at my naked ring finger, then back at me.

"What happened?" she said.

I hesitated, crying. "She showed me who she is," I said, "and I accepted it."

"Well, good for you," Mama said. "Good for you."

"It hurts Mama," I said. "It hurts real bad."

"I know," she said. "Growing up always do."

"I love you, Mama. " I said.

"I love you too, son," she said. "Your mama loves you too."

She put her arms around me again and held me for a long time. Then I heard her whisper: "In a few months you will be twenty-one. But today you are a man."

IT'S ALL ABOUT THE MOON WHEN THE SUN AIN'T SHINING

ERNEST HILL

ABOUT THIS GUIDE

The suggested questions are intended to enhance your group's reading of this book by Ernest Hill.

DISCUSSION QUESTIONS

1. What is the significance of the title?

2. What is the central theme?

3. How would you characterize Omenita? And do you think that she and Maurice are compatible?

4. Compare and contrast the relationship that Maurice and Omenita have with their respective mothers. In what ways do the relationship they enjoy with their mothers affect their views of family, marriage, and self? Please explain.

5. On several different occasions, Maurice interacts with his father, his grandfather, and Omenita's father. What is the significance of those interactions and what impact did they have on his eventual metamorphosis?

6. On the day of the marriage ceremony between Maurice and Omenita, Grandpa Luke reads a passage from the Bible. Why does he select that particular passage, and what impact does it have on Maurice, if any?

7. The confrontation in the parking lot offered insight into how people handle situations in perplexing times. What does this scene reveal about Danielle, Omenita, Maurice, and Gerald?

8. What are your perceptions of Danielle as a person and as a friend? Do you think her concern for Maurice is genuine or is there an ulterior motive?

9. Grandpa Luke is a pivotal character in the story. How does his presence impact the plot? And what is the significance of his camera?

10. What do you think of Miss Hattie's relationship with the Davenport family? What, if anything, does their relationship reveal about the "New South?"

11. How would you evaluate Miss Hattie as a parent?

12. Was there a proverbial straw that broke the camel's back in this story? If so, what was it? And how did it affect the outcome?

13. The ending of the book is quite emotional. What feelings does the ending evoke in you? Please explain.

14. What statement does this story make about love?